THE SAINT PLAYS
WITH FIRE

FOREWORD BY PAUL SIMPSON

THE ADVENTURES OF THE SAINT

Enter the Saint (1930), *The Saint Closes the Case* (1930),
The Avenging Saint (1930), *Featuring the Saint* (1931),
Alias the Saint (1931), *The Saint Meets His Match* (1931),
The Saint Versus Scotland Yard (1932), *The Saint's Getaway* (1932),
The Saint and Mr Teal (1933), *The Brighter Buccaneer* (1933),
The Saint in London (1934), *The Saint Intervenes* (1934),
The Saint Goes On (1934), *The Saint in New York* (1935),
Saint Overboard (1936), *The Saint in Action* (1937),
The Saint Bids Diamonds (1937), *The Saint Plays with Fire* (1938),
Follow the Saint (1938), *The Happy Highwayman* (1939),
The Saint in Miami (1940), *The Saint Goes West* (1942),
The Saint Steps In (1943), *The Saint on Guard* (1944),
The Saint Sees It Through (1946), *Call for the Saint* (1948),
Saint Errant (1948), *The Saint in Europe* (1953),
The Saint on the Spanish Main (1955), *The Saint Around the World* (1956),
Thanks to the Saint (1957), *Señor Saint* (1958), *Saint to the Rescue* (1959),
Trust the Saint (1962), *The Saint in the Sun* (1963),
Vendetta for the Saint (1964), *The Saint on TV* (1968),
The Saint Returns (1968), *The Saint and the Fiction Makers* (1968),
The Saint Abroad (1969), *The Saint in Pursuit* (1970),
The Saint and the People Importers (1971), *Catch the Saint* (1975),
The Saint and the Hapsburg Necklace (1976), *Send for the Saint* (1977),
The Saint in Trouble (1978), *The Saint and the Templar Treasure* (1978),
Count On the Saint (1980), *Salvage for the Saint* (1983)

THE SAINT PLAYS WITH FIRE

LESLIE CHARTERIS

SERIES EDITOR: IAN DICKERSON

THOMAS & MERCER

Text copyright © 2014 Interfund (London) Ltd.
Foreword © 2014 Paul Simpson
Publication History and Author Biography © 2014 Ian Dickerson
All rights reserved.

Published by Thomas & Mercer, Seattle

www.apub.com

ISBN-13: 9781477842782
ISBN-10: 1477842780

Cover design by David Drummond, www.salamanderhill.com

Printed in the United States of America.

To Bartlett Cormack

My Dear Bart,

*Once upon a time, when a chance letter of yours
dragged me into a dizzy whirl on the madman's
merry-go-round called Hollywood, I decided to
write a book called The Saint in Hollywood, and
I knew then that it must be dedicated to you.
But the years have ambled on, and somehow or
other that story still hasn't been started, and I'm
ashamed to keep you waiting any longer for what I
meant to give you so long ago. So will you take this
instead, with the same affection and gratitude as I
should have dedicated that unwritten adventure?*

Always,
Leslie Charteris

PUBLISHER'S NOTE

FOREWORD TO THE
NEW EDITION

For many fans of Leslie Charteris's writing, the 1930s saw the best Saint adventures appear in print. All-time favourites, including the Rayt Marius tales and the collections of short stories in which Simon Templar bamboozled the ungodly, made their debuts. But two full-length novels stand out above all the other pieces: *Getaway* and *The Saint Plays with Fire* (originally titled *Prelude for War*).

Getaway is a caper piece, adapted as *The Saint's Vacation* for the RKO series of movies. *The Saint Plays with Fire*, right from the start, is far more serious—or as serious as anything can be in the Saint's world, where there are damsels in distress to be rescued, Inspector Claud Eustace Teal's tummy to be prodded, and bad guys to threaten everything that Simon holds dear.

It contains some of Leslie Charteris's most evocative writing—I defy anyone to read the description of the Sons of France rally in the first few pages, and the picture that it evokes in Simon's mind, chronicled a little later, without feeling a chill. Remember, this was written in 1938, at a time when appeasement was God, America was isolationist, and very few people were willing to listen to the truth about Adolf Hitler and the Nazi creed. It's not an Indiana Jones adventure penned fifty years later, in which the Führer can sign the notebook Indy is carrying in Berlin, or a *Doctor Who* episode, where Hitler is thrown into a cupboard to get him out of the way of a regenerating River Song. This is an author stepping away from the heightened reality in which his character usually dwelt and dealing with a real creed of hatred, which stood for everything that the Saint—and, of course, his creator, Charteris—abhorred.

In some ways it's the last Saint novel. From hereon in, at least in the stories that Charteris penned himself, Simon is battling against the Nazis directly, more often than not, working for an unofficial part of the American government. Once he becomes part of the Establishment, no matter how obliquely, the Saint loses something of his edge. Here he is caught up in the madness purely by chance, but the more he learns, the angrier he gets. And, to borrow from a different franchise, you wouldn't like him when he's angry.

That's not to say that *The Saint Plays with Fire* isn't a fun novel—it's not the Saintly equivalent of a Bourne film, or Daniel Craig's oh-so-serious 007 in *Casino Royale* or *Quantum of Solace*. Any scene that involves Hoppy Uniatz (oh, if you've not met Hoppy yet, you're in for a treat) is guaranteed to raise a smile. The action sequences are told with Charteris's typical verve and style, giving no quarter to those who think that the English language should be used in as short sentences with as simple words as possible. The threat is credible, but even at the darkest hour, the "old Saintly smile" isn't far away.

The strength of the story can be gauged by the fact it's been adapted twice—so far—for other media. *The Saint Plays with Fire* was used for an early Roger Moore episode, with Simon battling neo- rather than real Nazis, but otherwise hardly changing the basic plot (unlike so many in the Moore series). It was one of three stories adapted for BBC Radio 4 in the mid-1990s. And with the growth of neo-Nazi movements around Europe as the Great Twenty-First-Century Recession bites, it's as relevant today as it was then if anyone's looking for a Saintly story on which to base a pilot film . . .

That's because it also makes a great introduction to Simon Templar. If this is your first Saint novel, then I envy you the journey of discovery you're about to embark upon. The year is 1938. The place: England . . .

—Paul Simpson

THE SAINT PLAYS
WITH FIRE

CHAPTER ONE:

HOW SIMON TEMPLAR WENT TO A FIRE AND PATRICIA HOLM HEARD OF A "FINANCIER"

1

Perhaps the story really began when Simon Templar switched on the radio. At least, before that everything was peaceful, and afterwards, for many memorable days which were to find an unforgettable place in his saga of hairbreadth adventure, there was no peace at all. But Simon Templar's life always seemed to run that way: his interludes of peace seemed to have something inescapably transient about them, some inborn predestined seed of dynamite that was foredoomed to blast him back into another of those amazing episodes which to him were the ever-recurrent breath of life.

He was not thinking of trouble or adventure or anything else exciting. He lounged back comfortably in the long-nosed rakish Hirondel, his fingertips barely seeming to caress the wheel as he nursed it over the dark winding roads at a mere whispering sixty, for he was in no hurry. Overhead a bright moon was shining, casting long shadows over the fields and silvering the leaves of passing trees and hedges. His blue eyes probed lazily the white reach of the headlights, and the unruffled calm of his brown face of a mocking buccaneer might have helped anyone to understand why in many places he was better known as "The Saint" than he was by his own name—without giving any clue to the disturbing fact that a mere mention of the Saint in initiated quarters was capable of reducing detectives and convicted criminals alike to a practically indistinguishable state of unprintable incoherence. None of the adventures that had left that almost incredible legend in their trail had left a mark on his face or in his mind: he was simply and serenely enjoying his interlude—even though he must have known, even then, that it could only be an interlude until the next adventure began, because Fate had ordained him for adventure . . .

"You know," he remarked idly, "much as I've cursed them in my time, there's something to be said for these kindergarten English licensing laws. Just think—if it wasn't for the way our professional grandmothers smack our bottoms and pack us off to bed when the clock strikes, we might still be swilling inferior champagne and deafening ourselves with saxophones in that revolting roadhouse, instead of doing our souls a bit of good with all this."

"When you start getting tolerant I'm always afraid you're sickening for something," said Patricia Holm sleepily.

He turned his head to smile at her. She looked very lovely leaning back at his side, with her blue eyes half-closed and her lips softly shaped with humour: he was always discovering her loveliness again with an exciting sense of surprise, as if it had so many facets that it was never twice the same. She was something that was always changing and yet never changed; as much a part of him as his oldest memory, and yet always new; wherever he went and whatever other adventures he found, she was the one unending and exquisite adventure.

He touched the spun gold of her hair.

"All right," he said. "You can have the saxophones."

And that was when he switched on the radio.

The little dial on the dashboard glowed alight out of the darkness, and for a few seconds there was silence while the set warmed up. And then, with an eerie suddenness, there were no saxophones, but a loud brassy voice speaking in French. The set picked it out of the air in the middle of a sentence, flung it gratingly at them as it rose in a snarling crescendo.

"*. . . to crush them like vermin, to destroy them like rats who would carry their plague germs through our fair land! The blood of a million Frenchmen, dead on the fields of glory, cries out to you to show yourselves worthy of their sacrifice. Rise up and arm yourselves against this peril that threatens you from within; stamp out these cowardly Pacifists, these skulking traitors, these godless anarchists, these alien Jews who are betraying our country for a handful of gold . . . Sons of France, I call you to arms. Fling yourselves into the fight with a song on your lips and glory in your hearts, for only in the blood and fire of battle will our nation be purified and find once more her true soul!*"

The brassy voice stopped speaking, and there was an instant's stillness. And then, like a thunderclap another sound burst in—a hoarse frenzied howl, shrill and hideous as the clamour of ten thousand hungry wolves maddened by the smell of blood, an inarticulate animal roar that scarcely seemed as if it could have come from human throats. Wild, savage, throbbing with a horrible bloodlust, it fouled the peaceful night with visions of flame and carnage, of mad mindless mobs, of torture and the crash of guns, of shattered broken buildings and the shattered broken bodies of men and women and children. For a full minute it swelled and pulsed on their ears. And then came the music.

It was not saxophones. It was brass and drums. Brass like the voice that had been speaking, blasting its brazen rhythm of ecstatic sacrifice in rasping fanfares that lashed clean through the filmy gloss of civilisation to clog the blood with intolerable tension. Drums thudding the maddening pulse-beats of a modern but more potent voodoo, hammering their insensate strum into the brain until the mind was stunned and battered with their merciless insistence. Brass shouting and shrieking its melodic echo of the clash of steel and the scream of human torment. Drums pattering their glib mutter of the rattle of firearms and the rumble of rolling iron. Brass blaring its hypnotic hymn of heroic death. Drums thumping like giant hearts. Brass and drums. Brass and drums. Brass and drums . . .

"Turn it off," said Patricia sharply, abruptly. "Stop it, Simon. It's horrible!"

He could feel her shiver.

"No," he said. "Listen."

He was tense himself, his nerves drawn to threads of quivering steel. The music had done that to him. The music went on, drowning out the incoherent voices until there were no more voices but only the crystallised blare and beat that was one voice for all. Brass and drums. And now into it, in time with it, growing with it, swelling above it, came a new sound—the unmistakable monotonous crunch of booted feet. Left, right, left, right, left. The terrible juggernaut tramp of masses of marching men. Legs swinging like synchronised machinery. Heels falling together steadily, heavily, irresistibly, like leaden pile-drivers pounding the bruised earth . . .

The Saint was in one of his queer moments of vision. He went on speaking, his voice curiously low against the background clamour of brass and drums and marching feet.

"Yes, it's horrible, but you ought to listen. We ought to remember what hangs over our peace . . . I've heard just the same thing before— one night when I was fiddling with the radio and I caught some Nazi anniversary jamboree in Nuremburg . . . This is the noise of a world gone mad. This is the climax of two thousand years of progress. This is why philosophers have searched for wisdom, and poets have revealed beauty, and martyrs have died for freedom—so that whole nations that call themselves intelligent human beings can exchange their brains for a brass band, and tax themselves to starvation to buy bombs and battleships, and live in a mental slavery that no physical slave in the old days was ever condemned to. And be so carried away by it that most of them really and honestly believe that they're proud crusaders building a new and glorious world . . . I know you can wipe out two thousand years of education with one generation of censorship and propaganda. But what is this sickness that makes one nation after another in Europe *want* to wipe them out?"

The bugles blared again and the feet marched against the tapping of the drums, in mocking denial of an answer. And then he touched the switch and the noise ceased.

Peace came back into the night with a strange softness, as if on tiptoe, fearful of a fresh intrusion. Once more there was only the murmuring hiss of the smooth-running engine and the rustle of the passing air, not even loud enough to blanket the hoot of an indignant owl scared from its perch on an overhanging bough, but it was a peace like waking from an ugly dream, with their ears still haunted by what they had heard before. It was some time before Patricia spoke, though Simon knew she was wide awake now.

"What was it?" she asked at last, in a voice too even to be wholly natural.

"That was the Sons of France—Colonel Marteau's blueshirt gang. You remember, they grew out of the break-up of the old Croix de Feu, only about ten times worse. They've been holding a midnight jamboree outside Paris, with torches and bonfires and flags and bands and everything. What we cut in on must have been the grand finale— Colonel Marteau's pep talk to the assembled cannon fodder."

He paused.

"First Russia, then Italy, then Germany, then Spain," he said soberly. "And now France is next. There, but for the grace of God, goes the next tin-pot dictator, on his way to make the world a little less fit to live in . . . There are almost enough of them now—marching mobs of idiots backwards and forwards and building guns and armies because they can't build anything else, and because it's the perfect solution to all economic problems so long as it lasts. How can you have peace and progress when fighting is the only gospel they've got to preach? . . . If you wanted to be pessimistic, you could feel that Nature had got the whole idea of progress licked from the start; because as soon as even the dumbest mass of people had just got educated to the futility of modern warfare and the stupidity of nationalism, she could turn round and come back with some strutting monomaniac to sell the old stock all over again under a new trademark and put the whole show back where it started from."

"*But why?*"

He shrugged.

"As far as the Sons of France are concerned, you could be pretty cynical if you wanted to. The present French socialist government is rather unpopular with some of our leading bloodsuckers because it's introducing a new set of laws on the same lines that Roosevelt started in America, to take all the profit out of war by nationalising all major industries directly it starts. The whole idea, of course, is too utterly Communistic and disgusting for words. Hence the Sons of France. All this blood and fire business tonight was probably part of the graft to get the Socialists chucked out and leave honest businessmen safe to make their fortunes out of murder. It's a lovely idea."

"And are they going to get away with it?"

"Who is to stop it?" asked the Saint bitterly.

And when he asked the question he could imagine no answer. But afterwards he would remember it. This was, as has been said, one of his precarious interludes of peace. Twice already in his lawless career he had helped to snatch away the threat of war and destruction from over the heads of an unsuspecting world, but this time the chance that the history of Europe could be altered by anything he did seemed too remote to be given thought. But in the same mood of grim clairvoyance into which the interruption had thrown him he gazed sombrely down the track of the headlights, still busy with his thoughts, and seeing the fulfilment of his half-spoken prophecy. He saw the streets swarming with arrogant strangely uniformed militia, the applauding headlines of a disciplined press, the new breed of sycophantic spies, the beginnings of fear, men who had once been free learning to look over their shoulders before they spoke their thoughts, neighbour betraying neighbour, the midnight arrests, the third degree, the secret tribunals, the fantastic confessions, the farcical trials, the concentration camps, and firing squads. He saw the hysterical ranting of yet another neurotic megalomaniac adding itself to the rising clamour of the crazy discords of Europe, the coming generations reared to believe in terrorism at home and war abroad as the apotheosis of a heroic destiny, children marching with toy guns as soon as they could walk, merging easily into the long crawling lines of new legions more pitiless than Caesar's. He saw the peaceful countryside before him gouged into swamps and craters where torn flesh rotted faster than the scavenging rats could eat; the long red tongues of the guns licking upwards into the dark as they thundered their dreadful litany; the first rose-pink glow of fire, deepening to crimson as it leaped up, flickering, spreading its red aura fanwise across the sky until the black silhouettes of trees could be seen clearly stamped against it . . . until with an odd sense of shock, as if he were coming out of another dream, the Saint realised that that at least was no vision—that his eyes really were seeing the scarlet reflection of swelling flame beyond the distant trees.

He pointed.

"Look."

Patricia sat up.

"Anyone would say it was a fire," she said interestedly.

Simon Templar grinned. His own reverie was swept away as quickly as it had begun—for that moment.

"I'll bet it is a fire," he said. "And in this neck of the woods the chances are that the nearest fire brigade is miles away. We'd better drift along and look it over."

He would never forget that fire. It was the beginning of the adventure.

2

As his foot came down on the accelerator his hand found the lever that opened the cut-out, and the whisper of the great car turned into a deep-throated roar. They were dragged against the back of the seat as it surged forward with a sudden terrific access of power, and the susurration of the tyres on the roadway rose to a shrill whine. It was as if an idly roaming tiger had suddenly been stung to vicious life.

The Saint had begun to drive.

He had no gift of second sight to tell him what that fire was to mean, but just as a fire it was sufficient. It might be fun, and he was going there—in a hurry now. And in his mercurial philosophy that was enough. His eyes had narrowed and come to life with the zest of the moment, and a shadow of his last smile lingered half-remembered on his lips . . . Half a mile further on a side road opened sharply to the right, leading in the direction of the red glow. As he approached it, the Saint shifted his foot from the accelerator to the brake and wrenched the wheel over: the rear wheels whipped round with a scream of skidding rubber, spun, bit the road again, took hold, and catapulted the car forward again at right angles to its previous course as the Saint's toe returned to the accelerator.

"That's how these racing blokes do it," he explained.

Patricia lighted two cigarettes.

"What do they do when they want to turn quickly?" she inquired tranquilly.

The way Simon slanted one of the cigarettes between his lips was its own impudent answer. The vivid red stain in the sky was almost straight ahead of them now, growing so that it blotted out the stars, and they were rushing towards it down the narrow lane with the speed of a hurricane. They squealed round another bend, and once more the Saint jammed on the brakes. On their left was a half-timbered lodge beside broad iron gates that opened on to a curving drive.

"This should be it," said the Saint, and again the great car seemed to pivot on its locked front wheels to make the turn.

In another moment they had the acrid smell of burning wood sharp in their nostrils. They swept round a semicircular channel of trees, and in an instant they were caught full in the red glare as if they had been picked up by quivering floodlights. Simon let the Hirondel coast to a breathless standstill beside a broad close-cropped lawn, and hitched himself up to sit on the back of the seat for a better view.

"It is a fire," he decided, with profound satisfaction.

It was. The whole lawn was lit up by it like a stage set, and a pall of black smoke hung over it like a billowing curtain. The house was one of those old historic mansions whose lining of massive beams and mellowed panelling could be diagnosed at a glance, and it was going up like a pile of tinder. The fire seemed to have started on the ground floor, for huge gusts of flame were spouting from the open windows along the terrace and climbing like wind-ripped banners towards the roof, roaring with a boisterous glee that could be clearly heard even above the reduced splutter of the Hirondel's exhaust. The Saint drew at his cigarette and settled more firmly into his conviction that, judged by any pyrotechnical standards, it was a beaut.

Across the lawn, figures in a grotesque assortment of deshabille were running with the erratic scurrying wildness of flushed rabbits.

"At least they all seem to have got out," said the Saint.

He switched off the engine and hitched his legs over the side of the car. Some of the scurrying figures, attracted perhaps like moths by the new blaze of the headlights, had started to run towards them. The first to arrive was a young man who carried a girl over his shoulder. He was large and blond and impressively moustached, and he wore blue and green striped pyjamas. He dumped the girl on the ground at the Saint's feet, rather like a retriever bringing in a bird, and stood over her for a moment breathing heavily.

"By Jove," he said. "Oh, by Jove! . . . Steady on, Val, old thing. It's all right now. You're quite safe."

He put out a hand to restrain her as she tried to get up, but with a quick movement she wriggled away from him and found her feet. She was dark and slender, but not so slender that the transparent nightgown which was her only covering lacked fascinating contours to cling to. The chiffon had slipped aside to bare one white shoulder and her curly hair was in wild disarray, but even the thoroughly petulant spoiled-child expression that pouted her face could not disguise its amazing beauty.

"All right, all right," she said impatiently. "You've rescued me now, and I'm very much obliged. But for heaven's sake stop pawing me and find me something to wear."

She seemed to regard the fire as an event arranged by a malicious fate solely for her own inconvenience. The young man looked somewhat startled.

"Dammit, Valerie," he said in an injured tone, "do you realise—"

"Of course she does," said the Saint soothingly. "She knows you're a little hero. She's just being practical. And while we're being practical, do you happen to know whether anybody else is left in the house?"

The young man turned. He looked at Simon rather blankly, as if taken aback at being interrupted so unceremoniously.

"Eh? What?" he said. "I dunno. I fetched Valerie out."

From the way he said it, one gathered that nobody mattered except Valerie.

Simon patted him on the back.

"Yes, we know," he said kindly. "We saw you. You're a hero. We'll give you a diploma. But just the same, wouldn't it be a good idea to round up the others and make sure that nobody's missing?"

Again the young man looked blank, and rather resentful. His expression indicated that having done his good deed for the day by rescuing Valerie, he expected to be set apart on a pedestal instead of being ordered about. But there was something about the Saint's cool assumption of command that eliminated argument.

"Oh, certainly. I see what you mean."

He moved reluctantly away, and presently people came straggling in from different parts of the lawn and gathered near Simon's car. There was a tall red-faced man with a white moustache and the stereotyped chutney-and-Scotch complexion of a professional soldier, a dour large-bosomed woman in a flannel dressing-gown who could have belonged to nobody else, an excited little fat man who came chattering pompously, the guardsmanly youth who had herded them together, and a fourth man who strolled up in the background. The reflection of the fire shone redly in their faces as they assembled in a group with an air of studied calm which proclaimed their consciousness of behaving like British aristocrats in an emergency.

Simon looked them over without reverence. He knew none of them by sight, and it was none of his business, but he was the only one present who seemed to have any coherent ideas. His voice stilled their chatter.

"Well," he said, "you ought to know. Are you all here?"

They glanced at each other in an awed and scared sort of way, and then turned and looked frightenedly at the blazing house and back again, as though it were the first time that any of their thoughts had gone beyond their own personal safety.

Suddenly the voice of the girl in the nightgown sounded shrilly behind Simon.

"No! They aren't all here! John isn't here! Where's Johnny?"

There was an awful stillness, in which realisation crawled horribly over chalky faces.

"B-but where can he be?" asked the short fat man, in a quavering voice. "He . . . he must have heard the alarm—"

The military-looking man turned round and raised his voice in a barrack-square bawl.

"Kennet!" he shouted. "Kennet!"

He sounded as if he was bellowing at a slovenly recruit who was late on parade.

The only answer was the derisive cackle of the leaping flames.

The large-bosomed woman shrieked. She opened her mouth wide and yelled at the top of her voice, her face contorted with an awful terror.

"No! No . . . it's too dreadful. He can't be still in there! You can't have—"

Her words broke off in a kind of gulp. For a couple of seconds her mouth went on opening and shutting like that of a fish out of water; then, without another sound, she collapsed like an empty sack.

"She's fainted," somebody said stupidly.

"So she has," said the Saint witheringly. "Now we all ought to gather round and hold her hands."

The military man, bending over her, turned up his purple face.

"By Gad, sir!" he burst out cholerically. "Haven't you—" He stopped. Another thought, overwhelming in its enormity, seemed to have erupted under his nose. He straightened up, glaring at the Saint as if he had just really become aware of his presence for the first time. "Anyway," he said, "what the devil are you doing here?"

The idea percolated into the brains of the others and brought them back to gaping stillness. And while they were staring in vacuous indignation, the man who had stayed in the background moved to the front. He was short and very broad-shouldered, with a square and rather flat face and very sunken shrewd dark eyes. "Unlike the others, he was fully dressed. There was no sign of flurry or alarm about him: with his powerful chin and thin straight mouth he looked as solid and impassive as a chunk of granite.

"Yes," he said, "who are you?"

Simon met his gaze with cold insouciance. The antagonism was instant and intuitive. Perhaps it was that that touched the Saint's swift mind with the queer itch of dissatisfaction that led to so many things. Perhaps it was then that the first wraith of suspicion took nebulous shape in his mind. But there was no time to dwell on the point just then. He only knew that something like a fine thread of steel wove through the plastic outlines of his attitude.

"At the moment," he said evenly, "I seem to be the only person who isn't behaving like a stuffed owl. Where does this man Kennet sleep?"

"I don't know," answered the square-built man. "Someone else will be able to tell you."

His face was expressionless; his tone was so expressionless as to sound almost ironical. There seemed to be a stony sort of amusement lurking at the back of his deep-set eyes. But that might have been an illusion created by the flickering firelight.

The girl Valerie supplied the information.

"He's in the end room on the left—that window there."

Simon looked.

The room was at the end of the house which was burning most fiercely—the end close to which the fire had probably started. Under it, the ground floor looked like an open furnace through which the draught from the open windows and the open front door was driving flames in long roaring streamers. The end upper window was about fifteen feet from the ground, but there was no way of reaching it from outside without a ladder.

The fat little man was wringing his hands.

"He can't still be there," he wailed. "He must have heard the alarm—"

"Suppose he got the wind up and fainted, or something?" suggested the large young man in the striped pyjamas helpfully.

Simon almost hit him.

"Do you know where there's a ladder, you amazing oaf?" he demanded.

The young man blinked at him dumbly. Nobody else answered. They all seemed to be in a fog.

Simon swung round to Patricia.

"Do what you can, darling," he said.

He turned away, and for a moment the others seemed to be held petrified.

"Stop him," bleated the fat little man suddenly. "For God's sake, stop him! It's suicide—"

"Hey!" bellowed the puce-faced militarist commandingly. "Come back!"

The queenly woman screeched indistinguishably and collapsed again.

Simon Templar heard none of these things. He was half-way across the lawn by that time, racing grimly towards the house.

3

The heat from the hall struck him like a physical blow as he plunged
through the front door; the air scorched his lungs like a gust from
a red-hot oven. At the far end of the hall long sheets of flame were
sweeping greedily up a huge pair of velvet curtains. Smaller flames
were dancing over a rug, and leaping with fiercer eagerness up the
blackening banisters of a wide staircase. The paint on the broad beams
crossing the high ceiling was bubbling and boiling under the heat, and
occasionally small drops of it fell in a scalding rain to take hold of new
sections of the floor.

The Saint hardly checked for an instant before he went on. He
dodged across the hall like a flitting shadow and leapt up the stairs four
at a time. Fire from the banisters snatched at him as he went up, stung
his nostrils with the smell of his own scorching clothes.

On the upper landing the smoke was thicker. It made his eyes
smart and filled his throat with coughing; his heart was hammering
with a dull force that jarred his ribs; he felt an iron band tightening
remorselessly around his temples. He stared blearily down the corridor
which led in the direction he had to go. Half-way along it, great gouts

THE SAINT PLAYS WITH FIRE

of flame were starting up from the floorboards, waving like monstrous flowers swaying in a blistering wind. It could only be a matter of seconds before the whole passage would plunge down into the incandescent inferno below.

The Saint went on.

It was not so much a deliberate effort as a yielding to instinctive momentum. He had no time to think about being heroic—or about anything else, for that matter. In that broiling nightmare a second's hesitation might have been fatal. But he had set out to do something, knowing what it might mean, and so long as there was any hope of doing it his only idea was to go on. He kept going with nothing to carry him on but the epic drive of a great heart that had never known what it was to turn back for the threat of danger.

He came out in a clear space on the other side of the flames, beating the sparks from his sleeves and trousers. Open doors and glimpses of disordered beds on either side of the passage showed where various rooms had been hastily vacated, but the door of the room at the very end was closed. He fell on the handle and turned it.

The door was locked.

He thundered on it with fists and feet.

"Kennet!" he shouted. "Kennet, wake up!"

His voice was a mere harsh croak that was lost in the hoarse roar of the fire. It brought no answer from behind the door.

He drew back across the corridor, braced himself momentarily, and flung himself forward again. Hurled by the muscles of a trained athlete, his shoulder crashed into the door with all the shattering-force of one hundred and seventy-five pounds of fighting weight behind it, in an impact that shook every bone in his body, but he might just as well have charged a steam roller. The floor might be cracking and crumbling under his feet, but that door was of tough old English oak, seasoned by two hundred years of history and still untouched by the fire. It would have taken an axe or a sledgehammer to break it down.

His eyes swept it desperately from top to bottom. And as he looked at it, two pink fingers of flame curled out from underneath it. The floor of the room was already taking fire.

But those little jagged fangs of flame meant that there was a small space between the bottom of the door and the floorboards. If he could push the key through so that it fell on the floor inside, he might be able to fish it out through the gap under the door. He whipped out his penknife and probed at the keyhole.

At the first attempt, the blade slipped right through the hole without encountering any resistance. The Saint bent down and brought his eye close to the aperture. There was enough firelight inside the room for him to be able to see the whole outline of the keyhole. And there was no key in it.

For one dizzy second his brain whirled. And then his lips thinned out, and a red glint came into his eyes that owed nothing to the reflections of the fire.

Again he fought his way incredibly through the hellish barrier of flame that shut off the end of the corridor. The charred boards gave ominously under his feet, but he hardly noticed it. He had remembered noticing something through the suffocating murk on the landing. As he beat out his smouldering clothes again he located it—a huge medieval battle-axe suspended from two hooks on the wall at the top of the stairs. He measured the distance and jumped, snatching eagerly. The axe came away, bringing the two hooks with it, and a shower of plaster fell on his face and half-blinded him.

That shower of grit probably saved his life. He slumped against the wall, trying to clear his streaming eyes, and that brief setback cheated Death for the hundredth time in its long duel with the Saint's guardian angel. For even as he straightened up again with the axe in his hands, about twenty feet of the passage plunged downwards with a heart-stopping crash in a swirl of flame, leaving nothing but a gaping chasm through which fire roared up in a fiendish fountain that sent him staggering back before its intolerable heat. The last chance of reaching that locked room was gone.

A great weariness fell on the Saint like a heavy blanket pressing him down. There was nothing more he could do.

He dropped the battle-axe and stumbled falteringly down the blazing stairs. There was no more battle now to keep him going. It was sheer blind automatism rather than any conscious effort on his part that guided him through another inferno to come reeling out through the front door, an amazing tatterdemalion outcast from the jaws of hell, to fall on his hands and knees on the terrace outside. In a dim faraway manner he was aware of hands raising him; of a remembered voice, low and musical, close to his ear.

"I know you like warm climates, boy, but couldn't you have got along with a trip to Africa?"

He smiled. Between him and Patricia there was no need for the things that other people would have had to say. They spoke their own language. Grimy, dishevelled, with his clothes blackened and singed and his eyes bloodshot and his body smarting from a dozen minor burns, the Saint smiled at her with all his old incomparable impudence.

"I was trying to economise," he said. "And now I shall probably catch my death of cold."

Already the cold night air, flowing like nectar into his parched lungs, was beginning to revive him, and in a few minutes his superb resilience would do the rest. He reviewed his injuries more systematically, and realised that comparatively speaking he was almost miraculously unscathed. The thing that had come nearest to downing him was the smoke and fumes of the fire, and the effects of that were dispersing themselves like magic now that he could breathe again without feeling as if he were inhaling molten ash.

He cocked an eye at the stolid country policeman who was holding his other arm.

"Do you have to be quite so professional, Reginald?" he murmured. "It makes me feel nervous."

The constable's hold relaxed reassuringly.

"I'd get along and see the doctor, sir, if I was you. He's in the lodge now with Lady Sangore."

"Is that the old trout's name? And I'll bet her husband is at least a General." The Saint was starting to get his bearings, and his legs began to feel as if they belonged to him again. He searched for a cigarette. "Thanks, but Lady Sangore can have him. I'd rather have a drink. I wonder if we could get any cooperation from the owner of this jolly little bonfire?"

"You mean Mr Fairweather, sir? That's him, coming along now."

While Simon had been inside the house, a number of other people had arrived on the scene, and another policeman and a sergeant were loudly ordering them to stand back. Paying no attention to this whatever, they swarmed excitedly round the Saint, all talking at once and completely frustrating the fat little Mr Fairweather, who seemed as if he was trying to make a speech. The voice of the General rose above the confused jabber like a foghorn.

"A fine effort, young man. A splendid effort, by Gad! But you shouldn't have tried it."

"Tell the band to strike up a tune," said the Saint shortly. "Did anybody find a ladder?"

With his strength rapidly coming back, he still fought against admitting defeat. His face was hard and set, and the blue in his eyes was icy as he glanced over the group.

"A ladder wouldn't be much use now," said a quiet voice. "The flames are pouring out of his window. There isn't a hope."

It was the square-jawed man who spoke, and again it seemed to Simon that there was a faint sneer in his dark eyes.

The Saint's eyes turned back to the house, and as if to confirm what the other had said, there came from the blaze a tremendous rumbling rending sound. Slowly, with massive deliberation, the roof began to bend inwards, sagging in the middle. Faster and faster it sagged, and then, with a shattering grinding roar like an avalanche, it crumpled up and vanished. A great shower of golden sparks shot upwards and fell in a brilliant rain over the lawns and garden.

"You see?" said the square man. "You did everything you could. But it's lucky you turned back when you did. If you had reached his room, the chances are that you'd never have got back."

Simon's eyes slanted slowly back to the heavy-set powerful face.

It was true that there was nothing more that he could do. But now, for the first time since the beginning of those last mad minutes, he could stop to think. And his mind went back to the chaotic questions that had swept through it for one vertiginous instant back there in the searing stench of the fire.

"But I did reach his room," he answered deliberately. "Only I couldn't get in. The door was locked. And the key wasn't in it."

"Really?"

The other's face expressed perfunctory concern. But his eyes no longer held their glimmer of cold amusement. They stared hard at Simon with a cool analytical steadiness, as if weighing him up, estimating his qualities, and methodically tabulating the information for future reference.

And once more that queer tingle of suspicion groped its way through the Saint's brain. Only this time it was more than a vague formless hunch. He knew now, beyond any shadow of doubt, with an uncanny certainty, that he was on the threshold of something which his inborn flair for the strange twists of adventure was physically incapable of leaving unexplored. And an electric ripple of sheer delight brought every fibre of his being to ecstatic life. His interlude of peace was over.

"Really," he affirmed flatly.

"Then perhaps you were even luckier than you realise," said the square man smoothly. If he meant to give the words any extra significance, he did it so subtly that there was no single syllable on which an accusation could have been pinned. In point of time it had only lasted for a moment, that silent and apparently unimportant exchange of glances, and after it there was nothing to show that a challenge had been thrown down and taken up. "If we can offer you what hospitality we have left—I'm sure Mr Fairweather—"

The Saint shook his head.

"Thanks," he said, "but I haven't got far to go, and I've got a suitcase in the car."

"Then I hope we shall be seeing more of you." The square man turned. I suppose we should get along to the lodge, Sir Robert. We can't be any more use here."

"Harrumph," said the General. "Er . . . yes. A splendid effort, young man. Splendid. Ought to have a medal. Harrumph."

He allowed himself to be led away, rumbling.

Mr Fairweather grasped the Saint's hand and pumped it vigorously up and down. He had recovered what must have been his normal tremendous dignity, and now he was also able to make himself heard.

"I shall take personal steps," he announced majestically, "to see that your heroism is suitably recognised."

He stalked off after the others, without stopping to inquire the Saint's name and address.

Clanging importantly, the first fire-engine swept up the gravel drive and came to a standstill in front of the terrace.

4

"I'm glad they got here in time to water the flowers," Simon observed rather bitterly.

He was wondering how much difference it might have made if they had arrived early enough to get a ladder to the window of that locked room. But the nearest town of any size was Anford, about seven miles away, and the possibility that they could have arrived much sooner was purely theoretical. From the moment a fire like that took hold, the house was inevitably doomed.

The policeman who had been holding his arm had moved off during the conversation, and the other spectators were simply standing around and gaping in the dumb bovine way in which spectators of catastrophe usually stand and gape.

Simon touched Patricia's arm.

"We might as well be floating along," he said. "The excitement seems to be over, and it's past our bedtime."

They had got half-way to the car when the police sergeant overtook them.

"Excuse me, sir."

"You are forgiven," said the Saint liberally. "What have you done?"

"How did you happen to be here, sir?"

"Me? I just happened to see the fire from the main road, so I beetled over to have a look at it."

"I see." The sergeant wrote busily in his note-book. "Anything else, sir?"

The Saint's hesitation was imperceptible. Undoubtedly there had been various things else, but it would have been very complicated to go into them. And when Simon Templar had got the scent of mystery in his nostrils, the last thing he wanted was to have the police blundering along the same keen trail—at least not before he had given a good deal of thought to the pros and cons.

"No," he said innocently. "Except that this bloke Kennet seemed to be still in the house, so I just had a dart at fishing him out. He wouldn't be any relation of the MP by any chance, would he?"

"His son, I believe, sir, from what I've heard in the village. Staying with Mr Fairweather for the weekend. He must have been suffocated in his sleep, pore devil—let's hope 'e was, anyway. It'll cause a bit of a stir, all right."

"I shouldn't be surprised," said the Saint thoughtfully.

The sergeant nodded sagely, no doubt squandering a moment on the satisfactory vision of his own name in the headlines. Then he returned to business.

"I'd better just have your name and address, sir, in case you're wanted for the inquest."

Simon felt in his pocket, produced a card, scribbled on it, and handed it over.

"That's where I'll be staying for the next few days." He started to move on, and then turned back. "By the way, who was that other fellow—the bloke who looks as if he'd been chopped out of a small piece of cuff?"

"You mean Mr Luker, sir?" He often comes down and stays with Mr Fairweather. He's a financier, or something like that, I believe."

"A financier, is he?" said the Saint slowly. "What fun!"

He walked on and climbed into the car with a new load of tangled thoughts. The engine started with a low whirr, and they drove back along the drive and slid round the corner into the road.

Presently the Saint said, inconsequentially, "Next time I go to a fire I'm going to wear some old clothes."

"You're better off than I am," said Patricia. "You've got some other things left. Lady Sangore and Valerie Woodchester between them have just about wrecked my suitcases. Lady Sangore practically told me that all my undies were immoral, but it didn't stop her helping herself to all she wanted. You know the sort. A pillar of the British Empire, and underpays her maids."

"I know," said the Saint feelingly. "What about the Woodchester girl?"

"Lady Valerie Woodchester, to be exact. All I know about her is that she picked all my most expensive things and didn't miss once."

"Did either of them tell you how the fire started?"

She shook her head.

"They didn't know. It's an old house, but it had modern automatic fire alarms. All they could tell me was that the alarms went off and everyone came tumbling out of bed. There seems to have been a good deal of confusion. Lady Sangore put the whole thing down to the Communists—but then, if she drops a stitch when she's knitting, she puts it down to the Communists. Valerie Woodchester was very peeved because the young Guardsman insisted on rescuing her without giving her time to put on a dressing gown. That's all I got out of her."

"Did you talk to anyone else?"

"Well, that man you were talking to—"

"Luker?"

"Yes. He said he thought it must have been a short circuit in the lighting system. But I couldn't pay much attention while you were in there. You know. I was too busy worrying about whether you were enjoying yourself."

The Saint chuckled absently.

"It was a bit dull at times," he said.

He drove on slowly. His smile faded, and a faint ridge of concentration formed between his brows. It was an insignificant betrayal of what was going on in his mind, for the truth was that he was thinking harder than he had done for a long time.

Patricia watched him without interrupting. She had that rare gift in a woman, the ability to leave a man to his silence, and she knew that the Saint would talk when he was ready. But there was nothing to stop her own thoughts. He had told her nothing, but in a puzzled bewildered way she knew that he had something startling to tell. The Saint when on the trail of trouble had something vivid and dynamic and transfiguring about him, as unmistakable as the quivering transformation of a hunting dog that has caught a new hot scent. Patricia knew all the signs. But now, with no idea of the reason for them, they gave her the eerie feeling of watching a dog bristling before an apparently empty room.

"Which only shows you that you never know," said the Saint presently, as if she should have known everything.

She knew that she would have to draw him out warily.

"They didn't seem to be a very brilliant crowd," she said. "I didn't seem to be able to get much more sense out of them than you could."

"I was afraid you wouldn't," he admitted. "Oh, no, they're not brilliant. But very respectable. In fact, just about what you'd expect to find at a place like that at the weekend. Lady Sangore, the typical army officer's wife, with her husband the typical army officer. Lady Valerie Woodchester, the bright young Society floozie, of the fearfully county huntin'-shootin'-an'-fishin' Woodchesters. Captain Whoosis of the Buffoon Guards, her dashing male equivalent, probably a nephew or something like that of old Sangore's, invited down to make an eligible partner for Lady Valerie. Comrade Fairweather, the nebulous sort of modern country squire, probably Something in the City in his spare time, and one of the bedrocks of the Conservative Party. A perfectly representative collection of English ladies and gentlemen of what we humorously call the Upper Classes. We can find out a bit more about them tomorrow—Peter's been living here long enough now to be able to dig up some extra dirt from the village, if he doesn't know it already. But I don't think we'll get anything sensational. People like that live in an even deeper rut than the fellow who goes to an office every morning, although they'd have a stroke if you told them. If only they hadn't invited Comrade Luker . . ."

"Who is he?"

Simon drew another cigarette to a bright glow from the stump of the last.

"If he's a financier, as the policeman said, and if he's the bloke I'm thinking of, I've heard of him. Which is more than most people have done. He moves in a mysterious way."

"Where does he move?"

"In the most distinguished international circles. He hobnobs with Foreign Secretaries and ambassadors and Prime Ministers, and calls dictators by their first names. But you never read about him in the newspapers, and there are never any photographers around when he pays his calls. They must like him just because he's such a charming guy. Of course, he's one of the biggest shareholders in the Stelling Steel Works in Germany, and the Siebel Arms Factory in France, and the Wolverhampton Ordnance Company in England, but you couldn't be so nasty as to think that that had anything to do with it. After all, he plays no favourites. In the last Spanish revolution, the rebels were mowing down Loyalists with Stelling machine-guns just as busily as the Government was bopping the rebels with Siebels. It was just about the same in the war between Bolivia and Paraguay, except that the Wolverhampton Ordnance Company was in on that as well—on both sides."

The knot around Patricia's heart seemed to tighten.

"Just one of Nature's altruists," she said mechanically.

"Oh, yes," said the Saint, with a kind of deadly and distant cheerfulness. "You couldn't say he was anything but impartial. For instance, he's one of the directors of the *Voix Populaire*, a French newspaper that spends most of its time howling about the menace of the Italo-German Fascist *entente*, and at the same time he's part owner of the *Deutscher Unterricht*, which lets off periodical blasts about the French threat to German recovery . . . At home, of course, he's a staunch patriot. He's one of the most generous subscribers to the Imperial Defence Society, which spends its time proclaiming that Britain must have bigger and better armaments to protect herself against all the European enemies of peace. In fact, the IDS takes a lot of credit for the latest fifteen-hundred-million-pound rearmament programme which our taxes are now paying for. And naturally it's just an unavoidable coincidence that the Wolverhampton Ordnance Company is now working night and day to carry out its Government contracts."

"I see," said Patricia, but it was only as if a fog had eddied and parted capriciously, giving her a glimpse of something huge and terrifyingly inhuman looming through shifting veils of mist.

Simon Templar's face was as dark and cold as graven copper.

"You know what I mean?" he said. "Kane Luker is probably the only serious rival that our old friend Rayt Marius ever had. And now that Angel Face is no longer with us, Luker stands alone—the king-pin of what somebody once called the Merchants of Death. It's interesting to have met him, because I've often thought that we may have to liquidate him one day."

The mists broke in Patricia's mind, so that for an instant she could see with blinding clarity. It was as if the whole interruption of the fire had never happened, as if she was still sitting in the car as she had been before, listening to the sounds that came over the radio, without a break, just as she had been listening. Their primitive stridency beat in her brain again as if they had never ceased—the lusting clangour of trumpets, the machine-like prattle of the drums. Brass and drums. And men marching like lines of ants, their boots thudding like the tick-tock of some monstrous clock eating up time. Left, right, left. In time with the brass and drums. And in time, too, now, with the hammer and clang of flaring forges and the deep rolling reverberation of stupendous armouries pouring out the iron tools of war—

She looked at the Saint and was aware of him in the midst of all that, like a shining light, a bright sword, a clear note of music in the thunder of brute destruction, following his amazing destiny. But the thunder went on.

She tried to shut it out.

She said, almost desperately, "That fellow who was left—in there. Why did you ask if he was any relation of the MP?"

"It just occurred to me. And he was. That's the funny part. Because unless my memory's all cockeyed, he's a flaming Red and a frightful thorn in the side of his respectable papa. He's the one part of the picture that doesn't fit in. Why should a really outstanding crop of old and young Diehards like that ask anyone like John Kennet down for a weekend?"

"He might have amused them."

"Would you credit them with that much sense of humour?"

"I don't know . . . But if it was a joke, they must be feeling pretty badly about it." She shuddered. "I know it's all over now, but I hope—

hope they were right—that the smoke did put him out before the fire got to him."

Simon's cigarette reddened again for a long moment before he answered.

"If there's one thing I'm sure of, I'm sure that the fire didn't hurt him," he said, and the way he said it stopped her breath for a moment.

The noise in her brain screamed up in an insane cacophony.

"You mean—"

"I mean—murder," said the Saint.

CHAPTER TWO:

HOW LADY VALERIE COMPLAINED ABOUT HEROES AND MR FAIRWEATHER DROPPED HIS HAT

1

"Seeing that time is flying," said Peter Quentin, "and since you have to attend an inquest this morning, I suppose you could use some extra nourishment."

"How right you are," said the Saint. "Some people have no respect for anything. It's a gloomy thought. Even when you're dead, you're liable to be lugged out of the morgue at the squeak of dawn to have your guts poked over by some revoltingly healthy jury of red-faced yokels."

"I like getting you up early," said Patricia. "It seems to lend a sort of ethereal delicacy to your ideas."

Simon Templar grinned, and watched Peter nipping the caps from a row of bottles of Carlsberg. As a matter of fact it was nearly ten o'clock, and for half an hour after breakfast they had been sitting in the sun on the porch outside Peter's dining-room. Two days had gone by since the fire, and it would have been hard to identify the supremely elegant Saint who sprawled in Peter's most comfortable deck chair with the blistered smoke-blackened scarecrow who had arrived there in the small hours of a certain morning with his grim foreboding.

He took the tall glass that Peter handed him and eyed it appreciatively.

"And while we're soothing our tender nerves with this ambrosia," he said, "I suppose we'd better just run over what we've found out about these people who roast their weekend guests."

"I might have known I should be let in for this," Peter said moodily. "I ought to have known better than to ask you down. This was the most peaceful place in England before you came near it, but wherever you go something unpleasant happens." He lifted his glass and drank. "However, as usual, I've been doing your dirty work. Our local gossip writer has been snooping and eavesdropping and will now present his report—such as it is."

He returned to his chair and lighted a cigarette before he went on.

"As you know, the house that provided the fireworks was called Whiteways. The owner is Mr A. S. Fairweather, a gentleman of wealth who is highly respected in local circles. For fifteen years he warmed a seat in the House of Commons as Conservative MP for Hamborough, and for one year just before he retired he held the job of Secretary of State for War. His abilities must have impressed some people more than they impressed the other members of that Cabinet, because as soon as he retired he was offered a place on the board of the Norfelt Chemical Company, where he has sat ever since. He has a town house in Grosvenor Square, a Rolls-Royce, and he has recently subscribed five hundred pounds towards the restoration of our local parish church—which means that he either has, or has not, a ripe sense of humour."

Down by the bottles, something stirred. It was something that looked rather like a reconstruction of the Piltdown Man might have looked if it had been first badly mauled with a sledgehammer and then encased in a brilliant check suit.

"I know a guy once what has a chemical factory," announced Hoppy Uniatz, with the happy interest of a big-game hunter who hears the conversation veering round to the subject of big game. "He makes a kind of liquor. Just say de woid, an' it's rye or Boigundy wit' all de labels an' everyting." A Thought appeared to strike him in a vital spot. "Say, maybe we got someting, boss. Maybe dis guy Fairwedder is in de same racket."

The Saint sighed.

Between Simon and Peter there was the understanding of men who had fought shoulder to shoulder in many battles. Between Simon and Hoppy Uniatz there was no such bond, since Nature, by some unfortunate oversight, had neglected to provide Mr Uniatz with any more grey matter than was required for the elementary functions of eating, drinking, and handling firearms. He was at once the joy and despair of Simon's life, but his dumb devotion to what he regarded as the positively supernatural genius of the Saint was so wistful that Simon had never had the heart to let him go.

"No, Hoppy," he said. "That stuff only burns your throat. The Norfelt product burns you all over."

"Chees," said Mr Uniatz admiringly. "Where do ya get dis stuff?"

"It's dropped from aeroplanes," explained Peter. "In large containers weighing about six hundred pounds each."

Mr Uniatz looked worried.

"But what happens when dey hit de ground?"

"They break," said Peter. "That's the whole idea. Think it over, Hoppy, while I go on with my gossip column."

He refreshed himself again, and continued.

"Brigadier-General Sir Robert Sangore has stayed with Fairweather before. During his last visit he delivered a stirring address to the Church Lads' Brigade, in which Comrade Fairweather takes a benevolent interest. He warned them particularly against Socialists, Communists, and Pacifists, and told them that the Great War was a glorious spree for everyone who fought in it. He graduated from Sandhurst in the year

Dot, served all over the place, got into the War Office in 1917, and stayed there until 1930, when he retired to become a director of the Wolverhampton Ordnance Company. He is an officer, a gentleman, and a member of the Cavalry Club."

"Lady Valerie Woodchester," said Patricia, "is the spoiled darling of London Society. She uses Mond's Vanishing Cream, Kissabel Lipstick, and Charmante Skin Tonic. She goes to all the right places at all the right times, and she has her photograph in the *Bystander* every week. She has also stolen all my best clothes."

"Don't worry about that, darling," said the Saint reassuringly. "I'll take them off her."

Pat made a face at him.

"That wouldn't surprise me a bit," she said calmly.

"The young hero who rescued Lady Valerie," resumed Peter, when order had been restored, "is Captain Donald Knightley of the Dragoon Guards. He has a fine seat on a horse and a set of membership cards to all the best night clubs. That's all I could find out about him . . . And that only leaves John Kennet, the man who didn't fit in anywhere."

"Yes," said the Saint thoughtfully. "The man who didn't fit in. And he seems to have been the most important one of all."

Patricia made a sharp restless movement.

"Are you sure?" she said, as if she was still fighting against conviction. "After all, if Fairweather has been in Parliament, he may have got friendly with Kennet's father—"

"I wouldn't argue. The old man may be a bit bothered about his aitches now and again, and he may still pretend that he belongs to the Labour Party, but he joined the National Government at the right time so of course all the Duchesses love him because they know his heart must be in the right place. If it had been the old man, it might have been all right. But it wasn't. It was young Kennet. And young Kennet was a Pacifist, an anti-blood-sporter, an anti-Capitalist, an anti-Fascist, and the Lord knows what not, and he once said publicly that his father had proved to be the arch-Judas of the working classes. Well, there may be all sorts of harmless reasons why a fellow like that should have been invited to join that congregation of worshippers of the golden calf, but you must admit that he still looks like the ideal burnt-offering."

There was a silence, in which the only interruption was the sound of Mr Uniatz cautiously uncorking his private bottle of Vat 69, while their thoughts went on.

Peter said, "Yes. But that isn't evidence. You've been very mysterious all this time, but you must have something more definite than that."

"I'll give you four things," said the Saint.

He stood up and leaned against one of the pillars of the porch facing them, very tall and dark and somehow deadly against the sunlit peace of the garden. Their eyes were drawn as if by a magnet.

"One: Kennet's door was locked."

Patricia stared at him.

"So you mentioned," Peter said slowly. "But if everybody who locked a door—"

"I can only think of two kinds of people who'd lock their bedroom doors when they were staying in a private house," said the Saint. "Frightened virgins and—frightened men."

"Maybe he was expecting a call from Lady Valerie," suggested Patricia half-heartedly.

"Maybe he was," agreed the Saint patiently. "But if that made him lock his door, he must have been a very undiscriminating young man. And in any case, that's only half of it. He not only locked his door, but he took the key out of the lock. Now, even assuming that anyone might lock a door, there's only one reason for taking the key out of the lock. And that's when you realise that an expert might be able to turn the key from the outside—in other words when you're really thinking hard along the lines of a pretty determined attempt to get at you."

"He might have been tight when he went to bed," Peter pointed out. "That would account for almost any weird thing he did. And besides that, it might account for him not hearing the fire alarm."

"It might," said the Saint bluntly. "But while you're at it, why don't you think of the other possibility? Suppose he didn't lock the door at all? Suppose somebody else did?"

They were silent again.

"Go on," said Patricia.

Simon looked at her.

"Two: during all the time we were there, did you see any signs of a servant?"

"It might have been their night out."

"Yes. And with a house that size, there must have been several of them. And Fairweather let them all go out together, on a Saturday night, when he had a house full of weekend visitors. And Valerie Woodchester cooked the dinner, and Lady Sangore washed the dishes. Why don't we make up some more brilliant theories? Maybe the servants were all burnt in the fire too, only nobody thought of mentioning it."

Peter sipped his beer abstractedly.

"What else?"

"Three: when we arrived, every door and window that I could see on the ground floor was wide open. Let me try and save your brains some of this fearful strain. Maybe that was because everybody who heard the alarm rushed out through a different window. Or maybe it was because they always went to bed with the ground-floor windows open so that if any burglars wanted to drop in they wouldn't have to break the glass. Of course, that's much more likely than that somebody wanted a good draught to make sure that the fire would burn up nice and fast."

This time there was no comment.

"Point Four," said the Saint quietly, "is only Luker. The man who ties Sangore and Fairweather together. And the man who perfectly represents the kind of bee that Kennet had in his bonnet . . . Do you really think I'm insane, or doesn't it all seem like too many coincidences even to you?"

They didn't answer. Incredulity, a traditional habit of mind, even in spite of the years that they had spent in wild pursuit of the fantastic visions that signposted the Saint's iconoclastic path, struggled desperately against the implications of belief. It would have been so much easier, so much more soothing, to let suspicion be lulled away by the uncritical rationalisations of ingrained convention, when to accept what the Saint argued meant—something so ominous and horrible that the mind instinctively recoiled from dwelling on it . . . But it seemed as if the unclouded sunlight darkened behind the Saint's tall disturbing figure while the echoes of his last words ran on through their protesting brains.

Mr Uniatz removed the neck of the bottle from his mouth with a faint squuck. The intermediate stages of the conversation had left as dim a blur on his consciousness as a discourse on the Quantum Theory would have left on an infants' class in arithmetic, but he had been told to think something over and he had been bravely obeying orders, even though thinking was an activity which always gave him a dull pain behind the eyes.

"Boss," he said, in a sudden wild bulge of inspiration. "I got it. It's some temperance outfit."

Simon blinked at him. There were occasions when the strange processes that went on inside the skull of Mr Uniatz were too occult even for him.

"What is?" he asked fearfully.

"De guys in de aeroplanes."

Simon clutched his head.

"What guys?"

"De guys," explained Mr Uniatz proudly, "who break de bottles of liquor."

2

The inquest was to be held at the Assembly Rooms in Anford, a largish building which served at various times for dances, whist drives, auctions, and a meeting-place for the Boy Scouts. When Simon arrived a small crowd had already started to gather, and three or four policemen were on duty to keep them back. Among the policemen Simon recognised the constable who had taken his arm on the night of the fire. He strolled across to him.

"Hullo, Reginald," he murmured. "What's new?"

"Oh, it's you, sir." The policeman lowered his voice confidentially. "Well, it all seems quite simple now. The pore devil never left 'is bed—'e come down, bed and all, right through into the libry. Shocking sight 'e was, too. But there, he couldn't've felt nothing. He must've bin spiflicated by the smoke before ever the fire reached 'im." He went on looking at the Saint with a certain amount of awe. "I didn't know 'oo you was till after you'd gorn, sir," he said apologetically.

"I'm sorry," said the Saint gravely. "But you can still arrest me if you want to, so there's no harm done."

"Arrest you?" repeated the policeman. "Wot—me?" A beaming grin split his face almost in half. "Why, I've read everythink they ever printed about you, and fair larfed myself sick sometimes, the way you put it over on those Smart Alecs at Scotland Yard. But I never thought I'd 'ave the pleasure of meeting you and not know it—though I did wonder 'ow you knew my name the other night."

"Your name?" said the Saint faintly.

"Yes, sir. Reginald. That was pretty good, that was. But I suppose you've got pretty near the 'ole police force of the country taped, haven't you?"

The Saint swallowed. He searched unavailingly for an adequate reply.

Fortunately his anguished efforts were cut short by the blessed advent of two large cars that rolled up to the steps at the entrance of the building, and a spontaneous movement of the crowd drew the policeman back to his job. The Saint took out his cigarette case with a feeling of precarious relief, and watched the cars disgorge the dignified shapes of Luker, Fairweather, Sir Robert and Lady Sangore, and Lady Valerie Woodchester.

"It must be wonderful to be famous," remarked Peter Quentin reverently.

"Get yourself some reflected glory," said the Saint. "Take Pat inside—I'm going to float around a bit."

He waited while they disappeared, and presently followed them in. Immediately inside the entrance was a fair-sized hall in which a number of people were standing about, conversing in cathedral mutters. There were single doors on each side, and a double pair facing the entrance which opened into the main room where the inquest was to take place. Near these farther doors Lady Valerie was standing alone, waiting, rather impatiently tapping the ground with one trim-shod foot. Simon went over to her.

"Good morning," he said.

She turned languidly and inspected him, one finely arched eyebrow slightly raised. She had lovely eyes, large and dark and sparkling, shaded by very long lashes. Her dark hair gleamed with a warm autumn richness. The poise of her exquisitely modelled head, the angle of her childishly tip-tilted nose, the curl of her pretty lips, proclaimed her utter and profound disinterest in Simon Templar.

"What's happened to Luker and the others?" Simon asked. "I saw them come in with you just now."

"They're in the office talking to the Coroner, if you want them," she said indifferently. Then suddenly she lost some of her indifference. "Are you a reporter?"

"No," said the Saint regretfully. "But I could get you one. May I compliment you on your taste in clothes? I always did like that dress."

He knew the dress very well, since he had helped Patricia to choose it.

Lady Valerie stared at him hard for a moment, and then her expression changed completely. It ceased altogether to be cold and disdainful: her features became animated with eagerness.

"Oh," she said. "How silly of me! Of course I remember you now. You're the hero, aren't you?"

"Am I?

She frowned a little.

"Not that I really hoot a lot about this hero business," she went on. "I daresay it's all very fine for great he-men to go rushing about dripping with sweat and doing noble things, but I think there ought to be special places set apart for them to perform in."

"You were rescued yourself the other night, weren't you?" said the Saint pleasantly.

"Rescued? My good man, I was simply thrown about like an old sack. When the fire alarm went off I didn't realise what it was for a moment, and then when Don Knightley came charging into my room with his hair standing on end and his eyes sticking out and his ears absolutely flapping with the most frightful emotion, I merely thought I was in for a fate worse than death, and believe me I was. I mean, all's fair in love and war and all that sort of thing, but to be heaved up by one arm and one leg and slung over a man's bony shoulder, and then to be galloped about over miles of lawn with your only garment flapping up around your neck . . ."

She seemed to be expecting sympathy.

Simon laughed.

"It must have been rather trying," he admitted. "I haven't seen my rival today, by the way—where is he?"

"He had to go and Change the Guard, or something dreary. But it doesn't matter. It's nice to see *you* again."

She might almost have meant it.

"Next time you want rescuing, you must drop me a line," said the Saint. "I'm told I have a very delicate touch with damsels in distress. Maybe I could give you more satisfaction."

She glanced sideways at him out of the corners of her eyes. Her lips twitched slightly.

"Maybe you could," she said.

"All the same," Simon continued resolutely, "it would have been even more trying if you'd been left in your room, wouldn't it?"

Again her expression changed like magic; in a moment she looked utterly woebegone.

"Yes," she said in a low voice. "Like . . . like John."

She turned wide distressed eyes on him.

"I . . . I can't think what could have happened," she said tremulously. "He . . . he must have heard the alarm, and I . . . I know he wasn't drunk or anything like that. He couldn't have committed suicide, could he? Nobody would commit suicide like . . . like that."

She seemed to be begging him to reassure her that Kennet had not committed suicide; there were actually tears in her eyes. Simon was puzzled.

"No, he didn't commit suicide," he answered. "I'll bet anything on that. But why should you think of it?"

"Well, we did have the most awful row, and . . . and I swore I'd never speak to him again, and he seemed to take it rather to heart. Of course I didn't really mean it, but I was getting awfully fed up with the whole silly business, and he was being terribly stupid and awkward and unreasonable."

"Were you engaged to him, or something like that?"

"Oh, no. Of course, he may have thought . . . But then, nobody takes those things seriously . . . Oh damn! It's all so hopelessly foul and horrible, and all just because of a silly bet."

"So he may have thought you were in love with him. You'd let him think so. Is that it?" Simon persisted.

"Yes, I suppose so, if you put it that way. But what else could I do?"

She stared at him indignantly, as if she were denying a thoroughly unjust accusation.

"I bet you wouldn't see a thousand-guinea fur coat that you were simply aching to have go slipping away just because you couldn't make a bit of an effort with a man," she said vehemently. "And it was in a good cause, too."

The Saint smiled systematically. He still hadn't much idea what she was talking about, but he knew with a tumultuous certainty that he was getting somewhere. Out of all that confusion, something clear and revealing must emerge within another minute or two—if only luck gave him that other minute. He was aware that his pulses were beating a shade faster.

"Was John going to give you a fur coat?" he inquired.

"John? My dear, don't be ridiculous. John would never have given me a fur coat. Why, he never even took me anywhere in a taxi."

She paused.

"He wasn't mean," she added quickly. "You mustn't think that. He was terribly generous, really, even though he didn't have much money. But he used to spend it all on frightfully earnest things, like books and lectures and Brotherhood of Man leagues and all that sort of thing." She shook her head dejectedly. "He used to work so hard and study such a lot and have such impossible ideals, and now . . . If only he'd had a good time first, it wouldn't seem quite so bad somehow," she said chokingly. "But he just wouldn't have a good time. He was much too earnest."

"He probably enjoyed himself in his own way," said the Saint consolingly. "But about this fur coat. Where was that coming from?"

"Oh, that was Mr Fairweather," she answered. "Of course, he's got simply lashings of money; a thousand guineas is simply nothing to him. You see, he thought it would be quite a good thing if John became reconciled with his father and stopped being stupid, and then he thought that if John was engaged to me—only in a sort of unofficial way, of course—I could make him stop being stupid. So he bet me a thousand-guinea fur coat to see if I could do it. So of course I had to try."

"Did you have any luck?"

She shook her head.

"No. He was terribly obstinate and silly. I wanted him to have a good time and forget all his stupid ideas, but he just wouldn't. Instead of enjoying himself like an ordinary person he'd just sit and talk to me for hours, and sometimes he'd bring along a fellow called Windlay that he lived with, and then they'd both talk to me."

"What did they talk about?"

She spread out her hands in a vague gesture.

54

"Politics—you know, *stupid* things. And he used to talk about a thing called the Ring, and Mr Luker, and General Sangore, and even his own father, and say the beastliest things about them. And there were newspapers, and factories, and some people called the Sons of France—"

The Saint was suddenly very rigid.

"What was that again?"

"The Sons of France—or something like that. I don't know what it was all about and I don't care. I know he used to say that he was going to upset everything in a few weeks, and make things uncomfortable for everybody, and I used to tell him not to be so damned selfish, because after all what's the point in upsetting everybody? Live and let live is my motto, and I wouldn't interfere with other people's private affairs if they'll leave mine alone."

The Saint put another cigarette between his lips and steadied his hands round his lighter.

"Have you any idea what he was going to do that was going to upset everybody so much?" he asked.

The girl shrugged her slim shoulders.

"I don't know—He had a lot of papers that he was going to publish and prove something. And just a week or two ago he was frightfully excited about some photographs that he'd got hold of. I don't know what they were, but both he and Windlay were frightfully worked up about it. But what does it matter, anyway?"

3

Simon Templar filled his lungs with smoke and let it out again in a trailing streamer that flowed with the unbroken evenness of a deep river. The shock that had brought him to conscious immobility had passed, letting the tenseness ebb out of his muscles to leave his natural lazy imperturbability apparently unchanged. But under his effortless and unruffled poise his brain was thrumming like an intoxicated dynamo.

He had fished for clues and he had brought them up in a pail. It didn't matter for the moment how they fitted together. Luker and the Arms Ring; Sangore, formerly of the War Office, now a director of the Wolverharnpton Ordnance Company; Fairweather, sometime Secretary for War, now on the board of Norfelt Chemicals; Kennet the Pacifist, the groping crusader. Papers, exposes, photographs. And the Sons of France. Whichever way you spilled them, they fell into some sort of pattern. The drums he had heard such a short while ago thundered in the Saint's temples; the blaring brass shrieked in his ears. He felt as if he were standing on the brink of a breathless precipice, watching the boiling of a hideously parturient abyss. The keen clear zenithal winds of destiny fanned through his hair.

He was conscious, in a curiously distant way, that the girl was still talking.

"I never used to listen very hard—I was too busy trying to think of ways to stop them. If I hadn't stopped them, they'd have gone on all night. So when I'd had enough of politics I'd say something like 'Let's go to the Berkeley and have a drink,' and then they'd both start talking about the snobbishness of big hotels, and how bad drink was for me, and I didn't mind that nearly so much, because I quite like talking about hotels and drink."

The Saint brought himself back to her with a deliberate effort. He could think afterwards; now, precious time was flying, and the inquest was already late. He could have no more than a few seconds to take advantage of what Providence had thrown into his lap.

He said, "But if Kennet hated Luker and Sangore so much, what made him come down here for the weekend?"

"I did. I thought that if he could come down here and see what they were really like, he might have given up his stupid ideas. And I knew they were going to offer him an awfully good job. Algy told me so."

"Who?"

"Algy. Algy Fairweather. Of *course* you know."

"Of course," said the Saint humbly. "And didn't Kennet appreciate it?"

"No. That's what made me so furious. When we got here he told me he was glad they wanted to see him, because he wanted to see them too, and instead of them giving him a job he was going to see that theirs were made so uncomfortable that they'd be glad to give them up. So I told him I thought he was a silly, stupid, narrow-minded, bigoted halfwit, and a crashing bore as well, and . . . and we parted. After dinner he went into the library to talk to them, and I went to the movies with Don Knightley, and I never saw John again." She gazed at the Saint appealingly. "D-do you really think it was my fault that all this happened?"

He considered her without smiling.

"I think you deserve a damned good hiding for leading Kennet up the garden," he said dispassionately. "And if I were Windlay I'd see that you got one."

She pouted. She seemed to be more disappointed that he could think of her like that than seriously annoyed by what he had said. And then, quite unanswerably, a gleeful little twinkle came into her eyes that made her look momentarily like a mischievous and very attractive child.

"You wouldn't say that if you knew Windlay," she giggled. "He's a very pale and skinny young man with glasses."

Simon gave up the struggle. Actually he felt a colder anger against the men who had used the girl as their tool. The possibility that she might have been something more than an unsuspecting instrument was one which he discarded almost at once. She had already told him far too much. And her mind, whatever its obvious failings, could never have worked that way.

"Where did Kennet and Windlay live?" he asked flatly.

"Oh, miles from anywhere, out in Notting Hill, in an awful place called Balaclava Mansions."

"Notting Hill isn't miles from anywhere," said the Saint. "The trouble with you is that you've never heard of any place outside the West End. You've got a brain: Why don't you get reckless and try using it?"

She sighed.

"My God," she said. "Now you're going to come over all earnest on me. You think I ought to have a good hiding for the way I treated Johnny. I suppose my intentions weren't serious enough. I oughtn't to have pretended something I didn't mean. Is that it?"

"More or less," he said bluntly.

He wondered what excuse she was going to make for herself.

She didn't make any excuse. She laughed.

"You have the nerve to stand there, in your beautiful clothes, with your dark hair and dashing blue eyes, and tell me that," she said startlingly. "I bet you've made love to heaps of women yourself, hundreds of times, and never meant a word of it."

The Saint stared at her. For a moment he was completely and irrevocably taken aback.

In that moment his first hasty estimate of her underwent a surprising reversal, although it made no difference to his belief in her innocence. But it gave him an insight into her mind which he had not been expecting. She might be feather-rained and spoiled, but she had something more in her head than he had credited her with. For the first time he found himself appreciating her.

"You win, darling," he said. The turn of his lips became impish. "Only I always mean it a little."

Then one of the side doors opened and he saw Lady Sangore surge out like a full-rigged ship putting out from harbour. Behind her, in a straggling flotilla, came Sir Robert, Kane Luker, and Mr Fairweather. Fairweather, peering round, caught sight of a ruddy-faced walrus-moustached man who looked like a builder's foreman dressed up in his Sunday suit, who got up from the bench where he had been sitting as the party emerged. They shook hands, and Fairweather spoke to him for a moment before he shepherded him into the office which they had just left and came puttering back to rejoin the wake of the fleet. Simon noted the incident as he watched the armada catch sight of Lady Valerie and set a course for her.

"My dear, I'm so sorry we've been such a long time," said Lady Sangore, as she hove to. "All this bother only makes everything to much worse."

She conveyed the impression that a fire in which somebody was burnt to death would not be nearly so distressing if it were not for the subsequent inconvenience which she personally had to suffer.

"I hope you haven't been too bored, my dear," said Fairweather, puffing through into the foreground.

Lady Valerie smiled.

"Oh, no," she said. "I've been very well looked after. You haven't forgotten the hero of the evening, have you?"

Fairweather blinked at the Saint.

"Of course—the gentleman who made that magnificent attempt to rescue poor old Kennet. I ought to have got in touch with you before, but . . . um, I'm sure you'll forgive us, everything has been so disorganised . . ." He shuffled his feet uneasily. "At any rate, it's a great relief to see that you don't look much the worse for your adventure."

The Saint smiled—and to anyone who knew him well, that smile would have seemed curiously like the smile on the face of a certain celebrated tiger.

He had been amazingly lucky. The return of Luker and Company had been delayed just long enough for him to coax out of Lady Valerie the whole incalculably important story which she had to tell; their reintroduction couldn't have been more desirably timed if he had arranged it himself. He could look for no more information, but he already had enough to keep his mind occupied for some time. Meanwhile, he could contribute something of his own which might add helpfully to the general embarrassment. He was only waiting for his chance.

"I come from a long line of salamanders," he said cheerfully. "Wasn't that Kennet's father I saw you speaking to just now?"

"Er . . . yes. I've known him for a long time, of course."

"This inquest isn't being heard in camera by any chance, is it?"

"Er . . . no. Why should it be?"

"It seems to involve rather a lot of private interviews."

"Um." Fairweather looked even more uncomfortable. He seemed to inflate himself determinedly. "I fear I have never had any experience of these things. But of course it's the Coroner's job to save as much of the Court's time as possible."

Simon toyed gently with his cigarette.

"Lady Valerie and I were just talking it over," he said. "She seemed to have an idea that Kennet might have committed suicide."

"Suicide?" boomed General Sangore with gruff authority. "No, no, my dear fellow, that wouldn't do at all. We can't possibly have any sort of scandal. Think what it would mean to the poor chap's father. No. Accidental death is the verdict, eh?"

He spoke as if the matter was all arranged. Fairweather supported him.

"That's the only possible verdict," he said. "We've got to avoid any silly gossip. You know what these beastly newspapers are like—they'd give anything for the chance to make a sensation out of a case like this. Luckily the Coroner is a sensible man. He won't stand any nonsense."

"Isn't that splendid?" said the Saint.

They all looked at him at once with a new intentness. The edge in his voice was as fine as a razor, but it cut through the threads of their complacency in a way that left them clammily suspended in an uncharted void. Before that, disarmed by his appearance and accent, they had taken him for granted as a slightly unusual member of a familiar species—their own species. Now they stared at him suspiciously, as they might have stared at an intruding foreigner.

"Are we to understand that you would disagree with that verdict, Mr Templar?" Luker inquired suavely.

He was the only one who had remained immune to that involuntary stiffening. But he had had a chance to measure the Saint before—when, for one intangible moment, they had crossed swords in the garden during the fire.

Simon's gaze sought him out with a sparkle of wicked sapphire.

"Simon Templar is the full name," he said deliberately. "While you were finding out who I was, you should have talked to one of the policemen. He could have refreshed your memory. When you've read about me in the papers, I've usually been called the Saint."

He might have dropped a bomb under their feet with a short fuse sizzling. There were times when the effects of revealing his identity gave him an indescribable delight, and this was one of them.

Lady Valerie Woodchester let out a little squeal. Lady Sangore's mouth opened, and then closed like a trap. The General's florid face added a tint of bright magenta to its varied hues. Fairweather dropped his hat, and it settled on the floor with an ear-splitting *ploff*. Only Luker remained motionless, with his dark sunken eyes riveted on the Saint . . .

And the Saint went on smiling.

There was a general eddy towards the entrance of the courtroom, and a red-faced constable took up his position beside the doors and began to intone self-consciously from a tattered piece of paper.

"Oyez! Oyez! Oyez! All manner of persons having anything to do at this court, before the King's Coroner for this county, touching the death of John Kennet, draw near and give your attendance, and if anyone can give evidence on behalf of our Sovereign Lord the King, when, how, and by what means John Kennet came to his death, let him come forward and he shall be heard, and you good men of this county summoned to appear here this day to enquire for our Sovereign Lord the King, when, how, and by what means John Kennet came to his death, answer to your names as they shall be called, every man at first call, on the pains and penalties that may fail thereon. God save the King!"

4

The courtroom was not crowded, in perceptible contrast with the encouraging throng of gapers that Simon, had seen outside, so that he knew at once that some steps must have been taken to discourage the influx of the vulgar mob. Those of the public who had been able to gain admittance were accommodated in rows of hard wooden chairs set across the room with an aisle down the centre. Simon located Peter and Patricia among them, but he took a seat by himself on the other side of the gangway. His eyes met Patricia's for a moment of elusive mockery, and then went on to take in the rest of his bearings.

The first two rows on the right were occupied by the party from Whiteways, the Sangores, Luker, Fairweather, and Lady Valerie, mingled with a few other people of the same obvious class who all seemed to know each other. They had an air of being apart from the remainder of the public, among them, but not of them, a small party of gentlefolk, self-contained and self-sufficient, only vaguely conscious that there were other people present.

The first two rows on the left had been reserved for the Press, and there was not a vacant chair among them. In front of them, and at right angles to the general public, sat the Coroner's jury, five good men of the county and two women. There was an attitude of respectful decorum about them, as if they had been in church. The Saint sized them up as being a representative panel of local shop-keepers. Only one of them was markedly different from the others—a little black-bearded man who seemed to resent being in court at all.

The Coroner was a well-fed, well-scrubbed looking man with close-cropped grey hair and a close-cropped grey moustache. He wore a dark suit, with a stiff white collar and a blue bow tie with small white spots on it. While the jury was being sworn, he shuffled over a small batch of papers on his table, which occupied the centre of a dais at the very end of the room.

When the jury were seated again, he cleared his throat noisily and addressed them.

"We are here to inquire into the circumstances attending the death of the late John Kennet. It is your duty to listen carefully to the evidence which will be put before you, and to return a verdict in accordance with that evidence. The facts concerning which evidence will be given as follows. On the night of the seventeenth, the house known as Whiteways, the property of Mr Fairweather, was burnt to the ground. Various people were in the house when the fire started, including Mr Fairweather himself, General Sir Robert Sangore and Lady Sangore, Mr Kane Luker, Lady Valerie Woodchester, Captain Donald Knightley, and the deceased. All of them except Captain Knightley are in court today. They will tell you that after they had left the building they discovered that John Kennet was missing. An attempt to reach his room was unsuccessful owing to the rapid spread of the fire, and on the following day his charred remains were found in the wreckage of the house."

His manner was brusque and important; quite plainly, nobody could tell him anything about how to run an inquest, and equally plainly he regarded a jury as nothing but a necessary evil, to be kept firmly in its place.

"If you wish to do so you are entitled to view the body. Do you wish to view the body?" He paused perhaps long enough to take another breath, and said, "Very well, then. We shall proceed to hear evidence of how the body was found. Call the first witness."

The sergeant standing beside him consulted a list of names and called out, "Theodore Bream."

A man who looked rather like a retired carthorse lumbered up on to the dais, sweating profusely, and took the oath. The Coroner leaned back in his chair and looked him over like a schoolmaster inspecting a new pupil.

"You are the captain of the Anford Fire Brigade?"

"Yessir."

"On the morning of the eighteenth you examined the ruins of Whiteways."

"Yessir."

"What did you find?"

"In the ruins of the library, among a lot of daybree, I found the body of the deceased."

"Did you find anything else?"

"Yessir. I found bits of a burned-up bedstead—coil springs and suchlike."

"What deductions did you make from the position of the body and the burned fragments of the bedstead?"

"Well, sir, I come to the conclusion that they'd dropped through the ceiling from one of the rooms above."

The Coroner rubbed his chin.

"I see. You came to the conclusion that the bed, with the deceased in it, had dropped through the ceiling from one of the rooms above the library when the floor collapsed in the fire."

"Yessir."

"That seems quite plain. Did you find anything to suggest what might have been the cause of the fire?"

"No, sir. It might've bin anything. The place was burned out so bad, there wasn't enough left to show how it started."

The Coroner turned to the jury.

"Have you any questions to ask this witness?"

Hardly giving them any time to answer, he turned again to the sergeant.

"Next witness, please."

"Algernon Sidney Fairweather."

Fairweather went up on to the platform and took the oath. The Coroner's manner became less peremptory. He clearly regarded it as a pleasant relief to be able to examine a witness of his own class.

"You are the owner of Whiteways, Mr Fairweather?"

"I am."

"The deceased was a guest in your house on the night of the seventeenth."

"He was."

"Which room was he occupying?"

"The end bedroom in the west wing, directly above the library."

"So that in the event of the collapse of the floor of his rooms his bed would fall through into the library."

"It would."

The Coroner glanced at the jury triumphantly, as much as to say, "There you are, you see." Then he turned back to Fairweather even more deferentially.

"Would you give us your account of what occurred on the night of the fire, Mr Fairweather?"

Fairweather clasped his hands in front of him, frowning seriously with the expression of a man who is carefully and conscientiously marshalling his memories.

"We had dinner a little early that night—at about seven o'clock—because Captain Knightley and Lady Valerie were going to the cinema. They left immediately after dinner, and shortly afterwards Lady Sangore went to her room to write some letters. The rest of us sat and talked in the library until about half past ten, when Kennet went to bed. That was the last time any of us saw him. At about a quarter past eleven Captain Knightley and Lady Valerie returned, and I should think we stayed up for not more than another quarter of an hour. Then we all went to bed.

"Some time later—I should imagine it was about half past twelve—I was awakened by the clanging of the fire alarms. I put on a pair of trousers and left my room. At once it became obvious to me that the fire was serious. There was a great deal of smoke on the stairs, and from the sound of the flames and the light they gave I could see that the fire must have taken a firm hold on the ground floor.

"You must understand that I had just been suddenly woken up, and I was somewhat bewildered. As I hesitated, I saw Captain Knightley come along the passage carrying Lady Valerie. Then I heard General Sangore's voice outside, shouting 'Hurry up and get out, everybody!' I started to follow Captain Knightley, and I was half-way down the stairs when I met Mr Luker coming up. He said, 'Oh, that's all right—I was afraid you hadn't heard. The others are all out.'"

"And then?"

"I ran out into the garden with him. That's about all I can remember. It all happened so quickly that my recollections are a trifle hazy. I still don't know how we came to forget Kennet until it was too late, but I can only imagine that in the excitement Mr Luker and myself mutually misunderstood each other to have accounted for the people we had not seen. It was a tragic mistake which has haunted me ever since."

The Coroner wagged his head sympathetically, as if he could feel everything that Fairweather must have suffered.

"I'm sure that we all appreciate your feelings," he said. He turned to the papers on his table, and went on, as though apologising for bringing back any more painful memories: "Have you any idea as to how the fire could have started?"

"None. It may have been a faulty piece of electric wiring, or a cigarette end carelessly dropped somewhere. It must have been something like that."

"Thank you, Mr Fairweather," said the Coroner. "Next witness, please."

There was an interruption. Before the sergeant could call out the next name, the little black-bearded juryman opened his mouth.

" 'Arf a mo," he said. "I've got some questions I'd like to ask."

The Coroner stared at him as if he had been guilty of some indecency. He seemed to find it extraordinary that a member of the jury should wish to ask a question.

The little juryman returned his stare defiantly. He had the air of Ajax defying the lightning.

"And what is your question?" asked the Coroner, in a supercilious patronising tone.

"Didn't the witness 'ave no servants?"

"Er . . . several," Fairweather said mildly. "But I had given them all leave to attend a dance in Reading, and they did not get back until the fire was practically over. The only one left was my chauffeur, who lives in the lodge, about three hundred yards away from the main building."

"Didn't nobody try to put the fire out?"

"It was hardly possible. It spread too rapidly, and we had nothing to tackle it with."

"Thank you," said the Coroner. "Next witness, please."

He contrived to be mildly apologetic and contemptuously crushing at the same time. He seemed to apologise to Fairweather for the trouble and distress he had been caused in answering two altogether ridiculous and irrelevant questions, and simultaneously to point out the little juryman as a pest and a nuisance who would be well advised to shut up and behave himself.

"Kane Luker," called the sergeant.

Luker gave his evidence in a quiet precise voice. He had been sitting up reading when he heard the fire alarm. He left his room and went downstairs, where he discovered that the fire appeared to have started in the library, but it was already too fierce for him to be able to get near it. He opened the front door, and while he was doing so Sir Robert and Lady Sangore came downstairs. He told them to get outside and shout up at the bedroom windows. He started to go down to the lodge to telephone for the Fire Brigade. He met the chauffeur on the way and sent him back to make the call, and himself returned to the house. As he reached it, Knightley carried Lady Valerie out. He went in and started to climb the stairs, where he met Fairweather. He was sure that everyone must have heard the alarms.

"I said, 'Do you know if the others are all out?' and I thought he gave some affirmative answer. It's only since then that I've realised that he must have missed my first words, and thought that I said, 'The others are all out.' But I agree with him that it will be hard for us to forgive ourselves for the tragic results of our misunderstanding."

"I don't think that any blame can be attached to you," observed the Coroner benignly. "All of us have made similar mistakes even in normal circumstances, and in a moment of excitement like that they are still more understandable. The tragic results of the mistake were due to a combination of causes for which you and Mr Fairweather can scarcely be held responsible."

He turned pointedly and challengingly towards the jury.

"Any questions?" he barked.

He seemed to be daring them to ask any questions.

"Yus," said the black-bearded little man.

The Coroner discovered him again with fresh evidence of distaste. His brows drew together ominously, as if it had just occurred to him to wonder who had been responsible for including such an impossible person in the quorum, and as if he was making a mental note to issue a severe reprimand to the party concerned. He tapped impatiently on the table with his fingertips.

"Well?"

"I suppose you all 'ad wine with your dinner, and when you went into the libry you 'ad more drinks," said the little juryman. " 'Ow many drinks did you 'ave and 'ow many did Mr Kennet 'ave?"

Luker shrugged.

"Some of us had a little wine with dinner, certainly, and after dinner there was whisky and soda in the library. I can't say exactly how much we had, but it was certainly a very moderate amount."

"Kennet wasn't drunk, was 'e?"

"Certainly not."

"Then why didn't 'e 'ear the alarm?"

Luker looked appealingly at the Coroner, who said, "That is hardly a question which the witness can be expected to answer."

He looked at the jury as if inviting them to dissociate themselves from their one discreditable member, and the foreman, a smeary individual with a lock of hair plastered down over his forehead, said ingratiatingly, "He might've been a heavy sleeper."

"From the evidence, it seems to be the only reasonable explanation," said the Coroner firmly. "Thank you, Mr Luker."

General Sangore and his wife briefly corroborated what had been told before. They had been wakened by the fire alarms, they left the house, and it was not until later that they realised that Kennet was missing. Lady Valerie gave evidence of being rescued by Captain Knightley, and of being the first to notice that Kennet was not outside. The chauffeur gave evidence of having met Luker on the drive, and of having gone back to call the Fire Brigade. He had had a lot of difficulty in getting through, and consequently had been detained too long to see much of what went on at the house.

None of these witnesses were questioned. The black-bearded juryman, temporarily discouraged, had relapsed into frustrated scowling.

The Coroner shuffled his papers again with an air of returning equanimity. No doubt he was feeling that he had now got the situation well in hand.

"Next witness, please."

"Simon Templar," called the sergeant.

CHAPTER THREE:

HOW SIMON TEMPLAR DROVE TO LONDON AND GENERAL SANGORE EXPERIENCED AN IMPEDIMENT IN HIS SPEECH

1

There was a stir of excitement in the Press seats as Simon Templar walked up on to the platform and took the oath. Even if the party from Whiteways had failed to recognise his name, there was no such obtuseness among the reporters. The Saint had provided them with too many good stories in the past for them to forget him, and their air of professional boredom gave way to a sudden and unexpected alertness. A subdued hum of speculation swept over them, and spread to one or two other parts of the room where the name had also revived recollections. The black-bearded little juryman sat forward and stared.

While Simon was taking the oath, he noticed that the Coroner was pouring intently over a scrap of paper which had somehow come into his hands. When he raised his eyes from it, they came to rest on the Saint with a new wariness. He folded the note and tucked it away in his breast pocket without shifting his gaze, and his manner became very brisk again.

"I understand, Mr Templar, that you arrived on the scene of the fire sometime after it had started."

"I have no idea," said the Saint carefully. "I only saw it a very short time before I got there. And I was there in time to hear Lady Valerie say that Kennet was missing."

The Coroner rubbed his chin. He seemed to be weighing his words with particular circumspection.

"Then you went into the house to try to get him out."

"Yes."

"In what condition was the house when you entered it? I mean, how far had the fire progressed?"

"The whole place was blazing," Simon answered. "It was worst in the part which I now gather was called the west wing. There was fire in the hall, and the stairs had begun to burn. Part of the passage I had to go down to reach Kennet's room was also alight."

"I take it that with all that fire there would be a great deal of smoke and fumes."

"There was quite a bit."

"I understand that you were quite . . . er . . . groggy when you came out."

"Only for a moment. It passed off very quickly."

"But I take it that if you had stayed in the house any longer than you did, you would inevitably have been overcome by the smoke and fumes and lost consciousness."

"I suppose so, eventually."

"To look at you, Mr Templar, one would certainly get the impression that your physical condition was exceptionally good."

"I've always got around all right."

There was a pause. The Coroner turned to the jury.

"Mr Templar modestly tells us that he gets around all right," he stated. "You can see for yourselves that he has the build and bearing of an unusually strong and athletic man. You will therefore agree that his powers of resistance to such things as smoke and fumes are probably higher than the average, and certainly immeasurably greater than those of a slightly-built sedentary type such as the late Mr Kennet, whose constitution I am told was always somewhat delicate. I want you to bear this in mind a little later on."

He turned back to the Saint.

"You appear to have acted with singular courage, Mr Templar," he said. "I'm sure that that is quite obvious to all of us here in spite of the modest way in which you have told your story. I should like to compliment you on your extremely gallant attempt to save this unfortunate young man's life. Next witness, please."

A glint of steel came into the Saint's eyes. He knew that the Coroner had had a good talk with the party from Whiteways, and it had been evident from the start of the proceedings that everything was laid out to lead up to a verdict of accidental death with as little fuss as possible. That was all very well, and the Saint had quite enjoyed himself while he was waiting for his turn. But now he realised that he was not intended to have a turn. His own evidence had been adroitly manoeuvred towards bolstering up the desired verdict, and the Coroner, warned about him in time, was getting rid of him with a pontifical pat on the back before he had a chance to derange the well-oiled machinery. Which was not by any means the Saint's idea.

"Haven't the jury any questions?" he asked breezily.

He turned towards them and looked hard at the black-bearded little man, who was sitting slumped disconsolately in his chair. There was something compelling about his direct gaze.

The black-bearded little man's figure straightened, and an eager light came into his eyes. He rose.

"Yus," he said defiantly. "I've got some questions."

The Coroner's hands tightened together.

"Very well," he snapped. "Go on and ask your questions."

The way in which he spoke explained to the entire audience that the questions could only be a pointless waste of their time as much as his own.

The little man turned to Simon.

"You're the chap they call the Saint, ain't you?" he said. "You've 'ad a lot of experience of crime—murders, and that sort o' thing."

Before Simon could answer, the Coroner intervened.

"Mr Templar's past life, and any nickname by which he may be known to the public, are not subjects which we have to consider at this inquiry. Kindly confine your questions to facts relevant to the case."

There was an awkward pause. The little juryman's attitude was still undaunted, but he didn't seem to know what to say next. He looked about him desperately, as if searching the room for inspiration. Finally he spoke.

"Do you think there was something fishy about this fire?" he demanded.

"Mr Templar's personal opinions are not matters which concern this court," interrupted the Coroner sternly.

The Saint smiled. He looked at the little juryman, and spoke very clearly and distinctly.

"Yes," he said. "I think there were a lot of very fishy things about it."

There was a moment of silence so heavy that it seemed almost solid. And then it broke in a babble of twittering speculation that surged over the room as if a swarm of bees had been turned loose. There was a craning of necks all over the court, a quick rustling of notebooks among the reporters.

Simon stood at his ease, absorbing the pleasant radiations of the sensation he had created. Well, he reflected, he had certainly done it now. He glanced at the rows of seats where the party from Whiteways was sitting. Luker's expression had not changed; he wore his usual cold stony mask. Fairweather looked acutely unhappy; he could not meet the Saint's gaze. The General and Lady Sangore had adopted an indignant pose of having nothing to do with what was going on; they sat as if red-hot pokers had been inserted into their backs and they were pretending not to notice it.

Simon's glance travelled on and found the faces of Peter and Patricia among the scatter of pink blobs that were turned up to him. He held their eyes for a moment with a message of impenitent devilry.

The jury were goggling at him open-mouthed, with the sole exception of the small black-bearded man, who had taken up a Napoleonic posture with his arms proudly folded and a radiance of anarchistic joy on his face. The Coroner had gone slightly purple; he banged on the table in front of him.

"Silence!" he shouted. "Silence, or I'll have the court cleared!"

He turned angrily on Simon.

"We are not interested in your theories, Mr Templar, and you had no right to make such a statement. You will please remember that this is a court of law."

"I'm trying to," said the Saint unflinchingly. "I thought I was summoned here to give evidence. I haven't had the chance to give any yet. I'm not offering theories. I'm trying to draw attention to one or two very curious and even fishy facts which I have not been allowed to mention."

"What are they?" chirped the little juryman exultantly, before the Coroner could speak again.

"For instance," said the Saint, "there is the fact which I noticed, which the lady who was with me noticed, and which even the police who were on the scene must have noticed, that every ground-floor window in sight was open, producing a draught which must have materially helped the growth of the fire."

Fairweather stood up.

"I could have explained that if it had been brought up before," he said. "It is true that most of the windows were probably open. It was a warm evening, and they had been open all day. It has always been the butler's duty to lock up the house before he retires, and it had completely escaped my attention that he was not there to do it that night when we went to bed. He would, of course, have locked up as soon as he came in, but unfortunately the fire started before that."

"Thank you, Mr Fairweather."

The Coroner shifted his papers on his desk again, with two or three aimless jerky movements, as if to gain time to re-establish his domination. Then he leaned back again to put his fingertips together and went on in a more trenchant voice.

"This is a regrettable but instructive example of the danger of jumping to rash conclusions. It is one very good reason why the personal opinions of witnesses are not admissible in evidence. There are some people whose warped minds are prone to place a malicious interpretation on anything of which the true explanation is beyond their limited intelligence. There are also persons whose desire for cheap notoriety leads them to distort and exaggerate without restraint when they find themselves temporarily in the public eye, in the hope of attracting more attention to themselves. It is the duty of a court to protect the reputations of other witnesses, and the open-mindedness of the jury, from the harm which may be done by such irresponsible insinuations . . . In this case, an insignificant fact which is not contested has been brought up with much ado. But so far from supporting the suggestion that there is something 'fishy' involved, to any normal and intelligent person it merely confines the chain of mischances through which the deceased lost his life."

"All right," said the Saint, through his teeth. "Then why was Kennet's door locked?"

The Coroner lost his head for a moment.

"How do you know it was locked?"

"Because I saw it. I got as far as his room, and I could have got him out if I could have got in. But it was locked, and it was too strong to break down. I went back to get an axe, but the floor of the corridor caved in before I could get back."

"Well, supposing his door was locked—what of it?" demanded the Coroner in an exasperated voice. "Why shouldn't he lock his door?"

Simon spoke very gently and evenly.

"I imagine he had every reason for locking it," he replied. "When a man goes to stay in a house full of his bitterest enemies, people whom he's fighting with all the resources at his command, people to whom wholesale slaughter is merely a matter of business, he's a fool if he doesn't lock his door. But it hasn't been proved that he did lock it. I simply said that his door was locked, and I might add that the key was not in it."

"Beg pardon, sir." The captain of the Fire Brigade stood up at the far end of the room. "I found a door key among the daybree in the libry."

There was a hushed pause.

"Exactly," said the Coroner, with sarcastic emphasis. "Kennet locked his door and took out the key. I fail to see any sinister implications in that—in fact, I have frequently done it myself."

"And have you frequently held inquests without bringing any evidence to establish the cause of death?" retorted the Saint recklessly.

For an instant he thought that even he had gone too far. When he thought about it afterwards, in cold blood, the consequences that he had invited with it brought him out in a dank sweat. But at that moment he was too furious to care.

The Coroner had gone white around the nostrils.

"Mr Templar, you will withdraw that remark at once."

"I apologise," said the Saint immediately. It was the only thing to do. "Of course I withdraw it."

"I have seen the body myself," said the Coroner tightly. "And in a straightforward case like this, where there is absolutely no evidence to justify a suspicion of foul play, it is not thought necessary to add to the suffering of the relatives of the deceased by ordering an autopsy."

He moved his hands over his blotter, looking down at them, and then he brought his eyes back to the Saint with grim decisiveness.

"I do not wish to repeat my previous remarks. But I cannot too strongly express the grave view which I take of such wild and unfounded accusations as you have made. I have only refrained from committing you for contempt of court because I prefer not to give you the publicity which you are doubtless seeking. But you had better go back to your seat at once, before I change my mind."

Simon hesitated. Every instinct he had revolted against obedience. But he knew that there was nothing else he could do. He was as helpless as a fly caught in the meshes of a remorseless machine.

He bowed stiffly, and walked down from the dais into the midst of a silence in which the fall of a feather would have sounded deafening.

None of the party from Whiteways even looked at him. But he noticed, with one lonely tingle of hope, that Lady Valerie's eyes were narrowed in an expression of intense concentrated thought. She seemed to be considering astounding possibilities.

The Coroner consulted inaudibly with the police sergeant, and then he cleared his throat again as he had done when the court opened. His well-scoured face wore a more tranquil expression.

"I don't think we need to call any more witnesses," he said.

He went on to give his summing-up to the jury. He pointed out that fires usually started by accident, and usually from the most trivial and unsuspected causes. He drew their attention to the fact that a number of fortuitous circumstances, for none of which Mr Fairweather or his guests were to blame, such as the heavily timbered construction of the house and the pardonably forgotten open windows, had contributed to make the fire far more serious than it might otherwise have been. He reminded them that it was by no means unusual for some people to be such sound sleepers that even an earthquake would not waken them, and that in the haste and stress of an emergency a verbal misunderstanding was even less extraordinary than it was in everyday life. And he urged them to dismiss from their minds altogether the fantastic accusations with which the issue had been confused, and to consider the case solely on the very simple and coherent evidence which had been placed before them.

In twenty minutes the seven jurors, including the black-bearded little man, who looked vaguely disappointed, brought back a verdict of death by misadventure.

2

A hungry pack of reporters fell on the Saint as he left the building. They formed a close circle round him.

"Come on, Saint; give us the story!"

"What's the use?" Simon asked grittily. "You couldn't print it."

"Never mind that—tell us about it."

"Well, what do *you* think?"

One of them pushed his hat on to the back of his head.

"It looks easy enough. Maybe Kennet was dead drunk, but they'd want to keep that dark for the sake of the old man. It doesn't make much difference. It's pretty obvious that the whole lot of them lost their heads and just ran like hares and left him behind, but with a crowd like that it's bound to be hushed up. You couldn't do anything about it. What was the use of asking for trouble?"

For a moment there was sheer homicide in the Saint's eyes. So that was the net result of his desperate fight to block the whitewashing performance that had been put over not only under the very nose of Justice but with its vigorous co-operation. That was the entire product of the risks he had taken and the humiliation to which he had exposed himself—so that even a sensation-loving Press was inclined to regard him as having for once exhibited a somewhat egregious and unsophisticated stupidity.

And then he realised that that must not only be the Press but the general opinion. Whitewashing was understandable, something to whisper and wink knowingly about, but the truth that Simon Templar was convinced of was too much for them to swallow. Retired Generals, great financiers, and ex-Cabinet Ministers couldn't conspire to cover up murder: it was one of those things which simply did not happen.

His flash of rage died in a hopeless weariness.

"Maybe I like trouble," he rasped, and pushed his way out of the group.

He had seen Peter and Patricia coming out. He took their arms, one on each side of him, and led them silently across the road into the pub opposite.

They took their drinks at the bar, and carried them over to a quiet corner by the window. The room was deserted, and for a while nobody broke the silence. Patricia's face was struggling between thunder and tears.

"You were magnificent, boy," she said at last. "I could have murdered that Coroner."

"But what good could you do?" Peter asked helplessly.

Simon took a cigarette and lighted it with tense deliberate fingers. The bitterness had sunk deeper into him, condensing and coalescing into one white-hot drop of searing energy from which the savage power of its combustion was driving with transmuted fierceness through every inch of his being. Perhaps he had failed disastrously in the first round, but he was still on his feet, and the marrow of his bones had turned to iron. His first pull of smoke came back between lips that had settled into a relentless fighting line.

"None," he said curtly. "No good at all. But it had to be tried. And that lets us out. The rest of the argument is a free-for-all with no holds barred."

"What did you tell the reporters?" asked Peter.

"Nothing. They didn't want telling. They told me. As far as they're concerned, it was all just a routine set-up to gloss over the fact that the Whiteways gang were all too busy saving their own skins to worry about anybody else . . . It was instructive, too, now I come to think about it. I was wondering how they'd managed to fix that Coroner—dumb as he was. I think I can see it now. They let him think he was doing just what the reporters thought he was doing, and of course he was obviously the type who could be counted on to stand by the Old School . . . Not that it matters now, anyway. They got their verdict, and the case is officially closed."

"The fireman said that he found the key," Peter observed.

Simon nodded.

"That was the worst mistake I've made so far—I told Luker the key wasn't in the door when I was trying to get a reaction out of him on the night of the fire. If he'd overlooked that, he'd've had plenty of chances to sling it in through a window afterwards. But I don't think even that really made much difference."

Peter raised his tankard again and drank moodily.

Patricia emptied her glass.

She said presently, "I saw you get hold of your girlfriend, but I didn't see you take my clothes off her."

"It was rather a public place," said the Saint. "But she's a nice girl, and never goes out with the same man twice unless he's a millionaire. Or unless a millionaire asks her to. Which is why she was running around with young Kennet. Fairweather was the philanthropist who wanted him led back into the fold, and he was ready to buy a thousand-guinea fur coat to see it done. And Fairweather was the guy who arranged for him to come down for the weekend. I got that much—and more."

The first taut-strung intensity of his manner was passing off, giving way before the slow return of the old exhilarant zest of battle which the other two knew so well. What was past was past, but the fight went on. And he was still in it. He began to feel the familiar tingle of impetuous vitality creeping again along his nerves, and the smoke came again through the first tentative glimmer of a Saintly smile.

"We were right, boys and girl," he said, "our old friends the arms racketeers are on the warpath again. Luker, Fairweather, and Sangore, just as we sorted them out, with Luker pulling the strings and Fairweather and Sangore playing ball. The Sons of France are in it too, though I don't know how. But there's something big blowing up, and you can bet that whatever it is the arms manufacturers are going to end up in the money, even if a few million suckers do get killed in the process. Kennet had a bee about the arms racket; he'd been scratching around after them, and somehow or other he'd got on to something."

"What was it?" asked Patricia.

"I wish I knew. But we'll find out. It was something to do with papers and photographs. Lady Valerie didn't remember. She never paid any attention. The whole thing bored her. But it provides the one thing we didn't have before—the motive. Whatever it was, it was dynamite. It was big enough to mean that Kennet was too dangerous to be allowed to go on living. And he just wasn't smart enough, or tough enough. They got him."

"Somehow," said Peter, "I can't see Fairweather doing a job like that."

"Maybe he didn't. Maybe Sangore didn't, either. But Kennet died—very conveniently. They knew about it. Probably Luker did it himself. I can just see him telling them—'Leave it to me.'"

"He was taking a big risk."

"What risk? It would have been a cinch, except for the pure fluke that I happened to come along. You saw how the inquest went. There were a dozen ways he could have done it. Kennet could have been poisoned, or strangled, or had his throat cut or his skull cracked: almost anything short of chopping him up would have left damned little evidence on a body that had been through a fire like that. He could even have been just knocked out and locked in his room and left there for the fire to do the rest. We'll never know exactly how it was done, and we'll never be able to prove anything now, but I know that they murdered him. And I'm going to carry on from where Kennet left off. You can take your own choice, but I'm in this now—up to the neck."

They sat looking at him, and in their ears echoed the faint trumpets of the forlorn ventures in which they had followed him without question so many times before.

Patricia smiled.

"All right, boy," she said. "I'm with you."

"If he's made up his mind to get murdered, I suppose you can't stop him," Peter said resignedly. "Anyway, if they put him in another fire we shan't have to pay for a cremation. But what does he think he's going to do?"

Simon stood up and looked at the clock on the wall.

"I'm going to London," he said. "I found out from the girlfriend that Kennet lived with another Bolshevik named Windlay, who was in on the party with him. So I'm going to try and get hold of him before anyone else has the same idea. And I've wasted enough time already. If you two want to be useful, you can try and keep tabs on the Whiteways outfit while I'm away. Be good, and I'll call you later."

He waved to them and was gone, in a sudden irresistible urge of action, and the room seemed curiously drab and lifeless after he had gone. They had one more glimpse of him, at the wheel of the Hirondel, as the great car snaked past the window with a spluttering roar of power, and then there was only the fading thunder of his departure.

The Saint drove quickly. When he was in a hurry, speed limits were merely a trivial technicality to him, and he was in a hurry now. He did not like to dwell too much on the thought of how desperate his hurry might really be. His effortless touch threaded the car through winding roads and obstructing traffic with the deftness of an engraver etching an intricate pattern; the rush of the wind beating at his face and shoulders assuaged some of his hunger for primitive violence; the deep-throated drone of the exhaust was an elemental music that matched his mood. The clean-cut activity of driving, the concentration of judgment, and the ceaseless play of fine nerve responses, absorbed the forefront of mechanical consciousness, so that another part of his mind seemed to be set free, untrammelled by dimension, outside of time . . . to roam over the situation as he knew it and to try to probe into the future where it was leading. It was ninety-five miles from Anford to Notting Hill, and the clock on the dashboard told him that he made the distance in one hour and twenty-five minutes, but the ground that his mind covered in the same time would have taken much longer to account for.

The arrival in Notting Hill brought him back to reality. He stopped beside a postman who directed him to Balaclava Mansions, and when he caught sight of the building he was obliged to admit to himself that he might have been unduly harsh with Lady Valerie. It actually did look like an Awful Place, being one of those gloomy and architecturally arid concoctions of sooty stucco to which the London landlord is so congenitally prone to attach the title of "Mansions," presumably in the hope of persuading the miserable tenant that luxury is being poured into his humble lap. Just inside the front door, a number of grubby and almost indecipherable scraps of paper pinned and pasted to the peeling wall gave instructions for locating those of the inhabitants who were still sufficiently optimistic to believe that anyone might have any interest in finding them. From one of those pathetically neglected emblems of stubborn survival, Simon ascertained that John Kennet and Ralph Windlay had been the joint occupants of the rear ground-floor flat on the right.

He went through the cheerless dilapidated hall and raised his hand to knock on the indicated door. And in that position he stopped, with his knuckles poised, for the door was already ajar.

The Saint scarcely paused before he pushed it open with his foot and went in.

"Hullo there," he called, but there was no answer. It did not take him any time to discover why. He had come through into the one all-purpose room of which the habitable part of the flat was composed, and when he saw what was in it he knew that his fear had been justified, that he had indeed wasted too much time. Ralph Windlay was already dead.

3

A bullet fired at close range had helped to shorten his life and had done it without making a great deal of mess. He lay flat on his back hardly a yard inside the doorway, with his arms spread wide and his mouth stupidly open. Lady Valerie's description of him was quite recognisable. He still wore his glasses. He couldn't have been much more than twenty-five, and his pale thin face looked as if it might once have been intellectual. The only mark on it was a black-rimmed hole between the eyes, but his head lay in the middle of a sticky dark red mess on the threadbare carpet, and Simon knew that the back of his skull would not be nice for a squeamish person to look at.

The room had been ransacked. The two divans had been ripped to pieces, and the upholstery of the chairs had been cut open. Cupboards were open, and drawers had been pulled out and left where they fell. A shabby old roll-top desk in one corner looked as if a crowbar had been used on it. The table and the floor were strewn with papers.

Simon saw that much, and then there was a sound of tramping footsteps in the hall. Automatically he pushed the door to behind him, subconsciously thinking that it would only be some other occupants of the building passing through; his brain was too busy with what he was looking at to think very hard. Before he realised his mistake the footsteps were right behind him, and he was seized roughly from behind.

He whirled round with his muscles instantly awake and one fist driving out mechanically as he turned. And then, with some superhuman effort, he checked the blow in mid-flight.

In that delirious instant his brain reversed itself with such fantastic speed that everything else seemed to have a nightmare slowness by comparison. He watched the trajectory of his hand as if from a vast distance, and it was exactly like sitting in a car with catastrophe leaping up ahead, with brakes jammed on to the limit and nothing left to do but to hold on and hope that they would do their work in time. And with a kind of hysterical relief he saw his zooming fist slow up and stop a bare inch from the round face of the man who had grabbed him. For another split second he simply stood blankly staring, and then suddenly he went weak with laughter.

"You shouldn't give me these shocks, Claud," he said. "My nerves aren't what they used to be."

The man on the other side of his fist went on gaping at him, with his baby-blue eyes dilating with a ferment of emotions which whole volumes might be written to describe. And a tinge of royal purple crept into his plump cherubic visage.

The reasons for that regal hue were only distantly connected with the onrush of that pile-driving fist which had been so miraculously held back from its mark. To Chief Inspector Claud Eustace Teal, a man who had never set any exaggerated value on his beauty, a punch on the nose would only have been a more or less unpleasant incident to be endured with fortitude in the execution of his duty, and in that stoical spirit he had in his younger days suffered more drastic forms of assault and battery than that. A punch on the nose, indeed, would have been almost a joyous and desirable experience compared with the spasm of unmitigated woe that speared through Mr Teal's cosmogony when he saw the face of the Saint. It was a pang that summed up, in one poignant instant, all the years through which Chief Inspector Teal had fought his hopelessly losing battle with that elusive buccaneer, all the disappointments and disasters and infuriating bafflements, all the wrath and sarcasm that his efforts had brought down upon him from his superiors, all the impudent mockeries of the Saint himself, the Saint's disrespectful forefinger prodding the rotundity of his stomach and the Assistant Commissioner's acidulated sniff. It was a sharp stab of memory that brought back all the occasions when Mr Teal had seen triumph dangling in front of his nose, only to have it jerked away by invisible strings at the very moment when he thought his hands were closing round it, and with it came a, revival of the barren desolation that followed so many of those episodes, when Mr Teal had felt that he was merely the dumb quarry of an unjust destiny, doomed to be harried through eternity with the stars themselves conspiring against him. And at the same time it was pervaded with the realisation that the identical story was starting all over again.

All these accumulated indignations and despairs drained through Mr Teal's intestines in one corrosive moment of appalling stillness before he finally wrenched a response out of his vocal chords.

"How the hell did you get here?" he glurked.

It was not, perhaps, the most fluent and comprehensive speech that Mr Teal had ever made. But it conveyed, with succinctness which more rounded oratory might well have failed to achieve, the distilled essence of what was seething through the overloaded cauldrons of his mind. Its most serious defect was in the enunciation, which lacked much of that flute-like clarity which is favoured by the cognoscenti of the science of elocution. It sounded, in fact, as if his throat was full of hot porridge.

Simon smiled at him rather thoughtfully. He also had his memories, and the prime deduction which they offered him was that that unexpected intrusion of Chief Inspector Teal, at that particular moment of all moments, was definitely an added complication in an affair that was already complicated enough. But the sublimely bantering slant of his brows never wavered.

"I might ask you the same," he murmured, "But I see that your feet are looking as flat as ever, so I suppose you're still wearing them down."

The detective's face, under his staid bowler hat, remained a glaring purple, but his inflated china-blue eyes were receding fractionally.

"I noticed your car outside," he said.

He was a liar. He had seen it, but not noticed it. That shining cream-and-red monster was something that it would have been almost impossible to overlook in any landscape, but Mr Teal's thoughts had been far away from any subject so disturbing as the Saint. They had simply been moving in a fool's paradise where detectives from Scotland Yard were allowed to plod along investigating ordinary crimes committed by ordinary criminals, without even a hint of such fantastic freaks as Simon Templar to mar the serenity of their dutiful labours. But Mr Teal had to say something like that to try and recover the majestic dominance from which in the agony of the moment he had so ruinously lapsed.

The Saint dissected his effort with a sardonically generous tolerance that made the detective's collar feel as if it were shrinking into his neck like a garrotte.

"Of course, Claud," he said mildly, "Of course you did. I was forgetting what a sleuth you were. And while we're on the subject of sleuthing, I must say that you seem to have arrived in the nick of time. I don't know whether you've noticed it yet, but there's a dead man on the floor behind me. Without pretending to your encyclopedic knowledge of crime, I should say that he appears to have been murdered."

"That's right," Teal said raspingly. "And I should say that I knew who did it."

The Saint raised his eyebrows.

"I don't want to seem unduly sensitive," he remarked, "but there's something about your tone of voice that makes me feel uncomfortable. Can you by any chance be suggesting—"

"We'll see about that," Teal retorted. He stepped aside out of the doorway. "Search him!" he barked.

Behind him, a lanky uniformed sergeant unfolded himself into full view. Somewhat apprehensively, he stepped up to the Saint and went over his coat pockets. He took out a platinum cigarette case, a wallet, an automatic lighter, and a fountain pen, and an expression of outraged astonishment came over his face.

" 'Ere," he said suspiciously. "What've you done with that gun?"

"What gun?" asked the Saint puzzledly. "You don't think I'd carry a gun in a suit like this, do you? I've got too much respect for my tailor. Anderson would be horrified, and Sheppard would probably throw a fit."

"Search his hip pockets, you fool," snarled Mr Teal. "And under his armpits. That's where he's most likely to have it."

"And don't tickle," said the Saint severely. "It makes me go all girlish."

Breathing heavily, the sergeant searched as instructed and continued to find nothing.

Simon lowered his arms.

"After which little formality," he said amiably, "let us get back to business. As I was tactfully trying to mention, Claud, there seems to be a sort of corpse lying about on the floor. Do you think we ought to do something about it, or shall we shove it into the bathroom and pretend we haven't seen it?"

Chief Inspector Teal's lower jaw moved in a ponderous surge like the first lurch of the pistons of a locomotive getting under way, as he dislodged a forgotten bolus of chewing gum from behind his wisdom teeth. The purple tinge was dying out of his face, allowing it to revert a little closer to its normal chubby pink. The negative results of the sergeant's search had almost thrown him back on his heels, but the shock had something homeopathic in its effect. It had jarred him into taking one wild superhuman clutch at the vanishing tail of his self-control, and now he found himself clinging on to it with the frenzied fervour of a man who has inadvertently taken hold of the steering end of a starving alligator.

Behind him, while the search was proceeding, a number of other persons had sidled cautiously into the room—a melancholy plain-clothes sergeant, a bald-headed man with a camera, a small sandy man with a black bag, a constable in uniform. To the experienced eye, they identified themselves as the members of a CID murder squad as unmistakably as if they had been labelled.

Simon had watched their entrance with interest. He was doing some rapid reconstruction of his own. Teal's advent had been far too flabbergastingly apt to be pure coincidence, and the presence of that compact covey of supporters was extra confirmation of the fact. Even Chief Inspectors didn't go forth with a retinue of that kind unless they were on a particular and major assignment. And Simon located the origin of the assignment a moment later, in the shape of a fat blowzy woman with stringy grey hair who was hovering nervously in the least exposed part of the background.

Teal turned and looked for her.

"Have you seen this man before?" he demanded. She gulped.

"N-no. But I bet 'e done it, just the sime. 'E looks just like one o' them narsty Capitalists as pore Mr Windlay was always talkin' abaht."

Simon's gaze rested on her.

"Do you live in these parts?" he inquired politely.

She bridled.

"This 'ere is my property, young man, so you mind yer tongue. I come 'ere every week to collect the rent, not that I 'aven't wasted me time coining 'ere the larst two weeks."

"You came here today and found the body?"

"Yes, I did."

"How long ago was that?"

"Not 'arf an hour ago, it wasn't. You oughter know."

"And then you went straight out for the police, I suppose."

"I went an' phoned Scotland Yard, that's wot I done knowing as it's their business to catch murderers, an' a good thing too. They got you, all right."

"You didn't scream or anything?" Simon asked interestedly.

The woman snorted.

"Wot, me? Me scream an' 'ave all the neighbours in, an' get me 'ouse a bad nime? Not likely. This is a respectable place, this is, or it was before you came to it." A twinge of grief shot through her suety frame and made it quiver. "An' now ooze going ter pie me rent, that's wot I wanter know."

The Saint extracted a cigarette from his case. The minor details of the situation were satisfactorily cleared up—the remarkably prompt arrival of the CID combined with the absence of a crowd outside. The fact that that exceptional conjunction of circumstances had resulted in his present predicament unfortunately remained unaltered, but it was some consolation to know that his first wild surmise was wrong, and that Teal hadn't been led there in some fantastic way on a definite search for him. It made the odds look rather more encouraging.

"Madam," he said helpfully, "I should think you might do rather well for a while by inviting the public to drop in and charging them sixpence admission. X marks the spot where the body was found, and they can see the original pool of blood on the mat. With Inspector Teal's bowler hat on the mantelpiece in a glass case, and a plaster cast of his tummy in the hall—"

Mr Teal thrust himself sizzlingly forward. He signed to his plain-clothes sergeant.

"Take her outside and get her statement," he gritted.

Then he turned back to the Saint. His eyelids drooped as he fought frantically to maintain some vestige of the pose of somnolent boredom which had been his lifelong defence against all calamities.

"And while that's being done, I'd like to hear what you've got to say."

"Say?" repeated the Saint vaguely. He searched for his lighter. "Why, Claud, I can only say that it all looks most mysterious. But I'm sure it'll all turn out all right. With that brilliant detective genius of yours—"

"Never mind that," Teal said pungently. "I want to hear what you've got to say for yourself. I came here and found you standing over the body."

The Saint shrugged.

"Exactly," he said.

"What do you mean—'exactly'?"

Mr Teal's voice was not quite so monotonous as he wanted it to be. It tended to slide off its notes into a kind of squawk. But that was something that the Saint's ineffable sangfroid always did to him. It was something that always brought Mr Teal to the verge of an apoplectic seizure.

"What do you mean?" he squawked.

"My dear ass," said the Saint patiently, in the manner of one who explains a simple point to a small and dull-witted child, "you said it yourself. You came in and found me standing over the body. You know perfectly well that when I murder people you never come in and find me standing over the body. Now, do you?"

Mr Teal's eyes boggled in spite of the effort he made to control them. The hot porridge came back into his larynx.

"Are you trying to tell me you're in the clear because I came in and found you bending over the body?" he yawped. "Well, this is once when you're wrong! Perhaps I haven't done it before. But I've done it now. I've got you, Saint." The superb, delirious conviction grew upon him. "This is the one time you've made a mistake, and I've got you." Chief Inspector Teal drew himself up in the full pride of his magnificent climatic moment. "Simon Templar, I shall take you into custody on a charge of—"

"Wait a minute," said the Saint quietly.

The porridge bubbled underneath Teal's collar stud.

"What for?" he exploded.

"Because," said the Saint kindly, "in spite of all the rude ideas you've got about me, Claud, I like you. And it hurts me to see you going off like a damp squib. Didn't you hear the landlady say that she found the body half an hour ago?"

"Well?"

"Well, I should think we could safely give her the full half-hour—she could hardly have got to a telephone and got you here with all your stooges in much less than that. And we've been talking for some minutes already. And if I murdered this body, you must give me a few minutes to spare at the other end. Let's be very conservative and say that I could have murdered him forty minutes ago." Simon consulted his watch. "Well, it's now exactly a quarter to three."

"Are you starting to give me another of your alibis?"

"I am," said the Saint. "Because at twelve minutes past one I left the Golden Fleece in Anford, which is ninety-five miles from here. Quite a number of the natives and several disinterested visitors can vouch for that—including a member of the local police whose name, believe it or not, is Reginald. And I know I'm the hell of a driver, but even I can't drive ninety-five miles in fifty-three minutes over the antediluvian cart tracks that pass for roads in this country."

Over Chief Inspector Teal's ruddy features smeared the same expression that must have passed over the face of Sisyphus when, having at last heaved his rock to the very top of the hill, it turned round and rolled back again to the bottom. In it was the same chaotic blend of dismay, despair, agonised weariness, and sickening Incredulity.

He knew that the Saint must be telling the truth. He didn't have to take a step to verify it, although that would be done later as a matter of strict routine. But the Saint had never wasted time on an alibi that couldn't be checked to the last comma. How it was done, Teal never knew; if he had been a superstitious man he would have suspected witchcraft. But it was done, and had been done before, too often for him not to recognise every brush-stroke of the technique. And once again he knew that his insane triumph had been premature—that the Saint was slipping through his fingers for what seemed like the ten thousandth time . . .

He bent his pathetically weary eyes on the body again, as if that at least might take pity on him and provide him with the inspiration for a comeback. And a sudden flare of breathless realisation went through him.

"Look!" he almost yelped.

The Saint looked.

"Messy sort of business, isn't it?" he said chattily. "Some of these hoodlums have no respect for the furniture. There ought to be a correspondence course in Good Manners for Murderers—"

"That blood," Teal said incoherently, "It's drying . . ."

He went down clumsily on his knees beside the body, fumbled over it, and peered at the stain on the carpet. Then he got slowly to his feet, and his hot resentful eyes burned on the Saint with a feverish light.

"This man has been dead for three to six hours," he said. "You could have gone to Anford and back in that time!"

"I'm sorry," said the Saint regretfully.

"What for?"

Teal's voice was a hoarse bark.

Simon smiled.

"Because I spent all the morning in Anford."

"What were you doing there?"

"I was at an inquest."

"Whose inquest?"

"Some poor blighter by the name of John Kennet."

"Do you mean the Foreign Secretary's son—the man who was killed in that country house fire?" Teal asked sharply.

Simon regarded him benevolently.

"How you do keep up with the news, Claud," he murmured admiringly. "Sometimes I feel quite hopeful about you. It's not often, but it's so cheering when it happens. A kind of warm glow comes over me—"

"What were you doing at that inquest?" Teal said torridly.

The Saint moved his hands.

"Giving evidence. I was the hero of the proceedings, so I got nicely chewed up by the Coroner for a reward. You'll read all about it in the evening papers. I hate to disappoint you, dear old weasel, but I'm afraid I've been pretty well in the public eye since about half past ten."

Simon struck his lighter and made the delayed kindling of his cigarette.

"So with one thing and another, Claud," he said, "I'm afraid you're going to have to let me go."

Chief Inspector Teal barred his way. The leaden bitterness of defeat was curdling in his stomach, but there was a sultry smoulder in his eyes that was more relentless and dangerous than his first unimpeded blaze of wrath. He might have suffered ten thousand failures, but he had never given up. And now there was a grim lourd determination in him that tightened his teeth crushingly on his battered scrap of spearmint.

"You still haven't told me what you're doing here," he said stolidly.

Simon Templar trickled smoke through momentarily sober lips.

"I came to see Windlay," he said. "I wanted to see him before somebody else did. Only I was too late. You can believe it or not as you like. But the late John Kennet shared this place with him."

The detective's eyes went curiously opaque. He stood with a wooden stillness.

"What was the verdict at this inquest?"

"Accidental death."

"Do you think there was anything wrong with that?"

Simon's glance travelled again over the disordered room.

"Someone seems to have been looking for something," he said aimlessly. "I wonder if he found what he was after?"

Casually, as if performing some quite idle action, he leaned forward and picked up a crumpled sheet of newspaper from the litter scattered over the floor. It was a French newspaper, five days old, and a passage in it had been heavily marked out in blue pencil.

"Well, well, well," he said. "Listen, Claud. What do you make of this? *'We should like your readers to ask themselves where this criminal association calling itself the Sons of France obtains its funds and the store of arms which Colonel Marteau has so often boasted that he has hidden away for the day when they will be needed. And we ask our readers, how long will they tolerate the existence of this terrorist organisation in their midst?'*"

He picked up a second scrap of paper from the floor. Again there was a blue-pencilled paragraph.

"*M. Roquambert, in a vitriolic speech to the Chamber of Deputies last night, urged on the Government the necessity for a greatly increased expenditure on armaments, 'Are we,' he demanded, 'to suffer the Boche to batter once more on the gates of Paris?'*" Simon let the cuttings flutter out of his fingers. "I seem to remember that Comrade Roquambert is one of the heads of the Sons of France," he said. "Doesn't that interest you?"

"What was wrong with that verdict?" Teal repeated.

The Saint looked at him, and for once there was no mockery in his eyes.

"I think it would be a good idea if you started investigating two murders instead of one," he said.

4

Which was undoubtedly a highly effective and dramatic exit line, Simon reflected, as the Hirondel roared westwards again towards Anford, but how wise it had been was another matter. It had been rather a case of meeting trouble half-way and taking the first smack at it. In the course of his inquiries, Teal would inevitably have discovered that Kennet had shared the flat with Windlay, and Simon knew only too well how the detective's mind would have worked on from there directly the inquest headlines hit the stands. The Saint had had no option about taking the bull by the horns, but he wondered now whether he might have achieved the same result without saying quite so much. Chief Inspector Teal's officially hidebound intelligence might sift slowly, but it sifted with a dour and dogged thoroughness . . . Simon realised at the same time that if he had an adequate alibi for the period during which Windlay might have been killed, Luker and his satellites had an alibi that was absolutely identical—it gave him an insight into the efficiency of the machinery that he had tampered with which was distinctly sobering, and he had plenty to think about on the return journey.

Patricia was waiting for him when he stopped the car on Peter's drive. He picked her up and kissed her.

"You look good enough to eat," he said. "And that reminds me, I haven't had any lunch. Where are the troops?"

"Peter's keeping an eye on your menagerie," she told him. "I came back and sent Hoppy over to keep him company. They're all at the Golden Fleece, and when Peter last phoned, Hoppy was just starting on his second bottle of whisky. Did you find Windlay?"

"I found him," said the Saint stonily. "But not soon enough."

In the kitchen, over a plate of cold beef and a tankard of ale, he told her the story in curt dispassionate sentences that brought it all into her mind as vividly as if she had been there herself.

"It only means that you were right, darling," he concluded. "Kennet had something that was big enough to commit murder for. There wasn't any accidental death hokum about Windlay. Somebody knocked on the door and gave him the works the minute he opened it. And the whole flat was torn into small pieces. It must have gone on while we were all footling about at that inquest acquiring beautiful alibis—these ungodly are professionals!"

"But did they find what they were looking for?"

"I wish I knew. But there's a hell of a good chance that they didn't, since they made a mess like that. I wish I knew exactly what the prize was. It seems to me that it must have been a fair-sized dossier—something that wouldn't be too easy to hide. And unless Kennet was a certifiable lunatic he wouldn't have brought that to Whiteways without leaving a duplicate somewhere. Hence the battle of Balaclava Mansions." He pushed his plate away and scowled at it. "If only that damned girl could remember a bit more of the things Kennet told her! He must have spouted like a fountain, and she simply didn't listen."

"Why don't you see her again?" suggested Patricia. "You might be able to jog her memory, or something. Anyway, you'd have a good time trying."

Simon looked up at her from under impenitently slanting brows.

"Are you insinuating that a man of my unparalleled purity—"

"You'll have to hurry if you want to catch her today," Patricia said practically. "Peter found out from one of the chauffeurs that they're starting back to London at five-thirty."

The Saint looked up restlessly.

"I think I'd better amble over," he said.

Again the Hirondel roared over the Anford road, and a few minutes later it swung in to a grinding stop in the small courtyard of the Golden Fleece. As Simon stopped the engine and hitched his long legs over the side, he glanced around for a glimpse of his confederates. The maternal laws of England being what they were, Hoppy must have been torn away from his second bottle about three hours ago, and it would be another half-hour before he would be allowed to return to it. Simon scanned the landscape for some likely place where the thirsty vigil might have been spent, and he became totteringly transfixed as his eyes settled on the window of an establishment on the opposite side of the road, next to the Assembly Rooms, over which ran the legend: Ye Village Goodie Shoppe.

Peter Quentin was stoically reading a magazine, but on the other side of the table, bulging over the top of a chocolate éclair, the frog-like eyes of Mr Uniatz ogled Simon through the plate glass with an indescribable expression of anguish and reproach that made the Saint turn hastily into the hotel entrance with his bones melting with helpless laughter.

The first person he saw was Valerie Woodchester herself. She was sitting alone on the arm of a chair in the lounge, smoking a cigarette and swinging one shapely leg disconsolately, but at the sight of him her face brightened.

"Oh, hullo," she said. "What's the matter?"

"Some things are too holy to talk about," said the Saint, sinking on to the chair opposite. "Never mind. Perhaps you can bring me back to earth. Are you always being left alone?"

"The others are upstairs having a business conference or something." She studied him with fresh and candid interest "Where have you been all the afternoon? You simply seem to vanish off the face of the globe. I was afraid I should have to go back to town without seeing you again."

"Then why go back to town?" he asked. "You could come over and join us at Peter Quentin's. There's a spare bed and a dartboard and plenty to drink, and we could see lots more of each other."

For a moment she looked a little hesitant. Then she shook her head quite decidedly.

"I couldn't do that. After all, two's company and all that sort of thing, you know, and anyhow I don't think it would be good for you to see much more of me than you did when we first met." A little smile touched her lips and gleamed in her dark eyes. "Besides, I'm quite sure Algy Fairweather wouldn't like it. He's been warning me against you. For some reason or other he doesn't seem to approve of you an awful lot."

"You amaze me," said the Saint solemnly. "But does it matter whether Comrade Fairweather approves or not?"

"Well," she said, "a girl has to struggle along somehow, and Comrade Fairweather is a great help. I mean, if he has a man coming to dinner, for instance, and he doesn't want him to concentrate too hard on business, he asks me along and pays me for it. And then I probably have to have a new dress as well, because of course you can't stop a businessman concentrating in an old piece of sackcloth, and I never seem to have any new clothes when I need them."

"In other words, you're his tame vamp, I take it."

She opened her eyes wide at him.

"Do you think I'm tame?"

The Saint surveyed her appraisingly. Again he experienced the bafflement of trying to probe beyond that pert childish beauty.

"Maybe not so tame," he corrected himself. "And what would be your fee for dining with a gent if it meant earning Comrade Fairweather's disapproval? For instance, what about having dinner with me on Thursday?"

She didn't answer for a moment. She sat looking downwards, swinging her leg idly, apparently absorbed in the movement of her foot.

Then she looked up at him and smiled.

"You've fallen for me in quite a big way, haven't you?" she said, a little ironically. "I mean, inviting me to dinner and offering to pay me for it."

"I fell passionately in love with you the moment I saw you," Simon declared shamelessly.

She nodded.

"I know. I couldn't help noticing the eager way you dashed off this morning when you thought you'd got all the information you could out of me. I mean, it was all too terribly romantic for anything."

"The audience made me bashful," said the Saint. "Now if only we'd been alone—"

Her dark eyes were mocking.

"Well!" she said, "I don't mean that I couldn't put up with having dinner with you if you paid me for it. After all, I've got to have dinner somewhere, and I've been out with a lot of people who weren't nearly so good-looking as you are even if they weren't nearly so bashful either. Algy used to pay me twenty guineas for entertaining his important clients."

"That must have helped to make things bearable," said the Saint in some awe.

"Of course," she went on innocently, "I should expect you to pay me a bit more than that, because after all I'm only a defenceless girl, and I know you must have some horrible motive for wanting me to have dinner with you."

Simon raised his eyebrows.

"You shock me," he said. "What horrible motive could I have for asking you out to dinner? I promise that you'll be as safe with me as you would be with your old Aunt Agatha."

She sighed.

"I know. That's just what I mean. If your eyes were foaming with unholy desire, or anything like that, I probably shouldn't charge you anything at all. After all, brief life is here our portion, and all that sort of thing, and a spot of unholy desire from the right sort of person and in the right sort of way—well, you see what I mean, don't you? But as things are, I don't think I could possibly let you off with less than fifty guineas."

Simon leaned towards her.

"You know," he said earnestly, "there's something about you— an innocence, a freshness, a sort of girlish appeal that attracts me irresistibly. You're so . . . so ingenuous and uncalculating. Will a cheque do, or shall you want it in cash?"

"Damn," she said in dismay. "I believe you'd have paid a hundred if I'd asked for it . . . Oh, well, I suppose a bargain's a bargain. A cheque will do."

The Saint grinned.

"Thursday, then, at eight o'clock. At the Berkeley, and since this is a business deal, I shall expect you to be punctual. The fee will go down one guinea for every minute I'm kept waiting."

She tossed the stub of her cigarette across the room into the empty fireplace.

"Well, now we've finished talking about business can't we enjoy ourselves? I was hoping we'd have a chance after the inquest, but Algy hustled me away before I could even look round. They were all as mad as hornets, and I can't blame them. After all, you did make rather an ass of yourself, didn't you?"

"Do you really think I was just playing the fool?" he asked curiously.

"I mean trying to make out that Johnny had been murdered and Algy set fire to the house and so on. I mean, it was all so ridiculous, wasn't it?"

This time he knew beyond doubt that her artlessness was not so naïve as it seemed. Her chatter was just a little too quick; besides, he had seen her face at one stage of the inquest.

He paused to consider his reply for a moment. If she knew what he had seen in London, it might startle something out of her. He felt that the move must be made with a fine hand.

He had no chance to make it in that way.

There was a sound of footsteps descending the stairs, reaching the entrance of the lounge. Simon glanced over his shoulder, and then rose leisurely to his feet.

"It's time you were getting ready, my dear—"

Fairweather's thinly jovial voice broke off sharply as he realised that there was someone else in the room. He stared at the Saint for a long moment, with his mouth slightly open, while his fat face turned into the likeness of a piece of lard. And then, without any acknowledgement of recognition, he turned deliberately to Lady Valerie.

"We shouldn't have left you so long," he said. "I hope you haven't been annoyed."

"Of course she's been annoyed!" General Sangore's stormy voice burst out without the subtlety of Fairweather's snub. "It's an insult for that feller to speak to any decent person after his behaviour this morning. Damned if I know what he meant by it, anyway."

Simon put his hands in his pockets and relaxed against a cabinet full of hideous porcelain.

"What I meant by it was that I believe Kennet was murdered," he said good-humouredly. "Now have I made myself quite clear?"

The General glared at him from under his bushy eyebrows. He seemed to expect Simon to melt like wax.

"By Gad, sir," he said truculently, "you're . . . you're a bounder! I've never heard such bad form in my life!"

"You mean that if it was murder you'd rather have it hushed up, don't you?" Simon said gently. "You didn't murder him yourself by any chance, did you?"

Sangore's complexion went a rich mottled puce. He tried to speak, but there seemed to be an obstruction in his throat.

Simon went on talking, and his voice was cool and pitiless.

"Last year, when there was a strike at the Pyrford Aviation Works, which is a subsidiary of the Wolverhampton Ordnance Company, you stated publicly that the ringleaders ought to be put up against a wall and shot. This year, addressing the Easter Rally of the Imperial Defence Society, you said, 'A great deal of nonsense has been talked about the horrors of war.' If you would have liked to kill half a dozen men for the sake of dividends, and if you think it's a great deal of nonsense to object to people being massacred in millions, I can't help feeling that you qualify as a good suspect. What do you think?"

What General Sangore thought could only be inferred; he was still choking impotently.

Lady Sangore came to his rescue. Her face had gone from white to scarlet, and her small eyes were glittering with vindictive passion.

"The man's a cad," she proclaimed tremblingly. "It's no use wasting words on him. He . . . he simply isn't a sahib!"

She appeared to be slightly appalled by her temerity, as if she had pronounced the ultimate unspeakable condemnation.

"It's . . . it's an outrage!" spluttered Fairweather. "The man is a well-known criminal. We're only lowering ourselves—"

The Saint's cold blue eyes picked him up like an insect on a pin.

"Let me see," he said. "I seem to remember that you played a forward part in getting a change made in the workings of the National Defence Contribution a few years ago. The sales talk was that the tax on excess profits would have paralysed business enterprise, but the truth is that it would have hit hardest against the firms that were booming on the strength of the new rearmament programme—of which, I think, Norfelt Chemicals was by no means the smallest. And you recently stated before a Royal Commission that 'The armament industry is one which provides employment for thousands of workers. The fact that its products are open to misuse can no more be held against the industry per se than can the production of drugs which would be poisonous if taken without medical advice.' If those are examples of your logic, I don't see why we shouldn't have you on the suspected list—do you?"

Luker stepped forward.

"Surely, Mr Templar," he remarked urbanely, "you aren't going to leave me out of your interesting summary."

"I can give you some news," he said. "That is, if you haven't heard it already. I spent the afternoon going to London to see if I could catch Ralph Windlay, the man Kennet lived with, before an accident happened to him. I'm sure you'll be cheered to know that everything went off without a hitch, and he was already dead when I got there."

There was a dead silence.

And then Lady Valerie Woodchester was tugging unconsciously at the Saint's arm. Her full lips were quivering, and there was an expression of dazed horror on her face.

"Not Ralph?" she was saying shakily. "No . . . no, he can't have been murdered too!"

The Saint's eyes went to her with an instant's brief compassion.

"I'm afraid so," he said. "Even our Coroner here couldn't make out it was an accident. He was shot right between the eyebrows, and his brains were all over the carpet."

"The use of the word 'too' is interesting." Luker's impassive voice came levelly through the stillness. "If Kennet was murdered, somebody killed him and then set fire to the house. Within a few minutes Mr Templar arrives on the scene. It is he who suggests foul play. Then Kennet's friend Windlay is murdered, and again Mr Templar is first on the scene; again it is he who discovers that there has been foul play. It certainly appears to be a coincidence to which the attention of the police should be called."

Simon's bleak gaze took him up.

"Or you might mention it to the Sons of France," he said.

It was a shot in the dark, but it hit a target somewhere. For the first time since he had known him, Simon saw Luker's graven mask slip for a fraction of a second. For that fleeting micron of time, the Saint saw the stark soul of the man to whom murder meant nothing.

CHAPTER FOUR:

HOW KANE LUKER SPOKE HIS MIND AND HOPPY UNIATZ DID THE BEST HE COULD WITH HIS

1

"I like this place," said Lady Valerie Woodchester, looking smugly around her. "It's one of the few places in London where civilised people can eat civilised food."

The Saint nodded. They had worked their way through three quarters of a menu selected with Simon Templar's own impeccable gastronomic artistry, and served with the deference which waiters always instinctively gave him, and he had watched her personality expand and ripen like an exotic flower coming into bloom. Undoubtedly she did the setting no less justice than it did to her. Her flawless shoulders and deliciously modelled head rose out of a plain but daringly cut evening gown like an orchid rising from a dark stem, with a startling loveliness that turned many envious eyes towards her; she knew it, and she was delighted, like a child who had been taken out on a special treat. A brighter sparkle had crept gradually into her eyes and a faint flush into her cheeks. It was fun, you felt, to be eating a good dinner, and to be in one of the best places among the best people, and to be with a man who was tall and dark and handsome and who could make waiters fuss about obsequiously. Her dazzling flow of gay senseless prattle had given the Saint no need to make trivial conversation while they ate, but now he hardened his heart.

"Yes," he agreed. "The food is good and the atmosphere is right. Also a stitch in time saves embarrassing exposure, and the horse is the noblest of animals. Now you've earned your bread and butter, and you can stop entertaining me. Let's be serious for a minute. Have you seen any of our friends today?"

She didn't answer at once. She was looking down at her plate, drawing, idle patterns with her fork. Her expression had become abstracted; her thoughts seemed to be very far away.

"Yes, I've seen them," she said vaguely.

"And how are they making out?"

She looked at him suddenly straight in the eyes.

"You remember what Luker said at the Golden Fleece? Well, I suppose if I'd got any sense I'd think the same, seeing what a reputation you've got. I suppose you could have got into the house somehow, and killed Johnny, and locked his bedroom door, and started the fire, and got out again, and then come back again and pretended to try and rescue him. And then of course you could easily have gone to London and shot Ralph Windlay."

"Easily," said the Saint. "But you don't believe I did, do you? Or do you?"

"I suppose not," she said. "In a way, I wish you had."

She pushed away her plate, and he offered her his cigarette case.

"Why do you wish I'd killed them? I didn't have any reason to."

"Well, it would have made everything so much easier. Of course, I suppose they'd have had to hang you, but everybody knows you're a criminal so that would have been all right. But then you went and upset it all at the inquest, and you made it sound frightfully convincing to me whatever anybody else thought, only it didn't seem quite real then. I mean, you know, it was all rather like something out of a book.

Blazing Mansion Mystery, and all that sort of thing. I was terribly sorry about it all, in a way, because I was quite fond of Johnny, but I wasn't going to be brokenhearted about it or anything like that. And then when Ralph was killed it wouldn't have made much difference, because he was a nice well-meaning boy but I never thought very much of him. After all, life's too short for one to be getting brokenhearted all the time, isn't it, and I'm sure it gives you circles under your eyes."

"You were too close up against it then to realise it properly," said the Saint shrewdly. "Now you've got away from it, your nerves are going back on you. I'm afraid I sympathise with you. What you need is another drink."

She pushed her glass forward.

"That's exactly what I do need." she said.

He poured her out the last of the wine, and she sipped it and put the glass down again.

"It's not really my nerves," she said, talking very quickly. "We modern girls have nerves of iron, you know, and we only swoon when we think a man needs a little encouragement. The point is, if I'd heard that Johnny had been killed in a railway accident I should have been terribly sorry whenever I thought about it, but I don't suppose I should have thought about it terribly often. You see, that would have been just one of those things that happen, and it would have been all over, and it wouldn't really have been anything to do with me."

"But you invited him down to Whiteways, and that makes it different."

She nodded feverishly.

"Of course, I told you that, didn't I?"

"The idea was that you were to get a fur coat if Johnny could be persuaded to keep his mouth shut," Simon pursued her ruthlessly. "He has been persuaded to keep his mouth shut. Do you get your fur coat?"

Her fingers tightened on the stem of her wine glass. Her face had gone very pale, but her eyes were burning.

"That's a filthy thing to say."

"Murder is a moderately filthy subject," answered the Saint brutally. "You can't play with it and keep your little girlie ribbons clean. Haven't you realised that yet?"

"Yes," she said.

She picked up her glass and drained it at one gulp. Then she sat back and laughed at him with a kind of brittle giddiness.

"Well?" he insisted.

"I'm a nice girl, aren't I?" she chattered. "I do the odd spot of gold-digging here and there, and in my spare time I lure men to their deaths. What would the dear vicar say if he knew?"

"I expect he'd say plenty. But that doesn't seem to matter so much as what you say. Do you enjoy luring men to their deaths?"

"I love it!"

"Then of course you'll be wanting another job soon. Why don't you advertise? There must be plenty of openings if you can produce proof of previous experience."

She sat looking at him and two scalding tears brimmed in her eyes.

"You swine!" she whispered.

"I'm sorry," he said cynically.

"What have you got to talk about anyway? I mean, you think Johnny was murdered. Well, why should you care? You've killed dozens of people yourself, haven't you?"

"Only people who really needed it. You know, there are some people who are vastly improved by death."

"If somebody murdered Johnny, perhaps they thought he needed it," she said. "I daresay the people you killed were pretty poisonous one way or another, but then who isn't? I mean, look at me for instance.

Supposing somebody murdered me. I suppose you'd think that was a damned good job."

"I should think it was a great pity," he said with surprising gentleness. "You see, you poor little idiot, I happen to like you."

"Isn't that thrilling?" she said, and then she suddenly put her face in her hands.

The Saint lighted a cigarette and watched her. She sat quite still, without sobbing. He knew that this was what he had been working for, the success of his relentless drive to break her down, and yet he felt sorry for her. An impulse of tenderness moved him that it was not easy to fight down. But he knew that on this moment might hang things too momentous to be thought about. His brain had to be cold, accurate, making no mistakes, even if he wanted to be kind . . .

"All right," she said huskily. "Damn you."

She put her hands down abruptly and looked at him, dry-eyed.

"But what's the use?" she said. "It's done now, isn't it? I did it. Well, that's all about it. If I were the right sort of girl I suppose I'd go and jump in the river, but I'm not the right sort of girl."

"That wouldn't help anybody very much." His voice was quiet now, understanding, not taunting. "It's done, but we can still do things about it. You can help me. We can go on with what Johnny was doing. But we've got to find out what it was all about. You've got to think. You've got to think back—think very hard. Try to remember what Johnny told you about Luker and Fairweather and Sangore. Try to remember what he'd got that was going to upset them all. You must remember something."

He tried to hammer his words into her brain with all the urgency that was in him, to awaken her with the warmth of his own intense sincerity. She must tell him now if she was to help him at all.

Her eyes stayed on him, and her hands opened and closed again.

She shook her head.

"I don't," she replied. "Really. But . . ."

She stopped, frowning. He held his breath.

"But what?" he prompted.

"Nothing," she said.

Simon turned an ash from his cigarette on to the edge of a plate with infinite restraint. The reaction had emptied him so that he had to make the movement with a deliberate effort.

And a waiter bustled up to the table and asked if they wanted coffee.

Simon felt as if a fire in him had been put out. He felt as if he had been led blindfold to the top of a mountain and then turned back and sent down again without being given a glimpse of the view. While he mechanically gave the order, he wondered, in an insanely cold-blooded sort of way, what would happen if he stood up and shot the waiter through the middle of his crisp complacent shirt-front. Probably it had made no ultimate difference, but it seemed as if that crowning clash of the banal had inscribed an irrevocable epilogue of frustration. The mood that might have meant so much was gone. Nothing would bring it back.

He sat without moving while coffee and balloon glasses were set before them.

Lady Valerie Woodchester stubbed out a half-smoked cigarette and lighted another. She tasted her brandy.

"It's a hard life," she observed moodily. "I suppose if one can't get exactly what one wants, the next best thing is to have bags of money. That's what I'm going to do."

"Who are you going to blackmail?" Simon inquired steadily.

Her eyes widened.

"What do you mean?" she asked in astonishment.

"Just that," he said.

She laughed. Her laughter sounded a trifle false.

She emptied her coffee cup and finished her brandy. She began to be very busy collecting her accoutrements and dabbing powder on her nose.

"You do say the weirdest things," she remarked. "I'm afraid I must go now. Thanks so much for the dinner. It's been a lovely evening— most of it."

"This is rather early for your bedtime, isn't it?" said the Saint slowly. "Don't you feel well, or are you a little bit scared?"

"I'm scared of getting wrinkles," she said. "I always do when I stay up late. And then I have to spend a small fortune to have them taken out, and that doesn't help a bit, what with one thing and another. But a girl's got to keep her looks even if she can't keep anything else, hasn't she?"

She stood up.

The Saint's hands rested on the arms of his chair. A dozen mad and utterly impossible urges coursed through his mind, but he knew that they were all futile. The whole atmosphere of the place, which had brought her once to a brief fascinating ripeness, was arraigned against him.

A lynx-eyed waiter ceremoniously laid a plate with a folded check on it in front of him.

Simon rose to his feet with unalterable grace, and spilled money on to it. He followed her out of the room and out of the hotel, and waited while the commissionaire produced a taxi and placed it before them with the regal gesture of a magician performing a unique and exclusive miracle.

"It's all right," she said. "You needn't bother to see me home."

Through the window of the cab, with the vestige of a sardonic bow, he handed her a sealed envelope.

"You forgot something," he murmured. "That isn't like you, I'm sure."

"Oh, yes," she said. "That."

She took the envelope, glanced at it, and put it in her bag. It didn't seem to interest her particularly.

She held out her hand again. He held it.

"If—" she began, and broke off raggedly.

"If what?" he asked.

She bit her lip.

"No," she said. "It wouldn't do any good. There's always the 'but.'"

"I'll buy it," said the Saint patiently. "What's the answer?"

She smiled at him rather wistfully.

"There isn't any answer. One just thinks, 'If something or other,' and then one thinks, 'But something else,' which makes it impossible," she explained lucidly. "As a matter of fact, I was thinking that you and I would make a marvellous combination."

"And why not?"

She made a little grimace. At that moment, even more inescapably than at any other, she looked as if she was on the point of bursting into tears.

"Oh, go to hell," she said.

Her hand slipped through his fingers, and she sank back into the corner of the cab. It moved away.

Simon Templar stood and watched it until the stream of traffic swallowed it up. And then he said, "Hell and damnation!" with a meticulous clarity which caused the commissionaire to unbend in a glance of entirely misdirected sympathy before he resumed his thaumaturgical production of taxis.

2

After which various things happened that Simon Templar would have been very edified to know about.

Mr Algernon Sidney Fairweather was sitting in the smoke-room of his paralysingly respectable and conservative club, finishing an excellent cigar and enjoying a sedate postprandial brandy and soda and the equally sedate postprandial conversation of an august bishop, a retired ambassador, and a senile and slightly lecherous baronet, when he was summoned to the telephone.

"This is Valerie," said the voice on the wire. "I'm frightfully sorry to bother you and all that, but I rather wanted your advice about something. Do you mind terribly? It's about Johnny."

"What exactly do you want my advice about?" asked Mr Fairweather uncomfortably. "That man Templar hasn't been pestering you again, I hope?"

"No—at least, not exactly," she answered. "I mean, he's quite easy to get on with really, and he simply throws money about, but he does ask rather a lot of questions."

Fairweather cleared his throat.

"The man is becoming a perfect nuisance," he said imperially. "But I think we can deal with him soon enough. I'm glad you told me about it. I'll have a word with the Commissioner of Police in the morning and see that he's taken care of."

"Oh, no, you mustn't do that," she said quickly. "I can take care of myself all right, and it's rather thrilling to be pestered by a famous character like the Saint. That isn't what I rang you up for. What I wanted was to ask your advice about something Johnny left with me."

"Something Kennet left with you?"

"Some papers he gave me to read only a week or two ago—a great thick wad of them."

Mr Fairweather experienced the curious sensation of feeling the walls close in on him, while at the same time the floor and the ceiling began to draw together. Since he was at that moment in a booth which had very little space to spare after enveloping his own ample circumference, the sensation was somewhat horrifying.

It had caught him so completely unprepared that for a few seconds he seemed to have mislaid his voice. A cold perspiration broke out on his forehead. He felt as if he was being suffocated, but he dared not open the door of the booth to let in the air for which his lungs were aching. In fact, he drew it tighter.

"Papers?" he got out hoarsely. "What papers? What were they about?"

"I don't know. Johnny seemed to think they were terribly important, but then, he thought so many things were terribly important that I just couldn't keep track of them all. So I didn't even read them."

The inward rush of the walls slackened for a moment. Mr Fairweather managed to snatch a handful of oxygen into his chest.

"You didn't read them?" he echoed weakly. "Well, I'd better have a look at those papers. It's a good thing you told me about them. I'll come round at once."

"But that wouldn't be any good," she said miserably. "You see, I haven't got the papers now. I don't even know where they are. That's what I wanted your advice about."

The accumulation of see-saw effects was making Mr Fairweather feel slightly seasick. He was very different from the staid and dignified gentleman who had been drinking a sedate brandy and soda only a few thousand years ago. He mopped his brow.

"You haven't got them?" he bleated shrilly. "Then who has got them?"

"Nobody. At least . . . it's frightfully difficult trying to tell you all at once. You see, what happened was something like this. John and I had been having a row—the usual row about you and his father and Mr Luker and all that. I was telling him not to be ridiculous, and he suddenly shoved a great envelope full of papers into my hands and told me to go through them and then say if I still thought he was being ridiculous. Then he stormed out of the place in a fearful rage, and I had lots of things to do, and I couldn't go on carrying a whacking great envelope about with me forever, so I dumped it somewhere and I didn't think any more about it until the other day."

"How do you mean, you *dumped* it?" squealed Fairweather, like a soul in torment. "You must have put it somewhere. Where is it?"

"That's just what I don't know," she said. "Of course, it must be somewhere; I mean, I didn't just drop it over the side of a bus, or anything like that. But I simply can't remember where I had it last. I've got a sort of idea that it might be in the cloakroom at Piccadilly Station, or I may have left it in the cloakroom at the Savoy. In fact, I'm pretty sure I did put it in a cloakroom somewhere."

Fairweather clung to the telephone bracket for support.

"Then you must have a ticket for it," he pointed out, with heart-rending logic. "Why don't you look for the ticket?"

"But I can't," she said plaintively. "It's a terrible bore. You see, if I had a ticket it was probably in my bag, and of course that was lost in the fire with all my other things."

"But—" said Fairweather.

The word 'but' is not commonly used to convey the more cosmic intensities of emotion, but Mr Fairweather's pronunciation imbued it with a depth and colour that can rarely if ever have been achieved before. The exasperation of a reasonable man who finds himself in an unreasonable and chaotic universe, the sharp horror of a prisoner on an excavating party who learns that he has kindly been allowed to dig his own grave, the outraged protest of a mathematician to whom has been demonstrated an insuperable fallacy in his proof that two and two make four—all these several shades of travail were summed up and vivified in Mr Fairweather's glorification of the word 'but.'

"I wondered if it might be a good chance to get Mr Templar to help me," Valerie went on. "I mean, he seems to have quite a crush on me, so he'd probably be glad to do it if I was nice to him, and he must have had loads of experience at ferreting about and detecting things."

"Grrr," said Mr Fairweather.

If possible, he improved on his performance with the word 'but.' This time, in one primitive ululation, he added to his symphonic integration of emotions the despairing dolour of the camel whose backbone is just giving way under the final straw, the shuddering panic of the hunted hyena which feels the tiger's fangs closing on its throat, the pitiful expiring gasp of the goldfish which has just been neatly hooked from its bowl by a hungry cat.

"Of course, I've been cursing myself for not thinking of it before," said Lady Valerie penitently. "I mean, if those papers really were important, I suppose I ought to have said something about them at the inquest. That's where I'd like your advice. Do you think I ought to ring up Scotland Yard and tell them about it?"

Mr Fairweather had no new deeps to plumb. He was a man who had already done all the gamut-running of which he was capable.

"Listen," he said with frightfully muted violence. "You must put that idea out of your head at once. The police have no discretion. Think . . . think of how it might hurt poor Johnny's father. And whatever happens, you mustn't say a word to Templar. You haven't told him about those papers yet, have you?"

"No, not definitely. But you know, I believe he guesses something about them. He's terribly suspicious. Two or three times this evening he asked me if Johnny had ever given me anything to keep for him, or if I knew where Johnny might have kept his private papers. But he can't do anything to me, because I thought I'd better be on the safe side and so I've taken plenty of precautions. You see, Celia Mallard probably knows where I left those papers, and I've written to her about them. She's at Cap d'Ail now, but I'll probably hear from her in a day or two."

"Celia Mallard knows where they are?" moaned Fairweather. "How the devil does she know?"

"'Well, I seem to remember that she was with me when I dumped them, and she's got a perfectly marvellous memory, so she'll probably remember all about it. I told her in my letter that they were worth thousands of pounds, and that the Saint was after them, and so if anything happened to me she was to go straight to the police. That ought to stop the Saint doing anything really awkward, oughtn't it?"

Mr Fairweather's mouth opened. After all his other vicissitudes, he underwent the culminating sensation of having been poured out of a frying pan into an ice-cold bath. The contrast steadied him for a moment, but he shivered.

"I suppose it might," he said. "But what made you say the papers were worth thousands of pounds?"

"I don't know. But I thought, if they really are terribly important, they're bound to be worth a lot of money to somebody, aren't they?" she said reasonably.

"That doesn't follow at all," Fairweather said firmly. "But . . . er . . . you know that I'd see you didn't lose by it, in any case. Now, will you let me know directly when you hear from Celia Mallard, or as soon as you remember what you did with them? And . . . urn . . . well, if it's a matter of money, you did tell me once that you needed a car to go with that fur coat, didn't you?"

"How could you?" she said pathetically. "To talk about that fur coat now, and remind me of poor Johnny . . . Please don't talk to me about it anymore; I don't think I can ever bear to hear it mentioned again. You're making me feel dreadfully morbid, Algy, and I've had such a tiring day. I think I'd better ring off now before I break down altogether. Goodbye."

The receiver clicked.

"Wait a minute," Fairweather said suddenly.

There was no answer.

Lady Valerie Woodchester was walking back across the bright modernistic sitting-room of her tiny apartment on Marsham Street. She fitted a cigarette into a long holder and picked up the drink she had put down when she telephoned. Over the rim of her glass she looked across to a small book-table where there was propped up the cheap unframed photograph of a dark and not unhappily serious young man.

"Poor old Johnny!" she said softly. "It was a lousy trick they played on you, my dear . . ."

Mr Algernon Sidney Fairweather jiggled the receiver hook. He took a coin out of his pocket and poised it over the slot, and then he hesitated, and finally put it back in his pocket. He left the booth and made his way to the bar, where he downed a double brandy with very little dilution of soda. His plump cheeks seemed to have gone flabby, and his hands twitched as they put down the glass.

Twenty minutes later he was waddling jerkily up and down the carpet of a luxurious room overlooking Grosvenor Square, blurting out his story under a coldly observant scrutiny that made him feel somehow like a beetle under a searchlight.

"Do you believe her when she says that she's lost this cloakroom ticket?" Luker asked.

He was as calm as Fairweather was agitated. He sat imperturbably behind the huge carved oak desk where he had been writing when Fairweather blundered in, and toyed with his fountain pen. The expression in his eyes was faintly contemptuous.

"I don't know what to believe," said Fairweather distractedly. "I . . . well, thinking it over, I doubt it. I've had enough dealings with her to know what her methods are, and personally I think she's fishing to see how much we're prepared to pay."

"Or how much Templar is prepared to pay," said Luker phlegmatically. "Did you know that she had dinner with him tonight at the Berkeley?"

Fairweather blinked as if he had been smacked on the nose.

"What?" he yelped. His voice had gone back on him again. "But I particularly told her to have nothing more to do with him!"

"That's probably why she did it," Luker replied unsympathetically. "I had an idea that something like this might happen—that's why I've been having them watched. For all you know, he may have put her up to this."

Fairweather swallowed.

"How much do you think she'll want?"

"I don't know. I don't think I care very much. It doesn't seem to be very important. Money is a very temporary solution—you never know how soon you may have to repeat the dose. This cloakroom story may be a myth from beginning to end. She might easily have these papers in her dressing-table drawer. She might easily have no papers at all. Her attitude is the thing that matters, and with this man Templar in the background it would be unwise to take chances." Luker shrugged. "No, my dear Algy—I'm afraid we shall have to take more permanent steps to deal with both of them."

"W-what sort of steps?" stammered Fairweather feebly. "H-how can we deal with them?"

That seemed to amuse Luker. The ghost of a smile dragged at the corners of his mouth.

"Do you really want to know?" he asked interestedly.

"You mean . . ." Fairweather didn't seem to know how to go on. His collar appeared to be choking him. He tugged at it in spasmodic efforts to loosen it. "I . . . I don't think so," he said. "I . . ."

Luker laughed outright.

"There's a sort of suburban piousness about you and Sangore that verges on the indecent," he remarked. "You're just like a couple of squeamish old maids who hold shares in a brothel. You want your money, but you're determined not to know how it's obtained. If anything unpleasant or drastic has to be done, that's all right with you so long as you don't have to do it yourselves. That's how you felt about getting rid of Kennet. Now it's Templar and Lady Valerie. Well, they've got to be murdered, haven't they?"

Fairweather wriggled, as if his clothes were full of ants. His face was glistening with sweat.

"I . . . Really, I don't—"

"I expect you think I'm excessively vulgar," Luker continued mercilessly. "I've got such a shockingly crude way of putting things, haven't I? I suppose you felt just the same when I offered you a place on the board of Norfelt Chemicals in return for certain items of business when you were Secretary of State for War. That's quite all right, my dear fellow. Go home and have a nice cup of tea and forget about it. There's no need for me to tell you to keep your mouth shut, is there? I know you're a worm, and you know you're a worm, but we won't let anybody else know you're a worm."

Fairweather gobbled.

"Really, Luker," he spluttered indignantly, "I . . . I . . ."

"Oh, go away," said Luker. "I've got work to do."

He spoke without impatience; if his voice carried any particular inflection, it was one of good-humoured tolerance. But there was no further argument. Fairweather went.

Luker remained sitting at the great carved desk after he had gone. Fairweather's emotional antics had made no impression on him at all. He had no illusions about his associates. He had long been familiar with the partiality that politicians, generals, and captains of industry have for squirming out of uncomfortable situations, with an air of being profoundly shocked by what has happened, and leaving somebody else to face the music. But that failing had its own compensation for him. Once started, the more drastic the measures he had to take, the stronger became his hold on them and the more blindly they would have to support him in whatever he did, as his safety became the more necessary to their own safety. The problems that he was considering were purely practical. He sat there, idly turning his fountain pen between his strong square fingers, until he had thought enough, and then he picked up the telephone and began to issue terse incisive orders.

3

"Did you have a nice dinner?" asked Patricia Holm. "And how was the new candidate for your harem?"

Simon Templar peeled off his coat, unbuttoned his shirt to the waist, and deposited himself at a restful angle on the chesterfield under the open windows. Through the curtains came the ceaseless grind of Piccadilly traffic and a stir of sultry air tainted with petrol fumes and grime, too thick and listless to be properly termed a breeze, but in spite of that the spacious apartment in Cornwall House which was the Saint's London headquarters attained an atmosphere of comparative peace and freshness.

"There are mugs of all kinds, but there are very special and superlative mugs who do their mugging in London, and we are it," he said gloomily. "I had a beautiful dinner, thanks. The *truites au bleu* were magnificent, and the *pigeons truffés* in aspic were a dream. The candidate was looking her best, which is pretty good. She went home early. Since then I've been drowning my sorrows at the Café Royal."

Patricia contemplated him discerningly.

"The dinner was beautiful, and the candidate was looking her best, and she went home early," she repeated. "What was the matter with her?"

"She wanted her beauty sleep," said the Saint. "After you with that barley water, Hoppy."

He stretched out a long arm and retrieved the bottle of Scotch from Mr Uniatz's jealous grasp.

"What Hoppy needs is compressed whisky, so he could get a bottle into a wineglass," he commented.

"Was it your scintillating conversation that made her yawn?" inquired Peter Quentin. "Or did she have the wrong kind of ideas about what sort of sleep would be good for her beauty?"

Simon splashed soda into his glass and drank meditatively.

"She's an attractive wench," he said. "I like her. She's so innocent and disarming, and as harmless as a hungry shark. The trouble is that if she's not careful she's going to wake up one day and find herself in a dark alley with her throat cut, and that will be a great pity for anyone with a face and figure like hers."

"Say, where do ya get dat stuff?" demanded Mr Uniatz loudly.

He sat forward on the edge of his chair, his ham-like hands practically obliterating his half-empty glass, with a deep frown corrugating the negligible clearance between his eyebrows and his hair, and his paleolithically rough-cast face chopped into masses of fearsome challenge.

Simon raised his head to stare at him. A criticism like that coming from Mr Uniatz, a man to whom any form of mental exercise was such excruciating torture that he had always been dumb with worship before the Saint's god-like ability to Think, had something awe-inspiring about it that numbed its audience. It was nothing like a rabbit turning round to bare its teeth at a greyhound. It was more like a Storm Trooper turning round and asking Hitler why he didn't stop strutting round and getting wise to himself. For one reeling instant the Saint wondered if history had been made that night, and the whisky which had for years been flowing in gargantuan quantities down Hoppy's asbestos throat had at long last soaked through to some hidden sensitive section of his entrails.

Mr Uniatz reddened bashfully under the stares that impinged upon him. He was unaccustomed to being the focus of so much attention. But he clung valiantly to his point.

"It sounds like a pipe-dream to me, boss," he said.

"Let me get this straight," said the Saint carefully. "I gather that you don't think that Valerie Woodchester runs any risk of getting her throat cut. Is that the idea?"

Mr Uniatz looked about him in dazed perplexity. He seemed to think that everyone had gone mad.

"I dunno, boss," he said, refusing to be sidetracked. "What I wanna know is where do ya get dat stuff?"

"What stuff?" asked Peter faintly.

"De compressed whisky," said Mr Uniatz.

There was a pregnant silence.

The Saint laid his head slowly back on the cushions and closed his eyes.

"Hoppy," he said solemnly, "I love you. When I die, the word 'Uniatz' will be found written on my heart."

"How about if de goil is selling it, boss?" ventured Mr Uniatz, tiptoeing into the dizzy realms of Theory. "Maybe she's in de racket too, woikin' for de chemical factory where dey make it."

Simon passed him the whisky bottle.

"Maybe she is, Hoppy," he said. "It's an idea, anyway. Give yourself some more nourishment while we think it over."

"Didn't you get anything useful out of her?" asked Patricia.

"She held out on me," said the Saint ruefully. "I did my best, but I might have saved myself the trouble. Amazing as it may seem, she wouldn't confide in me. The secrets of her girlish heart are still the secrets of her girlish heart so far as I'm concerned."

Peter clicked his tongue.

"You've met her four times now, and she hasn't confided in you," he said in accents of distress. "You must be losing your touch. They don't usually hold out so long."

"What do you mean by 'they?'" demanded the Saint un-blushingly.

"He means your harem candidates," said Patricia. "The wild flowers that droop shyly at you from the hedges as you pass by. This one must be pretty tough if she still hasn't given way to your manly charms."

Simon reached for a cigarette and flicked his thumbnail thoughtfully over a match.

"She's tough, all right," he said. "But I don't know how tough. She'll need all she's got to sit in on this game. She's sitting in, and I'm still wondering whether she really knows what the stakes are . . . There was one time tonight when I thought we were going to get somewhere, but she closed up again and went home."

"You started to get somewhere, then," said Peter. The Saint nodded.

"Oh, yes, I started. But I didn't finish, so we might just as well forget about it. She knows something, though—I found that out, even if she didn't admit it. But she's going to play her own hand, and so she'll probably get her throat cut, as I was saying. It makes everything very difficult."

He sat up in an access of unruly energy, and his blue eyes went over them with an almost angry light.

"Goddammit," he said quietly, "it's a complete and perfect set-up— with only the foundation missing. I've worked it all out a dozen times since we talked it over at Anford, and I expect you have too. We'll run over it again if you like, and get it all in one piece."

"All right," said Peter. "You run over it. We like hearing you listen to yourself."

"Here it is, then. We've got our friend Luker, the arms wangler. He's on a job. In this case he's in on it with a couple of his stooges named Sangore and Fairweather—two highly esteemed gentlemen with complete faith in their own respectability, but completely under his thumb for any dirty work he wants to put up. Also vaguely related is Lady Valerie, a sort of spare-time *entraîneuse* for Fairweather. Okay. On the other side you have well-meaning but not very agile professional Pacifists Kennet and Windlay. Somehow or other they dig up inside information about the job Luker is on. This is where their lack of agility shows up. They threaten exposure unless Luker drops it. Okay. Luker has no intention of dropping it. The first move is through Fairweather, to put Lady Valerie on to Kennet and see if she can seduce him from his irritating ideals. This fails. Lady Valerie is therefore used for the last time to lure Kennet down to Whiteways for a conference, where he meets with a fortunate accident. The Coroner, a staunch friend of the aristocracy, is probably persuaded that Kennet was caught in a drunken stupor, and keeps the inquest nicely hamstrung to save scandal. Everything goes off smoothly, and meanwhile Windlay is mysteriously murdered, apparently by some prowling thug. Okay again."

"And so soothing," said Peter. "Especially for the corpses."

"Unfortunately this isn't quite the end of it. The ungodly haven't found Kennet's incriminating evidence. Meanwhile Kennet has been partly overcome by Lady Valerie, at least enough to give her a little information about this evidence—either what it is, or where it is, or something. We now come to Lady Valerie's psychology."

"I thought we should come to that eventually," said Patricia.

Simon threw a cushion at her.

"She's not a bad kid, really," he said. "But she likes having a good time, and she has an almost infantile ability to rationalise anything that helps to get her what she thinks is a good time, to her own entire satisfaction. Nor is she anything like so dumb as she tries to make out. When Kennet meets with a highly suspicious accident, and Windlay is just obviously murdered, it wakes her up a bit—possibly with a certain amount of help from my own blundering bluntness. And maybe she even feels a genuine remorse. From the symptoms, I should say she did. She's absent-mindedly gone just a little further than she'd ever gone if she knew exactly what she was doing, and done something really nasty. She also realises that it's given her some sort of hold over Fairweather and the others. But she still doesn't want to confide in me. She's paddling her own canoe. And as far as I can see there are only two ways she can be heading. Either she's got some crazy idea of making amends by carrying on Kennet's work on her own, and taking some wild vengeance on the gang that used her for a cat's-paw; or else she simply means to blackmail them. And I may be daft, but it seems to me that her scheme might very well combine the two."

Peter Quentin got up and refilled his glass. He sat down again and looked at the Saint seriously.

"And she's the only link we've got with what's going on?" he said.

"The one and only. Kennet and Windlay are dead, and we shouldn't get anything out of Luker and Company unless we beat it out of them, which mightn't be so easy as it sounds. Meanwhile we're tied hand and foot. We're just sitting tight and twiddling our thumbs while she's playing her own fool game. What should we do? Use her for bait, and wait until something happens, with the risk of finding her as useful as John Kennet at the end of it? Or start again and try to cut in from another angle?"

"You tell us," said Patricia.

There was a pause in the intermittent glugging which had punctuated the conversation from the corner where Mr Uniatz was marooned with his consoling bottle in the midst of the uncharted wilderness of Thought. Mr Uniatz was no longer clear about why his purely sociable contribution to the pow-wow should have marooned him there, but in his last conscious moment he had been invited to join in thinking about something, and since then he had been submerged in his lonely struggle. Now, coming to the surface like a diver whose mates have suddenly remembered him and pulled him up, the anguished irregularities of his face dissolved into a radiant beam of heaven-sent inspiration.

"I got it, boss!" he announced ecstatically. "What we gotta do wit' dis wren is catch her at de aerodrome before she takes off."

"Before she takes off what?" asked the Saint foggily.

"Before she takes off wit' de compressed whisky." said Mr Uniatz proudly. "De stuff de temperance outfit she's woikin' for t'rows out of de aeroplanes." Mr Uniatz raised his bottle and washed out his throat with enthusiastic lavishness. His eyes glowed with the rapture of achievement. "Chees, boss, why didden we t'ink of dat before? It's in de bag!"

Simon looked at him for a moment, and then he bowed his head in speechless reverence.

And at that instant the telephone bell rang.

The sound jarred into the silence with a shrill unexpectedness that jolted them all into an unnatural stillness. There were many people among the Saint's large acquaintance who might have made a casual call at that hour, and yet for some illogical reason the abrupt summons gave him a queer intuitive tightening in his stomach. Perhaps it was the way his thoughts had been running. He lifted his head and looked at the faces of the others, but they were all expressionless with the same formless foreboding.

Simon picked up the microphone.

"Hullo," he said.

"Is that you, Simon darling?" it answered. "This is Valerie."

A feathery tingle passed up the Saint's spine, and was gone, and with it the tightness in his stomach was gone also. He could not have said exactly how he knew so much. Her voice was quite ordinary, and yet there was an indefinable tension in it that seemed to make everything quite clear. Suddenly his brain seemed to be abnormally cool and translucent.

"Hullo, darling," he said evenly. "And how are you?"

"I'm all right, thanks . . . Listen, Simon—you remember that cloakroom ticket I asked you to keep for me?"

Simon drew at his cigarette.

"Of course," he said without hesitation. "It's quite safe."

"That's good," she said. "You see, I'm afraid I've got to have it back at once. I'm awfully sorry to be such a nuisance, but it's frightfully important. I mean, could you bring it round right away? It's all frightfully thrilling, but I'll tell you all about it when you get here. Can you possibly manage it?"

"Easily," he said. "I was just looking for something useful to do."

"You know where I live, don't you?"

"I should think so. I looked it up in the phone book as soon as I got back to town, and I've just been waiting for an invitation."

"Well, you've got one now. And listen. Nobody must know you're coming to see me. I'll tell you why afterwards."

"No one shall even guess where I've gone," said the Saint, with his eyes on Patricia. "I'll be over in ten minutes."

"Thanks so much, darling," she said. "Do hurry."

"I will."

He laid the microphone gently back on its bracket, and stood up. The dance of his blue eyes was as if he had been asleep all the evening and had just become awake. He had no more doubts or problems. All the dammed-up, in-turned energy with which he had been straining was crystallised suddenly into the clean sharp leap of action. He was smiling.

"Did you get that, souls?" he said.

"She wants to see you," said Patricia. "Am I supposed to get excited?"

"She wants more than that," he said. "She wants a cloakroom ticket which she gave me to keep for her—which she never gave me. She wants it at once, and nobody's to know where I've gone. And somebody was listening on the wire all the time to make sure she said all the right things. So I don't see how I can refuse the date." The Saint's smile was dazzlingly seraphic. "I told you something was bound to happen, and it's starting now!"

4

"Excuse me a minute while I get into my shooting clothes," he said.

He vanished out of the nearest door, but the room had hardly had time to adapt itself to his disappearance when he was back again. The Saint could always make a professional quick-change artist look like an elderly dowager dressing for a state ball, and when he was in a hurry he could do things with clothes that bordered on the miraculous. He came back in a grey lounge suit whose sober hue had no counterpart in the way he wore it, which was with all the peculiarly rakish elegance that was subtly infused into anything he put on. His fresh shirt was buttoned and his tie was tied, and he was feeding a fully charged magazine into the butt of a shining Luger.

"You're not really going, are you?" asked Patricia hopelessly.

She knew when she said it that it was a waste of words, and the scapegrace slant of his brows was sufficient answer.

"Of course not, darling," he said. "These are my new pyjamas."

"But you're doing just what they want you to do!"

"Maybe. But do they know that I know it? I don't think so. That phone call was as straightforward as a baby's prayer—to the guy who was checking up on it. Only Valerie knows that she never gave me a cloakroom ticket, and she knows I know it. She's on the spot in her own flat, and that was the only way she could tip me off and call for help. Do you want me to stay home and knit?"

Patricia stood up. She kissed him.

"Be careful, boy," she said. "You know I look terrible in black."

Peter Quentin finished his drink, and rose. He buttoned his coat with a deep sigh.

"I suppose this is the end of our chance of a night's rest," he said pessimistically. "I ought to have stayed in Anford." He saluted Patricia. "Will you excuse Hoppy and me if we trot along to take care of the dragons while your problem child is striking attitudes in front of the heroine? We don't want anything to happen to him—it would make life so horribly quiet and peaceful."

Simon stopped at the door.

"Just a minute," he said. "There may be policemen and other emissaries of the ungodly prowling around outside. We'd better not take chances. Will you call down to Sam Outrell, Pat, and tell him to meet me in the garage?"

As they rode down in the elevator he felt the springy elation of the moment spreading its intoxication through his muscles. The lucid swiftness of his mind ran on, constructing a clear objective framework of action in which he moved with unhurried precision with each step unerringly laid out a fraction of time before he reached it.

Down in the basement garage Sam Outrell, the janitor, was waiting for him when the elevator doors opened, with a look of placid expectancy on his pleasant bucolic face. He fell in at the Saint's side as Simon walked across to where the Hirondel stood waiting in its private bay.

"Goin' out on business again, sir?" he queried, with the imperturbation of many years of experience of the Saint's unlawful occasions.

"I hope so, Sam." The Saint cocked his legs over the side while Peter and Hoppy climbed into their own seats. "I don't want to stage a big demonstration, but you might just do a quiet job of obstructing if anyone's waiting for us. Take your own heap and follow me up the ramp, and see that you stick tight on my tail. When I wave my hand, swing across the road and stall your engine. I'll only want two or three minutes."

The exhaust purred as he touched the starter. He pulled the Hirondel out to the foot of the ramp and held it there, warming the engine, until he saw Outrell's car behind him. Then he let in the clutch and roared up the slope, with the other car following as if it was nailed to his rear fenders.

At the top he whipped round in a screaming turn out into the narrow street that ran by the back of Cornwall House. There was a taxi parked close by the garage entrance, and a small sports car with a man reading a newspaper in it standing just behind; both of them might have been innocent, but if they were it would do them no harm to be obstructed for a few minutes.

The Saint raised one hand just above his head and made a slight movement.

He heard the squeal of Sam Outrell's brakes behind him, and grinned gently to himself as he locked the wheel for another split-arch turn into Half Moon Street. The snarl of the engine rose briefly, lulled, and then settled into a steady drone as they nosed into Piccadilly, shot across the front of a belated bus, and went humming down the westward slope towards Hyde Park Corner.

Peter Quentin settled deep into his seat and turned to Hoppy.

"I hope your insurance policies are all paid up, Hoppy," he said.

"I ain't never had none," said Mr Uniatz seriously. "I seen guys what try to sell me insurance, but I t'ought dey was all chiselers." He brooded anxiously over the idea. "Do ya t'ink I oughta get me some, boss?"

"I'm afraid it's too late now," said Peter encouragingly. "But perhaps it doesn't matter. You haven't got a lot of wives and things lying around, have you?"

Mr Uniatz scratched his head with a row of worried fingers.

"I dunno, boss," he said shyly. "Every time I get married I am not t'inking about it very much. So I never know if I have got married or not," he said, summarising his problem with a conciseness that could scarcely have been improved upon.

Peter pondered over the exposition until he felt himself getting slightly giddy, when he decided that it would probably be safer to leave it alone. And the Saint spun the wheel again and sent the Hirondel thundering down Grosvenor Place.

"When you two trollops have finished gloating over your sex life," he said, "you'd better try to remember what happens when we get to Marsham Street."

"But we know," said Peter, carefully continuing to refrain from looking at the road. "Don't we, Hoppy? If we ever get there alive, which is very unlikely, we jump about in the foreground and try to attract the bullets while the beauteous heroine swoons into Simon's arms."

Simon squeezed the car through on the wrong side of a crawling taxi which was hogging the centre of the road, and while he was doing it neatly swiped Peter's cigarette with his disengaged hand.

"That's something like the idea; except that as usual you'll be in the background. I'm just building on probabilities, but I think I've got it pretty straight. Two or more of the thugs will be in possession. When I ring the bell, one of them will come to the door. They can't all open it at once, and at least one of them will probably be busy keeping Valerie quiet, and in any case they won't want any noise that they can avoid. Besides, they'll be expecting me to walk in like a blindfolded lamb. Now, I think it can only break two ways. Either the warrior who opens the door will open it straight on to a gun . . ."

He went on, sketching possibilities in crisp comprehensive lines, dictating move and counter-move in quick sinewy sentences that strung the strides of a supreme tactician together into a connected chain on which even Hoppy Uniatz could not lose his grip. It might all seem very simple in the end, but in that panoramic grasp of detail lay the genius that made amazing audacities seem simple.

"Okay, skipper," Peter said soberly, as the car swooped into Marsham Street. "But don't forget you're responsible to Hoppy's widows and my orphans."

Ever since the few hectic moments of the ride they had been running with the cut-out closed, and the dying of the engine was scarcely perceptible as Simon turned the switch.

After the last turn they had slid up practically in silence to their destination, which was one of a row of modern apartment buildings that had not long ago transformed the topography of that once sombre district. One or two other cars were parked within sight, but otherwise the street seemed quiet and lifeless. Simon glanced up at the crossword design of light and dark windows as he stepped out of the car and crossed the pavement, with some attention to the softness of his footsteps, for he knew well how sounds could echo to the upper windows of a silent street at that hour of the night. He said nothing to the others, for all the ground had been covered in advance in his instructions. He read off the apartment number from the indicator in the empty lobby, and an automatic elevator carried them up to the top floor. The Saint was as cool as chromium, as accurate and self-contained as a machine. He left the elevator doors open and waited until Peter and Hoppy had taken up their positions flattened against the wall on either side of the door; then he put his knuckle against the bell.

There was an interval of perhaps ten seconds, and the door opened.

It opened, according to the Saint's first diagnosis, straight on to an awkward-looking silenced revolver in the hand of the stocky ape-faced man who unfastened the latch.

"Come in," he said.

Blank astonishment, anger, and incredulity chased themselves over the Saint's face—exactly as they were expected to chase themselves.

"What's the idea of this?" he demanded wrathfully. "And who the hell are you, anyway?"

"Come in," repeated the man coldly. "And put your hands up. And hurry up about it, before I give you something."

The Saint put his hands up and went in. But he went in with his shoulder-blades sliding along the door, so that the other was momentarily cut off from it. Then the man had to turn his back to the doorway when he started to close the door, so as to keep Simon covered at the same time. And that was part of the clockwork of the Saint's preorganised plan . . . Simon gave the signal with a gentle cough, and over the man's shoulder appeared the intent face of Peter Quentin, soundlessly, with a stiff rubber blackjack raised. There was a subdued clunk, and the man's eyes went comically glassy.

At that instant other things happened with the smooth timing of a well-rehearsed conjuring trick. The Saint's hands dropped like striking falcons on to the ape-faced man's gun, bent his wrists inwards towards the elbow, whipped the revolver out of the suddenly powerless fingers. Simultaneously Peter Quentin was moving aside, to be replaced by Hoppy Uniatz, whose massive paws closed on the man's throat in a gorilla grip faster than Peter himself could have put away his blackjack and taken the same hold. Meanwhile Peter slid round the man's side, received the revolver as Simon detached it, and jammed the silencer into the man's ribs. It was all done with a glossy perfection of team-work that would have dazed the eye of the beholder if there had been any beholder present, all within the space of a scant second, and then the Saint was talking into the man's ear.

"One whisper out of you, and they'll be able to thread you on a flagpole," he said. Then he stepped back a few inches. "Okay, Hoppy—let him breathe."

The crushing grasp of Mr Uniatz's fingers slackened just sufficiently to allow a saving infiltration of air. The delicately judged blow of the rubber blackjack had deadened the ape-faced man's brain for just long enough to allow the subsequent manoeuvres to take place, without stunning him permanently. Now he stared at the Saint with squeezed-out eyes in which there was a pallor of voiceless fear.

"Talk very quietly," said the Saint, in that ghostly intonation which barely travelled a hand's breadth beyond the ears of its intended audience. "What was supposed to happen next?"

"I was to take you in there—there's two chaps want to see you."

Simon's glance had already covered the tiny hall. The three doors that opened off it were all closed; the ape-faced man had indicated the centre one.

"Good enough," said the Saint. "Let's carry on as if nothing had happened."

He passed his own automatic to Peter, took away the silenced revolver, spilled the shells out into his palm and dropped them into Peter's pocket, and thrust the empty weapon back into the hand of its owner.

"Cover me with it and carry on," he ordered. "When we go in there, leave the door open. And remember this: my friends will be watching you from outside. If you breathe a word or bat an eyelid to let your reception committee know that everything isn't going according to plan, and any bother starts—you'll be the first dead hero of the evening." The Saint's voice was as caressing as velvet, but it was as cold and unsentimental as a polar sea. "Let's go . . ."

He turned his back and sauntered over to the middle door, and the ape-faced man, urged on by a last remembrancing prod from the muzzle of the murderous rod which Mr Uniatz had by that time added to the displayed collection of artillery, lurched helplessly after him.

Simon turned the handle and entered the room with his arms raised. On one side. Lady Valerie Woodchester was roughly tied to a chair, and one of the two men there was bending over her with a hand clamped over her mouth. The other man stood on the opposite side of the room, with a cigarette loosely held in one hand and a small automatic levelled in the other.

The Saint's eyes rambled interestedly over the scene.

"What ho, souls," he drawled. "And how are all the illegitimate Sons of France tonight?"

CHAPTER FIVE:

HOW SIMON TEMPLAR OBLIGED LADY VALERIE AND CHIEF INSPECTOR TEAL REFUSED BREAKFAST

1

The man who had been bending over Lady Valerie straightened up. He was slim and sallow, with black hair plastered down over his head until it looked as if it had been waxed. He had quick darting eyes and a sly slinking manner; his movements were abrupt and silent, like those of a lizard. One could imagine him lurking in dark corners for sinister purposes.

The Saint smiled at Lady Valerie as the lizard-like man withdrew his hand and her face became visible. The first expression on her face was a light of joy and relief, and then when she saw that he kept his hands up, and saw the ape-faced man follow him in with the silenced revolver screwed into his back, it changed through stark unbelief to hopeless dejection.

"Hullo, darling," he said. "You do have some nice friends, don't you?"

She didn't respond. She sat there and stared at him reproachfully: she seemed to be deeply disappointed in him. Simon realised that there was some excuse for her, but she would have to endure her unfounded disappointment for a little while longer.

He transferred his smile to the automatic and the cigarette.

"Nice weather we've been having, haven't we?" he murmured, keeping the conversational ball rolling single-handed.

This other man was bigger, and there was an air of conscious arrogance about him. He had the cold intolerant eyes and haughty moustache of a Prussian Guardsman. He gazed back at Simon with fish-like incuriosity, and made a gesture with his cigarette at the sallow man.

"Disarm and search him, Dumaire."

"So your name is Dumaire, is it?" said the Saint politely. "May I compliment you on your coiffure? I've never seen floor polish used on the head before. And while this is going on, won't you introduce me to your uncle?"

Dumaire said nothing; he simply proceeded to do what he was told and run through the Saint's pockets. Keys, cigarette case, lighter, money, handkerchief, wallet, fountain pen—he took out the commonplace articles one by one and laid them on a small table in front of the man who appeared to be in charge. While he was waiting for the collection to be assembled, the latter answered Simon's question.

"If it is of any interest to you," he said, "I am Major Bravache, a divisional commander of the Sons of France, about whom I think you said something just now."

He spoke English excellently, with only a trace of native accent.

"How perfectly splendid," said the Saint slowly. "But do you know what bad company you're in? This bird behind me, for instance, with the pea-shooter boring into my backbone—whatever he may have told you, I happen to know that his real name is Sam Pietri, and he has done three sentences for robbery with violence."

He felt the harmless gun quiver involuntarily against his spine, and chuckled inwardly over the awful anguish that must have been twinging through the tissues of the ape-faced man, not only compelled to be an impotent accomplice in snaring fresh victims into the net of his own downfall, but suffering the aftermath of a maltreated skull as well. Simon would have given much for a glimpse of his guardian's face, but he hoped that he was not betraying anything to the opposition. Fortunately, no one was paying any attention to Pietri. Dumaire, his job done, was leaning against the wall and watching Lady Valerie with reptilian eyes in which the only discernible expression had a brazen lewdness that quite plainly revealed his chief preoccupation; Bravache had simply ignored the Saint's last remarks as if he had not heard them. He was busily turning over the things on the table before him. He gave his most detailed attention to the wallet, and he had hardly started on it when a gleam of triumph flowed into his cold eyes. He held up a scrap of buff paper with a large number printed on it.

"Ah!" he said, with a deep satisfaction that was exaggerated by his slightly foreign handling of words. "The ticket. That is excellent!"

As a matter of fact, it was a ticket in an impromptu sweepstake organised over the weekend in Peter Quentin's favourite pub on the outskirts of Anford, but the Saint had known that it was there, and had left it there with the deliberate object of leading the comedy on as far as it would go in the hope of finding out exactly what was meant to be the end of it before he was forced to show his hand.

He waited to see how far his hopes would be fulfilled. Valerie Woodchester's eyes were like saucers: they looked at first as if they couldn't believe what they were seeing, and then a veiled half-comprehending half-perplexed expression passed over them which Simon hoped nobody would see. Bravache folded the ticket carefully and put it in his own wallet. Then he looked at Lady Valerie, and again the limp cigarette dangled between his fingers.

"We are very grateful, my dear lady," he said. "You have done a great service to the Sons of France. The Sons of France do not forget services. In future you will be under our protection." He paused,

155

smiling, and there was something wolfish about his smile. "Should anything happen to you—should you, for instance, be murdered by one of our enemies—you will be immediately avenged."

An arpeggio of spooky fingers stroked up the Saint's back into the roots of his hair. In spite of Bravache's stilted phrasing, the almost farcical old-fashioned melodrama in which his tongue roiled itself gloatingly around every word, there was something in his harsh voice that was by no means farcical, something which in combination with that wolfish smile was made more deeply horrible by the unreality of its enunciation. Simon realised for the first time in his life, in spite of everything he had believed, that it was actually possible for a villain to speak like that, in grotesquely serious conformity with the standard caricature of himself, and still keep the quality of terror: it was, after all the jokes were over, the natural self-expression of a certain type of man—a man who was cruel and unscrupulous and egotistical in too coarse a vein to play cat-and-mouse with the dignity that subtleness might give it, and yet whose vanity demanded that travesty of subtleness, and whose total lack even of the saving grace of humour made it possible for him to play the travesty with a perfectly straight face and made the farce more gruesome in the process. In that revealing instant the Saint had an insight into the mentalities of all the glorified Jew-baiters and overblown petty tyrants whose psychology had baffled him before.

He said lightly, "That'll be fun for you, won't it, Valerie?"

Bravache looked back at him, and again his eyes were cold and fishy.

"You have been attempting to discover the secrets of the Sons of France in order to betray them to our enemies," he said. "The penalty for that, as you know, is death."

"You must have been reading a book," said the Saint admiringly. "Or was that Luker's idea?"

The vulpine twist that was meant to be a smile remained on the other man's thin lips.

"I am acquainted with Mr Luker only as a sympathiser and supporter of our ideals to whom I have the honour to be attached as personal aide," he replied. "Your crime has been committed against an organisation of patriots known as the Sons of France, of which I am an officer. You are now a prisoner of the Sons of France. We have been informed that you are an unprincipled mercenary employed by the bandits of Moscow to spy upon and betray our organisation. Of that I have sufficient proof." He tapped the pocket where he had replaced his wallet with the sweepstake ticket in it. "It also appears that you have threatened Lady Valerie Woodchester, who is our friend. Therefore if you were to murder her, it would naturally be our duty to avenge her."

Simon's arms were beginning to ache and stiffen from being held up so long. But inside he felt tunelessly relaxed, and his mind was a cold pattern of crystalline understanding.

"You mean," he said unemotionally, "that the idea is to kill both of us, and arrange it so that you can try to spread the story that I murdered Lady Valerie and that the Sons of France killed me to avenge her."

"I am sure that the theory will find wide acceptance," answered Bravache complacently. "Lady Valerie is young and beautiful, whereas you are a notorious criminal. I think that a great many people will applaud our action, and that even the British police themselves will feel a secret relief which will tend to handicap their inquiries."

The Saint glanced at Lady Valerie. Her face had been blank with stupefaction; now it was drawn and frightened. Her big brown eyes were fixed on him in mute and hypnotised entreaty.

"I told you, you had charming friends, darling," Simon remarked.

He studied Bravache with cold-blooded interest. He felt that in the space of a few minutes he had come to know the man intimately, that he could take his soul apart and lay out all its components. How much of what Bravache had said was genuine fanaticism, or genuine self-deception, however wilful, he could not judge: in that kind of neurotic, the blend of idealism and conscienceless rationalisation became so homogeneous that it was practically impossible to draw a sharp cleavage. But he was not so much interested in the man individually as in the type, the matrix in which all the petty satraps of tyranny are cast. He had known it in Red Russia, in Fascist Italy, in Nazi Germany, and had known the imaginative horror of conceiving of life under a dynasty in which liberty and life itself lay at the caprice of men from that mould. Now he was finding the imprint of the same die on a Frenchman, the chilling prototypical hallmark of the breed from which secret police and authorised persecutors are recruited, and it gave him a grimmer measure of the thing he had set out to fight than anything else had done. If the Sons of France had progressed far enough to develop officers like Major Bravache, the wheels must be turning with nightmare speed—

"It all sounds very neat and jolly, my dear Major Cochon," he admitted. "Do we start right away?"

"I think we had better do so," said Bravache, still smiling with a face of marble. "We have already wasted enough time." He turned his head. "Dumaire, you know what to do. We will leave you to do it." He looked at the Saint again, with his lips drawn back from his white even teeth. "You, Mr Templar, will accompany Pietri and myself. If you resist or try to obstruct us you will be shot at once. I advise you to come quietly. I am hoping that as a reasonable man you will agree that the prospect of death in a number of hours is preferable to the certainty of death immediately. Besides"—the gleam of the white teeth was feline—"as a gentleman you will not wish to deprive me of the opportunity to answer some of your remarks which I have not had time to deal with here."

The Saint smiled.

"By no manner of means," he said. "Only I should rather like to take charge of the interview myself at this point—if you don't mind."

He stepped aside and backwards, and took hold of Pietri by the ear. The movement was so improbable and unexpected that it was completed before either Bravache or Dumaire could reorient their wits sufficiently to do anything about it. And by that time Pietri was securely held, like a writhing urchin in the grip of an old-fashioned schoolmarm, so that his body was between the Saint and Bravache, who was still trying to make up his mind whether to grab for the automatic which he had confidently left lying on the table a yard away.

Bravache's poise broke for a moment.

"Use your gun, you fool!" he thundered.

"He can't," said the Saint. "You tell them why, Sam."

An extra turn on the piece of gristle he was holding made his victim squeal like a mouse.

"There's nothing in it," wailed Pietri, with the revolver quivering futilely in his grasp. "They caught me outside—him and two other fellows—"

Bravache started to move then, and Simon's voice ripped out like a lash.

"I wouldn't," he said. "Really I wouldn't. It's dangerous."

And as he spoke, Peter and Hoppy came through the doorway.

Bravache stood very still. His face was cold and unmoved, but the veins on the backs of his clenched hands stood out in knotty blue cords. Dumaire, caught with one hand at the edge of his coat pocket, prudently let it fall back to his side. He flattened himself against the wall like a cornered rat, with his shoulders hunched up to the jaw level of his small ebony-capped head.

Simon released Pietri and strolled over to pick up Bravache's automatic and retrieve his cigarette case and lighter from among his strewn belongings on the table. With a cigarette between his lips and the lighter wick burning steadily, he looked at Bravache with cerulean mockery in his eyes.

"I'm hoping that as a reasonable man you will agree that the prospect of death in a number of hours is preferable to the certainty of death immediately," he said in a voice of satin. "Go on, Major—I don't want anything to interrupt our little chat."

2

The chat appeared to have been interrupted already, so far as Major Bravache was concerned. At any rate, he seemed disinclined to accept the Saint's invitation to proceed with his discourse. Or else the founts of eloquence had dried up within him. His lips closed down over his teeth until there was only a straight line to show where his mouth had been.

The Saint left him with a quizzically regretful shrug, and turned to untie Lady Valerie. She stood up and stretched herself, rather like a cat by the fire, and rubbed her chafed wrists. Then she went over to the table where her bag was, in search of the ineluctable restoratives of feminine sangfroid.

"You gave me some bad moments," she said, with an attempted nonchalance in which he could still see the signs of strain like carefully darned edges on a poor man's cuff. "For a long time I was thinking you'd let me down, but of course I ought to have remembered that you never let anyone down."

"What happened?" he asked.

She appeared from behind a card-sized mirror to point with the scarlet tip of a lipstick.

"He rang the bell and said you'd sent him round with something special to give me. I thought it was a bit funny, since we'd only said goodbye a little while ago, and he was a rather funny-looking person, but after all I thought a lot of funny things must go on in this life of crime, and I was quite intrigued. I mean, I just didn't think enough about how funny it was. So I started to let him in, and then these other two followed him in very quickly and there wasn't anything I could do. They tied me up and searched everywhere. This one was very nasty—he thought I might have the ticket on me, and he didn't miss anything."

She gazed vindictively at Dumaire, who was then having his hands efficiently taped behind his back by Peter Quentin, and kicked him thoughtfully on the shins.

"Then they made you ring me up?" Simon prompted her.

"Well, when they couldn't find the ticket they said they'd do horrible things to me unless I told them where it was. So I told them I'd given it to you to look after, and I was quite glad to be able to ring you up by that time. I . . . I sort of knew you'd catch on at once, because you're so frightfully clever and that's how things always happen in stories."

"It makes everything so easy, doesn't it?" said the Saint satirically. "We must talk some more about that—but I think we'll talk alone."

He watched while the taping of the other prisoners' wrists was completed; then he started exploring doors. He found one that communicated with the bedroom—a place of glass and natural woods and pale-blue sheets and pillows, with a pale-blue bathroom beyond it that gave an infinitesimally humorous shift to the alignment of his eyebrows. He left the door open and signed to Peter.

"Bring the menagerie in here," he said.

Dumaire, Pietri, and Bravache lurched suddenly in, urged on by the unarguable prodding of gun muzzles.

On his way in after them, Hoppy Uniatz stopped at the door. It is true, as has perhaps already been made superfluously clear, that there were situations in which the light of intelligence failed to coruscate on Mr Uniatz's ivorine brow; it is no less true that in the vasty oceans of philosophy and abstract Thought he wandered like a rudderless barque at the mercy of unpredictable winds, but in his own element he was immune to the distractions that might have afflicted lesser men, and his mental processes became invested with the indivagable simplicity of true greatness.

"Boss," said Mr Uniatz, with the placidity of a mahatma approaching the settlement of an overdue grocer's bill, "I t'ink ya better gimme dem shells."

"What shells?" asked the Saint lazily.

"De shells," explained Mr Uniatz, who was now flourishing Pietri's silenced revolver in addition to his own beloved Betsy, "you take outa de dumb cannon."

Simon blinked.

"What for?"

"It won't make no ners," explained Mr Uniatz, with a slight perplexity for such slowness on the uptake, "when we are giving dese guys de woiks."

The Saint swallowed.

"Peter'll give them to you when you need them," he said, and closed the door hastily on Mr Uniatz's back.

He went back and sat on the arm of a chair in front of Lady Valerie. He wanted to smile, but he had too many other things on his mind that were not smiling matters. The recent episode which had been absorbing all his nervous and intellectual energy was over, and his brain was moving on again with restless efficiency. It had not reached an end, but only a fresh beginning.

She had regained most of her composure. Her face was repaired, and she had lighted a cigarette herself. He had to admit that she possessed amazing recuperative powers. There was a naughty gleam in her eyes that would have amused him at any other time.

"You always seem to be catching me in these boudoir moments, don't you?" she said, smoothing her flimsy negligee. "I mean, first I was in my nightie at the fire, and then now. It must be fate, or something. The only trouble is, there won't be any thrills left when we get really friendly . . . Of course, I suppose I ought to thank you for rescuing me," she went on hurriedly. "Thanks very much, darling. It was sweet of you."

"Don't mention it," he said graciously. "It's been a pleasure. You must call me again any time you want a helping hand."

He got up restlessly, poured himself out a drink, and sat down again.

"Don't you think you'd better tell me what it's all about?" he said abruptly. "I could live through an explanation of this cloakroom-ticket gag."

"Oh, that," she said. She trimmed the end of her cigarette. "Well, you see, they thought I'd got a cloakroom ticket they wanted, so they came to look for it. That's all."

"It isn't anything like all," he said bluntly. "Why go on holding out on me? You've got something they want—probably some papers that Kennet gave you. You parked them in a cloakroom somewhere, and these birds knew it and wanted the ticket. Or do you want me to believe that they went to all this trouble to get a receipt for Luker's hat?"

She frowned at her knees, and then she shrugged.

"I suppose there's no reason why you shouldn't know, since you've guessed already," she said. "As a matter of fact, I have got some papers. I thought Algy might like to know, so I just mentioned it to him casually on the telephone tonight."

"Meaning what I was talking to you about at the Berkeley."

"What was that?"

"Blackmail."

"I don't understand."

"Don't make me tired. You were trying to sell him those papers."

"After all," she said, "a girl has to live."

"How long do you think you'd have lived tonight if it hadn't been for me?"

She hesitated.

"How was I to know Algy would do anything like this?" she said sulkily. "I told him I'd put the papers in a cloakroom and I wasn't sure where they were. He rang me up later on, just before the monkey-man got here, and offered me ten thousand pounds if I'd bring them round to him right away, but I thought they might be worth more than that, so I pretended I still couldn't remember what I'd done with them. Of course, I know where they are really."

The Saint's lips tightened.

"You poor little fly-brained moron," he exploded uncontrollably. "What makes you think you can cut in on a game like this? Haven't you had your lesson yet? You know what happened to Kennet and Windlay. You know what happened to you tonight. You heard what Bravache said. If I hadn't had everything organised, you were booked to go down the drain with me—plus any specialised unpleasantnesses that your boyfriend Dumaire could think of. Is that your idea of a good time?"

She shuddered almost imperceptibly.

"I know, that wasn't very nice. I never was one of those heroines who don't think life worth living unless bullets are whizzing past their ears and ships sinking under them and houses crashing in ruins about their heads and all that sort of thing. Personally I'm all for a life of selfish self-indulgence, and I don't care who knows it. If I could get a decent offer for those papers, I'd take it like a shot and skip off to Bermuda or somewhere and enjoy it. The trouble is, I don't know what they're worth. What do you think?"

She looked at him with limpid brown eyes big with artlessness.

"I'll give you a shilling for them," he said.

"Oh, I wasn't thinking of selling them to you," she said innocently. "What I was thinking was that if I went to a fairly decent pub tonight—the Carlton, for instance, where I should be perfectly safe—and then I rang up Algy and told him he could have the papers for fifteen thousand pounds, he'd most likely do something about it. I mean, after what's happened tonight, he ought to consider himself damned lucky to get them for fifteen thousand. Don't you think so?"

"Very lucky," said the Saint, with fine-drawn patience. "Where are the papers at the moment?"

She smiled.

"They're in a cloakroom all right. I've got the ticket somewhere, only I forget exactly where. But I expect I'll remember all right when I have to."

"I expect you will," he said coldly. "Even if somebody like Dumaire has to help you."

Suddenly he got up and went over to her and took both her hands. The coldness fell out of his voice.

"Valerie, why don't you stop being an idiot and let me get into the firing line?"

She looked at him speculatively for a while, for quite a long while. Her hands were small and soft. He kept still, and heard a taxi rattle past the end of the street. But she shook her head.

"I'd like to," she said sadly. "Especially after what you've done for me tonight—although if it comes to that, I expect you simply love dashing about rescuing people and doing your little hero act, so perhaps you ought to be a bit grateful to me for giving you such a good chance to do your stuff. And after all, if I just handed over the papers to you, that wouldn't do much good, would it? Of course, if you wanted to buy them—"

"To hell with buying them! Haven't you found out yet that there are some things in life that you can't measure in money? Haven't you realised that this is one of them? I don't know what there is in those papers—maybe you don't know either. But you must know that things like you've seen tonight don't get organised over scraps of paper with noughts and crosses on them—that men like Bravache and Fairweather and Luker don't take to systematic murder to stop anybody reading their old love-letters. These men are big. Anything that keeps them as busy as this is big. And I know what kind of bigness they deal in. The only way they can make what they call big money, the only way they can touch the power and glory that their perverted egos crave for, is in helping and schooling nations to slaughter and destroy. What hellish graft is at the back of this show called the Sons of France I don't know, but I can guess plenty of it. However it works, the only object it can have is to turn one more country aside from civilisation so that the market can be kept right for the men who sell guns and gas. Or else Luker wouldn't be in it. And he must know that there's an odds-on chance of bringing it off, or else he still wouldn't be in it. This may be the last cog in a machine that will wipe out twenty million lives, and you might have the knowledge that would break it up before it gets going. Doesn't that mean anything to you?"

She stood up slowly. And she freed her hands.

"I think I'll be getting along now," she said, and her voice was quite steady in spite of the reluctance in it. "It's been a lovely party, but even

the best of good times have to come to an end, and I need some sleep.
Do you think you could move those men out of the bedroom while I
put on some clothes?"

Simon looked at her.

The fire that had gone into his appeal was a glowing ingot within
him. It was a coiled spring that would drive him until it ran down,
without regard for sentiment or obstacles. It was a power transformer
for the ethereal vibrations of destiny. Earlier in the evening, the
atmosphere of the Berkeley had defeated him, but this was not the
Berkeley. He knew that there was only one solution, and there was too
much at stake for him to hesitate. He was amazed at his own madness,
and yet he was utterly calm, utterly resolute.

He nodded.

"Oh, yes," he said. "I was going to move them anyway. I didn't
think you'd want to keep them for domestic pets."

He went over and opened the bedroom door.

"Bring out the zoo," he said.

He stood there while the captives filed out, followed by Peter and
Hoppy, and waited until the door had closed again behind the girl. For
a few seconds he paced up and down the small room, intent on his own
thoughts. Then he picked up the telephone and dialled the number of
his apartment in Cornwall House.

Patricia answered the ring.

"Hullo, sweetheart," he said. His voice was level, too certain of its
words to show excitement. "Yes . . . No trouble at all. Everything went
according to plan, and we're all sitting pretty—except the deputation
from the ungodly. Now listen. I've got a job for you. Call Orace and
tell him to expect you. Then get out the Daimler, and tell Sam Outrell
to pull Stunt Number Three. As soon as you're sure you aren't followed,
come over here. Hustle it . . . No, I'll tell you when you arrive. There
are listeners . . . Okay, darling. Be seein' ya."

He put down the microphone and turned to Bravache. The pupils of his eyes were like chips of flint.

"So you were going to kill Lady Valerie and blame it on to me," he said with great gentleness. "That was as far as we'd got, wasn't it? The Sons of France avenge the murder of one of their sympathisers, and all sorts of high-minded nitwits wave banners. Do you see any good reason why you shouldn't take some of your own medicine?"

"You daren't do it!" said Bravache whitely. "The Sons of France will make you pay for my death a hundred times!"

Dumaire's face was yellow with fear.

Simon took him by the scruff of the neck and heaved him over to the window. He parted the curtains and pointed downwards.

"I suppose you came here in a car," he said, "Which of those cars is yours?"

The man shook like a leaf but did not answer.

Simon turned him round and hit him in the face. He held him by the lapels of his coat and brought him back to the window.

"Which of those cars is yours?"

"That one," blubbered Dumaire.

It was a small black sedan, far more suitable for the transport of unwilling passengers than the open Hirondel.

Simon released his informant, who tottered and almost fell when the Saint's supporting grip was removed. The Saint lighted another cigarette and spoke to Peter.

"You can use their car. Take them to Upper Berkeley Mews."

He looked up to find Hoppy Uniatz's questioning eyes upon him. There were times when Mr Uniatz had a tendency to fidget, and these times were usually when he felt that a very obvious and elementary move had been delayed too long. It was not that he was a naturally impatient man, but he liked to see things disposed of in the order of their importance. Now he grasped hopefully for the relief of the problem that was uppermost in his mind.

"Is dat where we give dem de woiks, boss?"

"That's where you give them the works," said the Saint. "Will you come outside for a minute, Peter?"

He took Peter out into the hall and gave him more detailed instructions.

"Did you hear enough while you were waiting to convince you that I haven't been raving?" he said.

"I always knew you couldn't be," Peter said sombrely, "because you sounded so much as if you were. I'm damned if I know how you do it, but it always seems to be the way."

"You'll see it through?"

"No," said Peter. "I'm going home to my mother." His face was serious, in spite of the way he spoke. "But aren't you taking an unnecessary risk with Bravache and friend? Of course, I'm not so bloodthirsty as Hoppy—"

The Saint drew at his cigarette.

"I know, old lad. Maybe I am a fool. But I don't see myself as a gangster. Do it the way I told you. And when you've finished, bring Hoppy back here and let him pick up the Hirondel and drive it down to Weybridge. You can stay in town and wait for developments—I expect there'll be plenty of them. Okay?"

"Okay, chief."

Simon's hand lay on Peter's shoulder, and they went back into the living-room together. The Saint's new sureness was like a steel blade, balanced and deadly.

3

"You can't do this!" babbled Bravache. Little specks of saliva sprayed from his mouth with his words. "It is a crime! You will be punished—hanged. You cannot commit murder in cold blood. Surely you can't do that!" His manner changed, became fawning, wheedling. "Look, you are a gentleman. You could not kill a defenceless man any more than I could. You have misunderstood my leetle joke. It was only to frighten you—"

"Put some tape on his mouth, Hoppy," ordered the Saint with cold distaste.

Pietri and Dumaire were gagged in the same way, and the three men were pushed on out of the flat and crowded into the lift. Simon left them with Peter and Hoppy in the foyer of the building while he went out to reconnoitre the car. It was nearly half past two by his watch, and the street was as still and lifeless as a graveyard. The Saint's rubber-soled shoes woke no echoes as they moved to their destination. There was a man dozing at the wheel of the small black sedan, and he started to rouse as the Saint opened the door beside him, but he was still not fully awake when the Saint's left hand reached in and took hold of him by the front of his coat and yanked him out like a puppy.

"Have you tried this for insomnia?" asked the Saint conversationally, and brought up his right hand in a smashing uppercut.

The man's teeth clicked together, his knees gave, he buckled forward without a sound, and Simon let him fall. He went back to the entrance of the building.

"All clear," he said in a low voice. "Make it snappy."

He led the way back to the black sedan and picked up his sleeping patient. There was a board fence on the opposite side of the road, above which rose the naked girders of another new apartment building under construction. Simon applied scientific leverage, and the patient rose into the air and disappeared from view. There was a dull thud in the darkness beyond.

Simon crossed the road again. The loading of freight had been completed with professional briskness while he was away. Already Peter Quentin was at the wheel, and Hoppy Uniatz, sitting crookedly beside him in the other seat, was covering the three men who were bundled together in the back. The engine whirred under the starter.

Simon looked in at the prisoners, and particularly at the staring cringing eyes of Bravache.

"It won't hurt much, Major," he said, "and you ought to be proud to be a martyr for the flag . . . On your way, boys."

He stood and watched the receding tail light of the car until it turned the corner at the end of the street, and then he strolled slowly back to the entrance of the building. He waited there less than five minutes before a dark Daimler limousine swept into the street and drew up in front of the door.

The Saint leaned in the open window beside the driver and kissed her.

"What's been happening?" asked Patricia.

In a few sentences he let her know as much as he knew himself, and while he was speaking he rummaged in the nearest side pocket of the car. He found what he was looking for—a blue chauffeur's cap—and set it at an angle on her curly head.

"I'll be back in a minute," he said.

When he re-entered the flat, Lady Valerie Woodchester was dressed. She came out of the bedroom carrying a small valise.

"What's happened to everyone?" she asked in surprise.

"Peter and Hoppy have removed the exhibits," he said irrepressibly. "They'll get what's coming to them somewhere else. We didn't want to make any more mess for you here."

The edges of pearly teeth showed on her under lip.

"Could you call me a taxi?"

"I could do better. I sent for one of my more ducal cars, and it's waiting outside now. You won't mind if I see you as far as the Carlton, will you? I don't want you to be put to the trouble of having to call me out again tonight."

For a moment he thought she was going to lose her temper, and almost hoped that she would. But she turned her back on him and sailed out into the corridor without a word, He followed her into the elevator, and they rode down in supercharged silence. At the door, he helped her into the Daimler and settled himself beside her. The car moved off.

They drove a couple of blocks without a word being spoken. Lady Valerie stared moodily out of the window on her side, scowling and biting her lips. The Saint was bubbling inside.

"A penny for them," he said at last.

She turned on him with sudden fury and looked him wrathfully up and down.

"You make me sick!" she flared.

The Saint's eyebrows rose one reproachful notch.

"Me?" he protested aggrievedly. "But why, at the moment? What have I done now?"

She shook her shoulders fretfully.

"Oh . . . nothing," she said. "I'm fed up, that's all."

"I'm sorry," said the Saint gravely. "Perhaps you've had a dull evening. You ought to get about more—go places, and meet people, and see things. It makes a tremendous difference."

"You think you're very funny, don't you?" she flashed. "You and your blonde girlfriend—the world's pet hero and heroine!" She paused, savouring the sting of her own acid. "She is nice looking—I'll give her that," she went on grudgingly. "But I just wish she'd never been born . . . Oh, well, perhaps we can't all be heroines, but there's no reason why the rest of us shouldn't have a pretty decent time. You'll be a bit fed up with yourself when Algy and Luker get those papers, won't you?"

"Are you quite sure you aren't going to give them to me?" he said.

She laughed.

"I suppose you think I ought to give them to you for saving my life," she jeered extravagantly. "With tears of gratitude streaming down my cheeks, I should stammer, 'Here they are—take them.' That's why you make me sick. You go about the place rescuing people and being the Robin Hood of modern crime, and then you go back to your blonde girlfriend and have a grand time being told how wonderful you are. So you may be, but it just makes me sick."

"Well, if you feel sick, don't keep on talking about it—be sick," said the Saint hospitably. "Don't worry about the car—we can always have it cleaned."

She gave him a withering glare and turned ostentatiously away. She seemed to want to make it quite clear that his conversation was beneath her contempt, and that even to endure his company was a martyrdom.

She huddled as far away from him as the width of the seat permitted, and resumed her pent-up scowling out of the window.

The Saint devoted himself to the tranquil enjoyment of his cigarette, and waited contentedly for the climax which he knew must come before long.

It came after another five minutes.

All at once her eyes, fixed vacantly on the window, froze into a strange expression. She sat bolt upright.

"Here," she blurted. "What the . . . Where are we going? This isn't the way to the Carlton!"

Obviously it wasn't; they were down at the Chelsea end of the Embankment, heading west.

"Have you noticed that already?" said the Saint imperturbably. "How observant you are, darling. Now I suppose I can't keep my secret any longer. The fact is, I'm not taking you to the Carlton."

She caught her breath.

"You . . . you're not taking me to the Carlton? But I want to go to the Carlton! Take me there at once! Tell the chauffeur to turn round—"

She leaned forward and tried to hammer on the glass partition. Quite effortlessly, the Saint pushed her back.

"Shut up," he said calmly, "You make me sick."

"W-what?" she said.

She stared at him with solemn wide-open eyes as if he were some strange monster that she was seeing for the first time.

"It's no use both of us being sick," he pointed out reasonably. "It would be a deafening duet."

"I don't know what good you think that is going to do you," she said haughtily. "If you think you're going to protect me, or anything like that—"

"Protect you?" he said, with bland incomprehension. "Who . . . me? Darling, that would never enter my head. I know you can look after yourself. But I want to take care of you for my own sake. You see, it wouldn't suit me at all if you sold those papers to Fairweather or Luker. I want them too much myself. So I just want to keep an eye on you until I get them."

"You . . . you mean you're kidnapping me?" she got out incredulously.

But somehow she did not sound quite so indignant.

"That's the idea," he said equably. "And it's my duty to tell you that if you try to scream or kick up any sort of fuss, I shall have to take steps to stop you. Quite gentle steps, of course. I shall just knock you cold."

"Oh!" She said.

She was sitting up very straight, one hand on the seat beside her, the other clutching the armrest at her side. Simon lounged at ease in his own corner, but he was watching her like a hawk, and his hands were ready for instant action. He had no wish to use violence, but he would have no compunction about it if it became necessary. He was fighting for something bigger than stereotyped chivalry, something bigger than the incidental hurt of any individual. He was the point of a million bayonets.

For a long moment she went on staring at him, and there was something in her face that he could not understand.

Then her muscles relaxed and she sank limply back.

"I think you're an unspeakable cad," she said.

"I am," said the Saint cheerfully. "And I fairly wallow in it."

Her mouth moved slightly, so that by the dim light of passing streetlamps it almost looked for one fleeting moment as though she were trying to stifle a smile. He reached over to crush his cigarette in the ashtray, so as to glance at her more closely, but she moved further away from him, and the expression on her face was surly and disdainful. He lay back and stretched out his legs and appeared to go to sleep.

But he was awake and vigilant for every minute of the drive, while the car whispered out of Putney and out on to the Portsmouth Road and down the long hill into Kingston. They went on to Hampton Court, and turned off over the bridge along the road by Hurst Park; in Walton they turned right again, and a few miles later they turned under a brick archway into what seemed like a dense wood. A few more turns, and the car swung into a circular drive and swept its headlights across the front of a big weather-tiled house set in a grove of tall pines and silver birches.

They pulled up with a crunch of gravel, and Simon opened the door.

"Here we are, darling," he said. "This is my nearest country seat. Thirty minutes from London if you don't worry about speed cops, and you might as well be in the middle of the New Forest. You'll like the air, too—it has oxygen in it."

He picked up her valise and stepped out. As she got out after him, she saw Patricia coming round the front of the car, pulling off her gloves, and her face went stony.

The Saint waved a casual hand.

"You remember Pat, don't you?" he murmured. "The girl with the wardrobe you liked so much. She'll chaperone you while you're here, and see that you have most of the things you want. Come along up, and I'll show you your quarters."

He led the way into the house, handing over the valise to Orace, who was standing on the steps. Without saying a word, Lady Valerie followed him up the broad oak staircase.

Upstairs, at the end of one wing, there was a self-contained suite consisting of sitting-room, bedroom, and bathroom. Simon indicated it all with a generous gesture.

"You couldn't do better at the Carlton," he said. "The windows don't open, and they're made of unbreakable glass, but it's all air-conditioned, so you'll be quite comfortable. And any time you get tired of the view, you've only got to tell me where that cloakroom ticket is, and I'll take you straight back to London."

Orace put down the valise and went out again with his peculiar strutting limp.

Lady Valerie turned round in a quick circle and stood in front of the Saint. Her face was blazing.

"You," she said incoherently. "You . . ."

She took a swift step forward and struck at him with her open hand. His cheek stung with the slap. Instinctively he grasped her wrist and held it, but she struggled in his arms like a wildcat, wriggling and kicking at his shins.

"Oh!" she sobbed. "I . . . I hate you!"

"You break my heart," said the Saint. "I thought it was the dawn of love."

She took a lot of holding; her slim body was strongly built, and her muscles were in excellent condition. In the struggle her hair had become disordered, and her breath came quickly between parted lips that were too close to his for serenity.

The Saint smiled, and kissed her.

She stopped struggling. Her breasts were tight against him; her lips were moist and desirous under his. One of her arms slid behind his neck.

The kiss lasted for some time. Then he put his hands on her shoulders and moved gently away.

"I'm sorry about that," he said. "I didn't really mean to force my vile attentions on you, but you asked for it."

"Did I?" she said.

She turned away from him towards a mirror, and began to pat her hair into place.

"You are a cad, aren't you?" she said.

Her eyes, seen in the mirror, held the same baffling expression that had puzzled him in the car, but now there was mockery with it. Her lips were stirred by a little smile of almost devilish satisfaction. She had a pleased air of feeling that she had done something very clever.

"I think you're a dangerous woman," he said with profound conviction.

She yawned delicately, and rubbed her eyes like a sleepy kitten.

"I don't know what you mean," she said. "Anyway, I'm too tired to argue. But you'll have to go on being nice to me now, won't you? I mean, what would Patricia do if I told her?"

"She'd write your name on the wall," said the Saint, "where we keep all the others. We're making a mural of them."

"Would she? Well, don't forget that I know what you've done with Bravache and those other men. When they've been bumped off, or whatever you call it, I shan't want you to get hanged for it if I go on liking you."

The Saint was grinning as he went out and locked the door. It was the first piece of unalloyed fun that had enriched the day.

At four that morning a young policeman on his beat noticed a suspicious cluster of shapes in a doorway in Grosvenor Square. He flashed his light on them and saw that they were the bodies of three men, with adhesive tape over their mouths and their hands fastened somehow behind them, sprawled against the door in grotesque attitudes. They were stripped to the waist and horrid red stains were smeared across their torsos.

Blood! . . . The young policeman's heart skipped a beat. In a confused vision, he saw himself gaining fame and promotion for unravelling a sensational murder mystery, becoming in rapid succession an Inspector, a Superintendent, and a Chief Commissioner.

He ran up the steps, and as he did so he became aware of a pungent odour that seemed oddly familiar. Then one of the bodies moved painfully, and he saw that they were not dead. Their bulging eyes blinked at his light, and strange nasal grunts came from them. And as he bent over them he discovered the reason for the red stains that had taken his breath away, and at the same time located the source of that hauntingly familiar perfume. It was paint. From brow to waist they were painted in zebra stripes of gaudy red and blue, with equal strips of their own white skins showing in between to complete the pattern. The decorative scheme had even been carried over the tops of their heads, which had been shaved for the purpose to the smoothness of billiard balls.

Hanging over them, on the door handle, was a card inscribed with hand-painted letters:

> THESE ANIMALS ARE
> THE PROPERTY OF
> Mr KANE LUKER
> PLEASE DO NOT TOUCH

4

Simon Templar was having breakfast in Cornwall House when a call on the telephone from the watchful Sam Outrell at his post in the lobby heralded the arrival of Chief Inspector Claud Eustace Teal a few seconds before the doorbell sounded under his pudgy finger.

Simon went to the door himself. The visitation was no surprise to him—as a matter of fact, he had been fatalistically expecting it for some hours. But he allowed his eyebrows to go up in genial surprise when the opening door revealed Teal's freshly laundered face like a harvest moon under a squarely planted bowler hat.

"Hail to thee, blithe spirit," he greeted the detective breezily. "I was wondering where you'd been hiding all these days. Come in and tell me all the news."

Teal came in like an advancing tank. There was an aura of portentous somnolence about him, as if he found the whole world so boring that it was hardly worthwhile to keep awake. Simon knew the signs like the geography of his own home. When Chief Inspector Teal looked as if he might easily fall asleep in a standing position at any moment, it meant that he had something more than usually heavy weighing on his mind, and on this particular morning it was not insuperably difficult for the Saint to guess what that load was. But his manner was seraphically conscience-free as he steered the detective into the living-room.

"Have some breakfast," he suggested convivially.

"I had my breakfast at breakfast time," Teal said with dignity.

He stood rather stiffly and sluggishly, holding his sedate black derby over his navel.

Simon lifted his shoulders in regret.

"There are times when you have an almost suburban smugness," he said deploringly. "Never mind. You'll excuse me if I go on with mine, won't you? Sit down, Claud. Take off your boots and make yourself at home. Why should these little things come between us?"

Teal sank heavily into a chair.

"I suppose you were up late last night," he said ponderously. "Is that why you're having breakfast so late this morning?"

"I don't know." The Saint punctured his second egg. "That wouldn't be a bad excuse, but why should I make excuses?" The Saint waved his fork oratorically. "One of the many troubles of this cockeyed age is the glorification of false virtues. The bank clerk gets up early because he has to. And consequently dozens of fortunate people who don't need to get up early drag themselves out of bed at insanitary hours because it makes them feel as virtuous as a bank clerk. Instead of aspiring towards freedom and emancipation, we make a virtue of assuming unnecessary restrictions. A man spends his life working to the position where he doesn't have to get to the office at nine o'clock, and then he boasts that he still gets up at seven-thirty every morning. Well, then, what was he working for? Why didn't he save his energy and remain a clerk? You might build an indictment of all our accepted values on that. Poor men nibble a crust of bread because that's all they've got, and millionaires go on a diet of dry crusts and soda-water—"

"What were you doing last night?" asked the detective implacably.

Simon looked shocked.

"Really, Claud! Have you no discretion? Or have you by any chance become a gossip writer?"

"I just want to know where you were last night," Teal said immovably. "I know you've got one of your usual alibis, but I'd like to hear it. And then perhaps you'll tell me why you did it."

"Did what?"

"You know what I'm talking about."

"I wish I did. It sounds so intriguing."

"What were you doing last night?"

Simon buttered a slice of toast.

"So far as I recollect, I spent a classically blameless evening. An archbishop could have followed in my footsteps without getting a single speck of mud on his reverend gaiters. Preceded by massed choirs in white surplices, and marshalled by a fatigue party from the Salvation Army."

"Let me tell you some of the things you did," Teal interrupted stolidly. "You dined at the Berkeley with Lady Valerie Woodchester. She left at about half past ten, and you went to the Café Royal. You got back here towards twelve-fifteen, and at five minutes past one you went out again. Your friends Quentin and Uniatz were with you, and you were careful to see that you weren't followed. At twenty-five minutes past two Miss Holm left here in another of your cars, and she was also very careful to see that she wasn't followed. At four-thirty this morning you came in alone. I want to know what you were doing between one-five and four-thirty."

"What a man you are, Claud!" said the Saint with admiration. "Nothing is hidden from you. Your house must be full of little birds."

"It's my business to know what people like you are doing."

"You know," said the Saint in an injured tone, "I believe you must have been having me watched. I don't call that very friendly of you. Have you lost your old faith in me?"

"What were you doing between one-five and four-thirty this morning?" Teal repeated tigerishly.

The Saint stirred his coffee with an air of shy discomfort.

"I really didn't want you to know about that," he confessed. "You see, much as I love you, you're always the professional policeman, and you have to take such a morbidly legal view of things. The fact is, Peter and Hoppy and I decided that we didn't feel tired, so we pushed off to a little club we wot of where they haven't any respect for the licensing laws, and we stayed there hardening our arteries and talking to loose women until nearly dawn."

"What's the name of this club?"

"That's just what I can't tell you, Claud. You see my point. If you knew where it was you'd feel you had to do something about closing it down, because any place in London where one might have a good time has to be closed down. And that would be a pity, because it's quite a cheery little spot now, and these places always become so dismal when they get infested with disguised policemen snooping for evidence and leaving the smell of Lifebuoy Soap in their wake—"

"All right," Teal said with frightful restraint. "That's your story. And now suppose you tell me about those men you painted red, white, and blue and left outside Luker's house."

The Saint put his coffee cup down. He wore the incredulous and appalled expression of a Presbyterian Elder who has been accused of operating an illicit still.

"Painted?" he said hollowly.

"Yes."

"Red, white, and blue?"

"Yes."

"Outside Luker's house?"

"Yes."

"Who were these men?"

"You know as well as I do. Their names are Bravache, Pietri, and Dumaire."

The Saint shook his head with great concern.

"Somebody must have been pulling your leg, Claud," he said. "I simply can't imagine myself doing a thing like that, even after a night at the place where I was. Did anybody see me paint them and leave them outside Luker's house? Do *they* say I painted them?"

Mr Teal unwrapped a springboard of spearmint with wearily deliberate fingers, as if he were undressing himself for bed after a hard day. He had already spent a bad hour in dire anticipation of this interview, and his forebodings had not been disappointed. But he had to go through with it. For an hour he had been preparing himself, wrestling with his soul, facing in prospect all the gibes and banter and infuriating mockery that he knew he would have to endure, drilling himself to the fulfilment of the vow that he would be calm, that he would be rock-like and masterful, that for this one lone historic occasion he would not let the Saint get under his skin and cut the suspenders of his self-control, as the Saint had done with fateful facility so often in the past, and the soul of Claud Eustace Teal had emerged tried and tempered from the annealing fires. Or nearly. He would triumph in the ordeal even though blood oozed from his pores.

"No," he said. "Nobody saw you do it. The men don't say it was you. They say they don't know who it was. But I know it was you!"

"Do you?" At that moment the Saint was as sleek as a seal. "What makes you think so?"

"I know it because Luker was one of the guests at that country house fire that you were meddling in, where John Kennet was killed, and I should think of you in connection with anything that happened to Luker now. Besides that, two of those men are Frenchmen. When I saw you at that place where Ralph Windlay was murdered, you read me two cuttings from French newspapers and talked about something called the Sons of France. Red, white, and blue are the French national colours. Painting those men like that and leaving them outside Luker's doorstep is just the sort of thing I'd expect of you. There's one connecting link all the way through—and you're it! "

Simon regarded him like a spot on the carpet.

"And that's your evidence, is it?"

Teal swallowed, but he nodded stubbornly.

"That's it."

"That's the collection of barefaced balderdash that's supposed to authorise you to take me into custody and lug me off to Vine Street. That's the immortal excretion of the best brains of Scotland Yard. Or have I misjudged you, Claud? Have you taken a pill and woken up to find you've got a genius for publicity? You'll certainly get a bale of it over this. Let's go on with it. What will the charge be? Wait a minute, I can see it all—'That he did feloniously and with malice aforethought assault the complainants with an unlawful instrument, to wit, a paintbrush—'"

"Did I say that?" asked Mr Teal.

It was quite a moment for Mr Teal. For the first time that he could remember he stopped the Saint short.

The Saint looked at him in wary surmise. A hundred disjointed ideas rocketed through his head, but they all arrived by devious paths at the same mark. And that was something compared with which a seven-headed dragon pirouetting on its tail would have been a perfectly commonplace phenomenon.

"Do you mean," he said foggily, "that you didn't come here to arrest me?"

"You ought to know enough about the law to know that I can't do anything if these men won't make a complaint."

Simon felt a trifle light-headed.

"You didn't come here to congratulate me, by any chance?"

"No."

"And you didn't come here for breakfast?"

"No."

"Well, what the devil did you come for?"

"I thought you might like to tell me something about it," Teal said woodenly. "What is all this about, and what has Luker got to do with it?"

The Saint reached for a cigarette.

"Quite apart from the fact that I don't see why I should be supposed to know—haven't you thought of asking him?"

"I have asked him. He said he'd never seen these men before, and they say they've never heard of him."

The Saint lighted his cigarette. He leaned back in his chair and stretched out his legs under the table.

"Then it certainly does look very mysterious," he said, but his blue eyes were quiet and searching.

Chief Inspector Teal turned his venerable bowler on his blue serge knees. He had got his spearmint nicely into condition now—a plastic nugget; malleable and yet resistant, still flavorous, crisp without being crumbly, glutinous without adhesion, obedient to the capricious patterning of his mobile tongue working in conjunction with the clockwork reciprocation of his teeth, polymorphous, ductile. It was a great comfort to him. He would have been lost without it. What he had to do was not easy.

"I know," he said. "That's why I came to see you. I thought you might be able to give me a lead."

The Saint stared at him for several moments in a silence of gull-winged eyebrows and wide absorbent eyes, while that cataclysmic statement sank through the diverse layers of his comprehension.

"Well, I will be a cynocephalic mandrill scratching my blue bottom on the ramparts of Timbuctoo," he said finally. "Or am I one already? I thought I'd seen every kind and sample of human nerve in my time, but this is the last immortal syllable. You treat me as a suspicious character; you habitually accuse me of every crime that's committed in England that you're too thick-headed to solve; you threaten me three times a week with penal servitude and bodily violence; you persecute me at every conceivable opportunity; you disturb my slumbers and hound me at my own breakfast table; and then you have the unmitigated gall to sit there, with your great waistcoat full of stomach, and ask me to help you!"

It was a bitter draught for Mr Teal to get past his uvula, but he managed it, even though his gorge threatened to suffocate him. Perhaps it was one of the most prodigious victories of self-discipline that he had ever achieved in his life.

"That's what I want," he said, with a superhuman effort of carelessness that made him look as if he was about to lapse into an apoplectic coma. "Why should we go on fighting each other? We're both really out for the same thing, and this is a case where we could work together and you could save yourself getting into trouble as well. I'll be quite frank with you. I remembered everything you said at Windlay's place, and I made some inquiries on my own responsibility. I've seen a verbatim report of the Kennet inquest, and I've talked with one of the reporters who was there. I agree with you that it was conducted in a very unsatisfactory way. I put it to the Chief Commissioner that we ought to consider reopening the case. He agreed with me then, but yesterday evening he told me I'd better drop it. I'm pretty sure there's pressure being put on him to leave well alone—the kind of pressure he can't afford to ignore. But I don't like dropping cases. If there's anything fishy about this it ought to come out. Now, you said something to me about the Sons of France, didn't you?"

"I may have mentioned them," Simon admitted cautiously. "But—"

Chief Inspector Teal suddenly opened his baby-blue eyes, and they were not bored or comatose or stupid, but unexpectedly clear and penetrating in the round placidity of his face.

"Well, that's why I came to see you. You may have something that puts the whole puzzle together. Bravache and Dumaire are Frenchmen." Mr Teal paused. He fashioned his gum once into the shape of a spindle, and then clamped his teeth destructively down on it. "And I happen to have found out that John Kennet was a member of the Sons of France," he said.

CHAPTER SIX:

HOW MR FAIRWEATHER OPENED
HIS MOUTH AND MR UNIATZ PUT
HIS FOOT IN IT

1

"Kennet was a member of the Sons of France?" Simon repeated. "Are you sure?"

"Yes. His mother was French, and he was brought up with French as a second language. He spoke it perfectly. I told you I'd been making inquiries. I've established the fact that he joined the Sons of France six months ago under the name of Jean de la Paix. Incidentally, he was also a member of the French Communist Party." Teal went on watching the Saint, searchingly, and with a glint of malice. "I thought you'd have known that."

The Saint blew a geometrically faultless smoke-ring across the table. His face was tranquilly uncommunicative, relieved from blankness only by a faint inscrutable smile, but behind the mask his brain was running like a dynamo.

"I might have guessed," he said.

"Did you?"

"I'm a good guesser . . . 'Jean de la Paix', too—he had a sense of humour after all. And guts. For a registered member of the French Communist Party to join the Sons of France at all was guts, and he must have got further than just joining. That would only be another reason why he had to be cremated."

"What was the first reason?"

Simon looked down at his fingernails.

"You want to know a great deal," he said, and looked up again.

"Of course I do."

"Well, so do I." The Saint thought for a while, and made up his mind. "All right, Claud. You asked for it, and you can have it. For about the first time in my life I'll be perfectly frank with you. It'd be worthwhile if it only meant that I could get on with my job without having to cope with all your suspicions and persecutions as well as my own troubles. But I don't suppose it'll do any good, because as usual you probably won't believe me—You see, Claud, the fact is that I don't know any more than you do."

Teal's face darkened.

"I didn't come here to waste my time—"

"And I don't want you to waste mine. I told you, you wouldn't believe me. But there it is. I don't know any more than you do. The only difference is that not being a policeman I haven't got so many great open spaces in my brain to start with, so I don't need to know so much."

Mr Teal's spearmint, under the systematic massage of his molars, became in turn a sphere, an hour-glass, and something like a short-handled frying pan.

"Go on," he said lethargically. "Make allowances for my stupidity, and tell me how much I know."

"As you like. Let's start with Comrade Luker. As you know, he is the current top tycoon of the arms racket."

"I suppose so."

"Comrades Fairweather and Sangore are his stooges in a couple of British armaments firms which he controls."

"I don't—"

"Call them what you like, and they're still his stooges. Between them, those three are running a combine that practically constitutes a monopoly of the arms industry in this country. Their only job is manufacturing engines and instruments and gadgets that kill people, and the only way they can make good money is in having a good demand for their products. I shall also ask you to grasp the idea that one customer's money will buy as much champagne and caviar as another's, whoever he wants to kill. But under the laws we suffer from, there's nothing criminal in any of that—nothing that you could take any professional interest in. If a man gets drunk and kills somebody with his car, it's your job to put him in jail, but if he organises the killing of several thousand people they make him an earl, and it's your job to stop the traffic when he wants to cross the street. The technical name for that is civilisation. Correct?"

"Go on."

The Saint poured out some more coffee.

"Now let's go to France. There they have a political, Fascist organisation called the Sons of France. It may or may not be illegal. I seem to remember that they passed a law not long ago to ban all organisations of that kind, and the old Croix de Feu was disbanded on account of it. The Sons of France may have found a way to get round the law, or the law may not give a damn, or they may have too much pull already, or something, or they may be just illegal and proud of it, and even if that's the case it's nothing to do with you. It's a matter for the French police."

"I'm listening."

"That's something. Well, from one indication and another it seems pretty clear that Luker is backing the Sons of France. That's natural enough. Dictators always go in for rearmament in a big way, and therefore Fascist regimes are good for business. Besides which, if you can get enough synthetic Caesars thumping their chests and bellowing defiance at each other, it won't be long before you have a nice big war, which means a boom for the armourers. But it isn't a crime to finance a political party, or else half the titled people in England would be in the hoosegow. Unless the Sons of France are an illegal organisation, in which case it's still a matter for the French police and not for you."

"You haven't got down to Kennet yet," Teal said sluggishly.

"Kennet was a Pacifist, a Communist, and all kinds of idealistic 'ists.' He thought he could do a lot of good by showing up the arms racket. Old stuff. Dozens of people have done it before, and everybody says 'How shocking!' and 'Why can't something be done about it?' and then they go off and forget about it. But Kennet went on. He joined the Sons of France. And by some fluke he must have found out something that really was worth finding out, so he had an accident. But you still can't do anything about it."

"I can do something about wilful murder."

"I did say he was murdered, but that's just what seems obvious to me. I've no evidence at all. We both know how Windlay was murdered, but I've no evidence to pin it on any particular person, any more than you have. It's no good just saying that whoever did the actual jobs, we know that Luker was at the back of them. What are you going to tell a jury? With people like we're dealing with, you'd want an army of eye-witnesses before you could even get a warrant. Even then I don't know if you could get it. They're too big. Look how you've already had the word from up top to lay off the case. British justice is the most incorruptible in the world, so they tell you, but you can always whitewash a crook if he's big enough because it isn't what they call 'in the public interest' that he should be shown up. And look at the circumstances of these Kennet and Windlay cases. It's a million to one that you could never get any conclusive evidence on either of them if you worked until you could tuck your beard into your boots."

Mr Teal rolled the pink wrapping of his chewing gum into a ball and went on rolling it. His china-blue eyes were still unwaveringly inquisitorial.

"I'll agree with some of that up to a point. But you know more than that. You know something else that you're still working on."

"Only one thing." Simon was calm and collected: he had made up his mind to be candid, and he was going through with it—it could do him no harm, only perhaps reduce the complications of Teal's interference. "Kennet fell pretty hard for Lady Valerie Woodchester, who was set on to him by Fairweather to try and steer him off. He talked to her a lot—I don't know how much he told her. And he left some of his evidence in writing. That's why the flat was torn apart when Windlay was murdered. They were looking for it. But it wasn't there. Lady Valerie has got it."

The detective's eyes suddenly opened wide.

"But—"

"I know," said the Saint wearily. "You're too brilliant, Claud, that's what's the matter with you. I know all about it. So all you've got to do is to go to Lady Valerie and say 'Where's that stuff that Kennet gave you?' Well, you try it. I have."

"But if she's concealing evidence—"

"Who said she was? She did. To me alone—without witnesses. If you pulled her into court, she could deny every word of it, and you couldn't prove anything different."

"But what is she doing it for?"

"Champagne coupons."

"What?"

"Dough. Geetus. Mazuma. Boodle. Crackle paper. She's in business for the money, the same as I used to be. And she knows that evidence is worth cash to Fairweather and Company. The only way you could break her down would be to talk her language, which means putting up more cash than the others will, which personally I don't propose to do and you in your job couldn't do." The Saint shook his head. "It's no good, Claud. You still aren't in the running. You can't even go after her and batter her with your sex appeal—not with a figure like yours. You're sunk. Why don't you pack up and go home to chivvying the poor little street bookmakers in Soho, where you can't go wrong?"

Chief Inspector Teal's ruminant jaws continued their monotonous mastication. The logic of the Saint's argument was irrefutable, but there was in Mr Teal an ineradicable scepticism, founded on years of bitter disappointment, that fought obstinately against the premises from which that logic took its flying start. The Saint might for once be telling the truth, but there had been many other occasions when he had been no less plausible when he was lying. All of Mr Teal's prejudices fought back from the dead end to which credulity inevitably led.

"That's all very well," he said doggedly. "But you're still working on something. And when did you stop thinking about money? Suppose you get this evidence—what's going to happen?"

"I wouldn't turn it over to you. I don't imagine it would help you. I only want it to make perfectly sure—to find out just how much there is behind this racket. I could deal with Luker and Company today, without it. Mind you, I don't want to put any ideas into your head, although there must be lots of room for them, but if Luker for instance should meet with a minor accident, such as falling off the roof of his house into Grosvenor Square—"

The telephone bell rang while the Saint was speaking.

He went over and picked it up, while Teal watched him with broody eyes.

Simon said, "Hullo," and then his eyebrows lifted. He said, "Speaking . . . Yes . . . Yes . . . Yes . . ."

Darkness gathered on Teal's lace. Something leaden crept into his light-blue eyes, like clear skies filling with thunder. Sudden brilliance flashed across them like the snap of lightning as a storm breaks. He came out of his chair like a whale breaking the surface. Surprisingly quick for his adipose dimensions, he plunged across the intervening space and snatched the microphone out of Simon's hand.

"Hullo!" he bawled. "Chief Inspector Teal speaking . . . No, that wasn't me before . . . Never mind that, go on . . . What? . . . What's that? . . . Yes . . . Yes. . ."

An indistinguishable mutter droned on from the receiver, and as Teal listened to it his cherubic round face grew hard and strained. His eyes stayed fixed upon the Saint, hot and jagged with a seethe of violent emotions of which the most accurately identifiable one was wrath rising to the temperature of incandescence. His mouth was a clenched trap in the lurid mauve of his face, which now and again opened just sufficiently to eject a sizzling monosyllable like a blob of molten quartz.

"All right," he bit out at last. "Stay there. I'll be round presently."

He slammed the instrument back on its bracket and stood glaring at the Saint like a gorilla that has just got up from sitting down on a drawing pin.

"Well?" he snarled. "Let's hear what you've got to say about that."

"What have I got to say?" Simon's voice was the honey of spotless innocence. "Well, Claud, since you ask me, it does seem to me that if you're going to turn this place into a club and tell your low friends to ring you up here, you oughtn't to mind my having a bit of fun out of—"

"I'll see that you get your fun! So you thought you were taking me in with all that slop you were giving me. You've been . . . You're—"

"You're getting incoherent, Claud. Take a deep breath and speak from the diaphragm."

Chief Inspector Teal took the deep breath, but it came out again like an explosion of compressed air.

"You heard enough on the telephone—"

"But I didn't. It just looked like getting interesting when you so rudely snatched it away. Apparently one of your minions had been out trying to persecute somebody who wasn't at home."

"I sent a man round to interview Lady Valerie Woodchester," said Mr Teal, speaking like a locomotive ascending a steep gradient. "I thought she might know more than she'd told anyone. No, she wasn't at home. But her maid was, and she'd already been wondering whether she ought to call the police. Apparently Lady Valerie went out last night and didn't come back. When her maid came in this morning, her bed hadn't been slept in, but the whole flat had been turned inside out and there were pieces of rope and sticking plaster on the floor as if someone had been tied up. It looks exactly as if she'd been kidnapped—and if she has been I'll know who did it!"

The Saint had sat down again on the edge of the table. He came off it as if it had turned red-hot under him.

"What!" he exclaimed in horrified amazement. "My God, if anything's happened to her—"

"You know damn well what's happened to her!" Teal's voice was thick with the rage of disillusion. "You've told me enough to make that obvious. That's why you were so sure I couldn't get her information! Well, you're wrong this time. I'm going to see that you're taken care of till we find her." Unconsciously Teal drew himself up, as he had done in those circumstances before, if he could only have remembered, so many fruitless times. "I shall take you into custody—"

Perhaps after all, as Mr Teal had so often been driven to believe in his more despondent moments, there was some fateful interdiction against his ever being permitted to complete that favourite sentence. At any rate, this was not the historic occasion on which completion was destined to be achieved. The sound of a bell cut him off in midflight, like a gong freezing a prize-fighter poised for a knockout punch.

This time it was not the telephone, but a subdued and decorous trill that belonged unmistakably to the front door.

Teal looked over his shoulder at the sound. And as the Saint started to move, he moved faster.

"You stay here," he flung out roughly. "I'll see who it is."

Simon sat down again philosophically and lighted another cigarette. His first smoke-ring from that new source was still on its way to the ceiling when Mr Teal came back. After him came Mr Algernon Sidney Fairweather.

2

Mr Fairweather wore a dark suit with a gold watch-chain looped across the place where in his youth he might once have kept his waist. He carried a light grey homburg and a tightly rolled umbrella with a gold handle. He looked exactly as if a Rolls-Royce had just brought him away from an important board meeting.

The Saint inspected him with sober admiration mingled with cordial surprise, and neither of these expressions conveyed one per cent of what was really going on in his mind.

"Algy," he said softly, "what have I done to deserve the honour of seeing you darken my proletarian doors?"

"I . . . er . . . um!" said Mr Fairweather, as if he had not made up his mind what else to say.

Teal interposed himself between them.

"I was just about to take Mr Templar under arrest," he explained grimly.

"You were . . . um! Were you? May I ask what the charge was, Inspector?"

"I suspect him of being concerned in kidnapping Lady Valerie Woodchester."

Fairweather started.

"Lady—" He swallowed. "Kidnapped? But—"

"Lady Valerie Woodchester has disappeared, and her apartment has been ransacked," Teal said solidly. "I'm glad you came here, sir. You may be able to give me some information. You knew her well, I believe?"

"Er . . . yes, I suppose I knew her quite well."

"Did she ever say anything to make you think that she was afraid of anyone—that she considered herself in any sort of danger?"

Fairweather hesitated. He glanced nervously at the Saint.

"She did mention once that she was frightened of Mr Templar," he affirmed reluctantly. "But I'm afraid I didn't pay much attention to it at the time. The idea seemed so . . . But you surely don't think that anything serious has really happened to her?"

"I know damn well that something has happened to her—I don't know how serious it is." Teal turned on the Saint like a congealed cyclone. "That's what you'd better tell me! I might have known you couldn't be trusted to tell the truth for two minutes together. But you've told me too much already. You told me that Lady Valerie had something you wanted. Now she's disappeared, and her place has been ransacked. Ralph Windlay was murdered, and his flat was ransacked. In both places someone was looking for something, and from what you've told me the most likely person is you! "

The Saint sighed.

"Of course," he said patiently. "That's what they call Deduction. That's what they teach you at the Police College. I'm looking for something, and therefore everyone who is looking for something is me."

Teal set his teeth. The suspicions which had been held in check at the beginning of the interview were flooding back on him with the overwhelming turbulence of a typhoon. In all fairness to Mr Teal, than which there is nothing dearer to this chronicler's hardened heart, it must be admitted that there was some justification for his biased viewpoint. Mr Teal could make allowances for coincidence up to a point, but the swift succession of places and people where and to whom violent things had happened in close proximity to Simon Templar's presence on the scene was a little too much for him. And there was the curdling memory of many other similar coincidences to accelerate the acid fermentation of Mr Teal's misanthropic conclusions. The congenital runaway tendencies of his spleen were aggravated by the recollection of his own recent guilelessness.

"Lady Valerie didn't stay with you very long last night," he rapped. "Why did she leave you so early?"

"She was tired," said the Saint.

"Had you quarrelled with her?"

"Bitterly. I may be old-fashioned, Claud, but one thing I will not allow anybody to do is to be rude about my friends. They may have figures like sacks of dough and faces like giant tomatoes, but beauty is only skin deep and kind hearts are more than coronets and all that sort of thing, and just because a bloke is a policeman is no reason why any girl should make fun of him. That's what I told her. I said, 'Look here, Lady Valerie, just because poor old Claud Eustace has fallen arches and a bay window like the blunt end of the Normandie—'"

"Will you shut up?" roared the detective.

Simon shut up.

Mr Teal took a fresh grip on his gum.

"Why was Lady Valerie frightened of you?" he barked.

The Saint did not answer.

"Had you been threatening her?"

Simon remained mute. He made helpless clownish motions with his hands.

The detective's complexion was like that of an over-ripe prune.

"What the hell's the matter with you?" he bayed. "Can't you even talk anymore?"

"Of course not," said the Saint. "You told me to shut up. I am an oyster. Will you have me on the half shell, or creamed in white wine?"

Chief Inspector Teal looked as if he had swallowed a large live eel. His stomach appeared to be trying to reject this refractory diet, and he seemed to be having difficulty in keeping it down. His neck swelled with the fury of the struggle.

"Tell me why Lady Valerie was frightened of you," he said in a garotted gargle.

"I've no idea why she should have been," said the Saint. "I'd no idea she was. Why don't you ask Algy? He seems to know all about it. And while you're on the job, what about asking him why he came here and what he thought he was going to do?"

Fairweather sniffed into a white silk handkerchief, tucked it back into his breast pocket, and planted himself like a Minister in Parliament preparing to answer a question from the Opposition.

"I have not visited Mr Templar before," he said, "and I should not expect to do so again. The reason for my call this morning is quite simple. I had a tentative engagement to lunch with Lady Valerie today, and I rang her up not long ago to confirm it. She was not in, and her maid informed me in some agitation that she had apparently not slept at her apartment last night, and had left no message to give a clue to her whereabouts. Knowing that this was an extraordinary departure from her normal habits, I puzzled over it with some seriousness and recalled her mentioning that she was in some fear of Mr Templar, as I have told you. I telephoned again later, and could still hear no news of her, and on my way from the Club to the Savoy, where we were to have met, I recollected that she had told me she was dining with Mr Templar last night. My anxieties at once became graver, and since

I was at that moment close to this building, on an impulse—which was perhaps rash in conception, but which I now feel to have been very sensibly founded—I instructed my chauffeur to stop, and came up with the intention of—"

"Algy," said the Saint, with profound respect, "I don't wonder you got into the Cabinet. With your gift for making a collection of plain goddam lies sound like an archbishop's sermon, the only thing I can't understand is why they didn't make you Prime Minister."

Conviction hardened on Mr Teal like the new carapace on a moulted lobster. His eyes held on the Saint with dourly triumphant tenacity.

"I'll tell you why Lady Valerie was frightened of you," he said. "I expect she was thinking of what happened to Kennet and Windlay. She knew you were trying to make trouble for Mr Luker and Mr Fairweather, and since she was a friend of theirs—"

"Was Kennet a friend of theirs?" asked the Saint pungently.

Fairweather said, with solemn and unshakable pomposity, "He was a guest in my house. I think that should be sufficient answer."

Teal nodded implacably.

"You've pulled the wool over my eyes often enough, Templar, but you can't do it this time. What's the use of bluffing? There's enough circumstantial evidence already to put you away for a long time. If you want to be smart you won't make things any worse for yourself. Tell me what's happened to Lady Valerie Woodchester, and you may get off with eighteen months."

The Saint looked at him for several seconds. And then he laughed out loud.

"You poor pin-brained boob," he said.

The detective's face did not change.

"That won't—"

"Won't do me any good?" Simon completed the sentence for him. "Well, I'm not interested, I'm not trying to do myself good—I don't have to. I'm trying to do you some. You need it. Have you gone so completely daft that you've lost your memory? Have you ever known me to threaten, beat up, bump off, or otherwise raise hell with women? Have you ever had even the slightest reason to suspect me of it? But because you're too bat-eyed and pig-headed to see any further than the pimples on the end of your own nose, you want to believe that I've turned myself into an ogre for Lady Valerie's special benefit. What you need—"

"I don't need any of—"

"You need plenty." The Saint was cool, unflurried, but his curt sentences were edged like knives. "According to some ancient law which it doesn't look as if you'd ever heard of, a man in this country is presumed innocent until he can be proved guilty. Why don't you try being just half as credulous with me as you are with Algy? Because he was once a member of His Majesty's immortal Government. You pitiful cretin! In other words, he made his living for years out of making lies sound like sententious platitudes. Have you ever started to criticise what he's just told you? Lady Valerie wasn't home, and hadn't been home, when he phoned to check up on a lunch date. 'Knowing that this was an extra ordinary departure from her normal habits—'"

"I heard what Mr Fairweather said."

"And you gulped it down! This is the guy who knew Lady Valerie well. He didn't just assume that she'd been out on an all-party night and forgotten to come home. He 'puzzled over it with some seriousness.' Well, I don't want to be unkind about the girl, and I don't even ask you to believe me, but I'll bet you five thousand quid to fourpence that if you check back on her record you'll find that she's often done things like that before. Algy never thought of that. His 'anxieties at once became graver'—so grave that he dropped in here to ask me, a comparative stranger, what I thought about it. And while we're on the subject of lunch dates, I'll give you something else. Algy tells you that he had this date with Lady Valerie, and naturally you believe him. Well, he's got his ideas mixed. He didn't have this date—I had it. Now would you like to think that over for yourself, or shall I go on helping you?"

There was a candour, an ardent sincerity in the Saint's voice that would have arrested most listeners. Mr Teal was visibly shaken. In spite of himself, a new doubt joined the mad saraband that was taking place in his fevered brain. Certainly he had found it hard to believe that the Saint had done any harm to Lady Valerie: even he had to admit that such a crime would have been out of character. On the other hand, he found it equally hard to believe that such obviously respectable members of Society as Luker and Fairweather could be involved in any sinister motives. If he arrested the Saint after a speech that carried conviction, experience indicated that he would probably end up by making himself look highly ridiculous, but on the other hand experience also indicated that he usually ended up by looking quite ridiculous enough when he left the Saint at large. It was one of those situations in which Mr Teal habitually felt himself drowning in the turgid waters of an unfathomable *Weltschmerz*.

He glowered at Simon with a smouldering malevolence which he hoped would help to disguise the sinking foundations of his assurance.

"You're wasting your time," he said, but a keen ear could have detected the first loss of dominance in his voice, like the flattening note of a bell that has begun to crack. "Mr Fairweather's suspicions sound quite reasonable to me—"

"Suspicions?" The Saint was lethally sardonic. "Why don't you call them certainties and have done with it? That's what they'd look like to anyone who hadn't got such a one-track mind as yours. So Algy had a date with Lady Valerie for lunch. But he hasn't shown any signs of impatience to push along to the Savoy and see if she's waiting for him.

He didn't even go there first and see whether she turned up before he came here to see me. And he still doesn't have to wait and make sure she isn't there before he backs up this charge against me. He knows damn well she isn't going to be there! And how do you think he gets so damn sure about that?"

Teal's mouth opened a little. After a moment he turned his head. And for the first time he looked hard and invitingly at Mr Fairweather.

Mr Fairweather's chins wobbled with the working of his Adam's apple like rolls of soft raspberry jelly.

"Really," he stuttered, "Mr Templar's insinuations are so preposterous . . . I . . . I . . . Really, Inspector, you ought to . . . to do something to . . . um . . ."

"I quite understand, sir." Teal was polite and respectful, but his gum was starting on a new and interesting voyage. "At the same times if you gave me an explanation—"

"I should think the explanation would be obvious," Fairweather said stuffily. "If your imagination is unable to cope with such a simple problem, the Chief Commissioner might be interested to hear about it."

Had he been a better psychologist he would have known that that was the last thing he should have said. Mr Teal was still acutely conscious that he was addressing a former Cabinet Minister, but the set of his jaw took on an obstinate heaviness.

"I beg your pardon, sir," he said, "but the Chief Commissioner expects me to obtain definite statements in support of my imagination."

"Rubbish!" snorted Fairweather. "If you propose to treat me like a suspected criminal—"

"If you persist in this attitude, sir," Teal said courageously, "you may force me to do so."

Fairweather simply gaped at him.

And a great grandiose galumptious grin spread itself like Elysian honey over Simon Templar's eternal soul. The tables were turned completely. Fairweather was in the full centre of Teal's attention now—not himself. And Fairweather had assisted nobly in putting himself there. The moment contained all the refined ingredients of immortality. It shone with an austere magnificence that eclipsed every other consideration with its epic splendour. The Saint lay back in a chair and gave himself up to the exquisite absorption of its ambrosial glory.

And then the telephone bell rang again.

The Saint sat up, but this time Teal did not hesitate. Still preoccupied but still efficient, almost mechanically he picked up the microphone.

"Hullo," he said, and then. "Yes, speaking . . ."

Simon knew that he lied. He was simply playing back the trick that Simon had shown him before. But the circumstances were not quite the same. This call had come through on one of those exceptionally powerful connections that sometimes happen, and the raised voice of the speaker at the other end of the line did everything else that was necessary to produce a volume of sound in the receiver that was faintly but clearly audible across the room. Quite unmistakably it had said, "Is dat you, boss?"

Simon started to get up, spurred faster than thought by an irresistible premonition. But the agitation which had lent its penetrating pitch to Mr Uniatz's discordant voice was too quick for him. Hoppy's next utterance came through with the shattering clarity of a radio broadcast. "Listen, boss—de goil's got away!"

3

Teal put down the telephone with a sharp clunk of concentrated viciousness. Any reversal of emotion that he had suffered before was a childish tantrum compared with this. The Saint had not only been on the verge of making a monkey out of him for the second time in an hour—he had lured him on to the brink of affronting Fairweather in a way that might easily have cost him his job into the bargain. Whatever sentient faculties Mr Teal possessed at that moment were merely a curried hash of boiling vitriol. His face was congested to a deep shade of heliotrope, but his nostrils were livid with the whiteness of a berserk passion that would have been fuelled rather than assuaged by buckets of human blood.

He dug into his hip pocket and dragged out a pair of handcuffs as he lurched across towards the Saint.

"Come on," he said in a voice that could scarcely be recognised as his own. "You can write the rest of it down in Vine Street."

Simon watched him approach while he thought faster than he had ever done since this story began. Why and how Valerie Woodchester had escaped, and what momentous consequences that escape might bring after it, were questions that had to be crushed out of the activity of his mind. They could be dealt with afterwards; unless he forgot them now there would be no useful afterwards in which to deal with them.

This was a time when his fluent tongue would be no more use to him—he might as well have tried to argue Niagara to a standstill. From where he stood he could have reached a gun, but that would have been almost as useless. It would certainly have cowed Fairweather, but the paroxysm of cold rage that was propelling Teal across the floor would have kept him walking straight on into it until it blasted him down. And the Saint knew that he would never be capable of using a gun on Claud Eustace Teal for anything more than a bluff. Equally beyond doubt, he knew that he would never be capable of letting himself be handcuffed and taken to Vine Street without knowing how he was going to get out again—

He said, "Wait a minute, Claud. You win. I'll give you Lady Valerie."

It was the only thing he could have said that the detective would even have heard. It stopped Teal a yard from him, with the handcuffs held out.

"Where is she?"

Simon gazed at him with a sad wistful smile.

"It's been a good long scrap and a lot of fun, hasn't it, Claud?" he said. "But I suppose you were bound to come out on top in the end . . . Oh, well, let's make a clean sheet of it while we're at it. Hoppy was getting excited about nothing. Lady Valerie hasn't got away. I took her away myself, only I didn't have time to tell him. She's here in this apartment now, only about half a dozen yards away from you."

Teal gawped at him.

"Here?"

"Yes. You didn't think of that, did you? Well, you'll find her perfectly safe and sound, without even a speck of powder brushed off her nose."

"Where?"

"Come through the bedroom and I'll show you."

He turned away with an air of stoical resolution and sauntered steadily towards the door. Teal followed on his heels. Fairweather grasped his umbrella and followed Teal. As they entered the room, where the bed was still disordered from the Saint's recent rising, Simon said, "You've always suspected that I had a collection of secret passages and things here. You were pretty close to the mark, too. This ought to amuse you."

He indicated a door to one side of the bed.

Teal jerked it open. It revealed the interior of a big built-in cupboard in which an assortment of suits from the Saint's unlimited wardrobe hung on a long rail like a file of thin soldiers.

The Saint sat dejectedly on the side of the bed.

"Just push the wall at the end, and it opens," he said listlessly.

Teal shoved himself grimly in, shouldering the rank of suits aside. Fairweather stepped up to the door and peeped in after him.

What happened next was a succession of startling events of which Mr Fairweather's subsequent recollections were inclined to be confused. It seemed to him that without any warning the back of his collar and the seat of his pants were seized by the grappling mechanism of a kind of bimanual travelling crane. He rose from the ground and moved forward without any effort of his own into the ulterior of the cupboard, letting out a thin plaintive squeal as he did so. Then his advancing abdomen collided with breath-taking violence with the unyielding posterior of Chief Inspector Teal; the cupboard door slammed behind him; the light overhead went out; darkness descended; there was the sound of a key turning in the lock, and after that there was as much empty and unhelpful silence as Teal's sporadic sputtering of inspired profanity left room for . . .

Simon Templar moved swiftly out of the bedroom and locked that door also after him.

Now he was in it up to the neck, but he felt only an exuberant elation. As soon as Teal and Fairweather got out, which they must do in a comparatively short time, he would be a hunted man with all the nationwide networks of the Law spread out to catch him, but he only felt as if a burden had been taken off his shoulders. He had lived like that in the old days, when every man's hand was against him and death or ignominious defeat waited for him around every carelessly turned corner, and in those days he had known life at its keenest rapture, with a fullness that men who led safe humdrum existences could never know. Now at least the issues were clean-cut and unevadable. Perhaps he had been respectable for too long . . .

The telephone was ringing again. He picked it up.

"Hi, boss," said Mr Uniatz plaintively. "We got cut off."

"We didn't," said the Saint tersely. "That was your old friend Claud Eustace Teal you were talking to."

There was a long silence.

"Did I hear what you said, boss?"

"I hope so."

"You mean he hears what I say about de goil?"

"Yes."

"But I ask him is he you and he says he is," complained Hoppy, as if appalled by this revelation of the depths of perfidy to which a human being could sink.

Words rose to Simon's lips—short Anglo-Saxon words, colourful and expressive. But what was the use? Dull thudding noises reminiscent of an enraged crocodile lashing its tail in a wooden crate reached him through the walls. His time was short.

"Never mind," he said. "It's done now. Let me talk to Patricia."

"She ain't got back yet, boss. She goes out in de baby car just now to buy some more Scotch, and she is out when dis happens."

"When did it happen?"

"Just two, t'ree minutes back, boss. It's like dis. I am taking lunch up to de wren, and when I go in she says 'Lookit, de rug is boining.' It is boining, at dat. I go out for de extinguisher and squoit it on de fire, arid when I have been squoiting it for some time I see de broad has beat it."

"I suppose you left the door open for her."

"I dunno, boss," said Mr Uniatz aggrievedly. He seemed to feel that Lady Valerie had taken an unfair advantage of him. "Anyway, de door is open and she has hung it on de limb. I beat it downstairs and I hear a car going off outside, and when I open de door she is lamming out of here wit' your Daimler. So I call you up" said Mr Uniatz, conscientiously completing his narrative.

Simon opened his cigarette case on the telephone table.

"All right," he said crisply. "Now listen. Hell is going to pop over this party, and it's going to pop at you. You'd better get out from under. Stick around till Patricia gets back, and tell her what's happened. Then pile yourself and Orace into the pram and tell her to take you to the station. Buy tickets to Southampton and make enough fuss about it so they'll remember you at the booking office. Come out the other side of the station with the next crop of passengers, walk back to Brooklands, get out the old kite, and fly over to Heston. Peter will be there waiting for you. Do just what he tells you. Have you got it?"

"Ya mean we all do dis act?"

"Yes. All three of you. Teal will trace your call as soon as he gets back into action, and Weybridge will be no place for any of you to be seen alive in. You can take the Scotch with you, so you won't be hungry. Happy landings."

"Okay, boss—"

Simon put his finger on the contact breaker.

He lifted it again and lighted a cigarette while he dialled the number of Peter Quentin's apartment. The dull thudding behind him seemed louder, and splintering noises were beginning to blend with it. The Saint blew smoke-rings.

"Peter? . . . Good boy. This is Simon . . . Nothing, except that a small flock of balloons have gone up . . . No, but they will. In other words, Claud Eustace was here this morning to sing his theme song, as we expected, and meanwhile our protégé has pulled the bung. Hoppy rang up to tell me about it, and Teal took the call."

There was a pause while Peter assimilated this.

"Which police station are you speaking from, old boy?" he inquired cautiously, at last.

"None of them yet. But I expect they'll all be inviting me as soon as Teal gets out of the wardrobe where I've got him warming up at the moment. And they won't leave you out, either."

"As soon as—"

Peter's voice sounded faint and expiring.

The Saint grinned.

"Yes. Now listen, old son. Pat and Hoppy and Orace will be on their way to Heston with the Monospar at any moment, I've told them to pick you up there. Get on your way, and don't leave any tracks behind you. You can take off at once and hop to Deauville; take the train to Paris, and I'll get in touch with you later at the Hotel Raphael."

There was another pause.

"That's all very well" said Peter. "But suppose I don't feel like going abroad?"

"Think how it would broaden your mind," said the Saint. "Don't be heroic, Peter. I'll be harder to catch on my own, and there's nothing for you to do here. I shan't be staying long myself. I've got a pretty sound idea that the last act of this 'ere thrilling mellerdrammer takes place in Paris, and I may want you there. I'll be seeing you."

He rang off before Peter could answer again.

The thundering in the next room was louder still; it could only be a matter of seconds now before the wardrobe door gave way. But the Saint stayed to refill his cigarette case before he went out and caught a descending lift that dropped him swiftly to the basement garage.

He was debonair and unhurried as he stepped into the Hirondel and woke the engine; the fighting vitality that was lilting recklessly through every cell in his body found an outlet only in the sapphire alertness of his eyes, and the dynamic economy of his movements and the ghost of an unrepentant smile that lurked in the corners of his mouth . . . There was the same taxi parked by the kerb at the top of the ramp, the same miniature sports car with the driver reading a newspaper spread over the wheel; this time Simon had no Sam Outrell in a following car to help him, but he was unconcerned. He shot past them and turned into Half Moon Street, heading north; in the mirror over the windshield he saw them coming after him. Simon worked his way into Park Lane, cruised up it until he saw a break of no more than half a dozen yards in the stream of traffic pounding down towards him; then he swung the wheel and sent the Hirondel screeching through the gap towards the pavement on the wrong side of the road. The cataract of vehicles swerved wildly out to avoid him, flowed on past him with curses and straining brakes, effectively barring the path of his pursuers. Simon bumped the kerb, straightened up, and crawled round the next corner into Mount Street. A couple of instants later he was whirling away with gathering speed, to zigzag round four more consecutive corners and obliterate the last clue to his direction in the rabbit-warren of Mayfair.

The tangle he had left behind him in Park Lane was still sorting itself out when he crossed Oxford Street and turned the Hirondel to the west.

He felt sure that he knew what Lady Valerie's first move would be now, and he felt almost as sure that London would be the place where she would make it. Both of the two most probable routes from Weybridge to London led through Putney, and he still had time to meet her there.

He crossed Putney High Street more decorously than he had crossed Park Lane, and backed into a side turning from which he could watch the crawling flow of London-bound traffic and pull out to join it with the minimum of delay. The Hirondel stood there like a great glistening jewel, and not for the first time since he had chosen its flamboyant colour scheme the Saint wished that his tastes had been more conservative. That plutocratic equipage, which drew every eye back for a second look, would do nothing to simplify his problems. A policeman strolled by and studied it with deep interest for fifty slow-paced yards; Simon's heart was in his mouth, but the constable passed on without stopping. Doubtless the alarm which must even then have been circulating had not yet reached him. For ten minutes the Saint endured a strain that would have worn many hardened nerves to shreds, and coupled with it was the continual gnawing fear that his guess might after all have been wrong, and Lady Valerie would not come that way. His tanned face gave no inkling of his thoughts, but when he saw the black Daimler glide past the end of his side road, with Lady Valerie at the wheel, looking straight ahead of her, it was as if a miracle had happened.

The start of the Hirondel's engine was scarcely audible. Almost instantaneously he let in the clutch, and cut in to the line of traffic only two cars behind her. Intent and expressionless as a stalking leopard, the Saint drove on after her.

4

Her first stop was at the South Kensington post office. The Saint's eyes went cold and brittle when he saw the Daimler slowing up: Exhibition Road was too wide and unfrequented for any car to be unnoticeable in it. Fortunately on that account he had let himself fall some distance behind her. He jammed on the brakes and whipped round into Imperial Institute Road, and felt that the gods had been kind to him when he saw that she crossed the sidewalk and entered the post office without looking round. Clearly it had not occurred to her that she could have been picked up by that time.

He made a U-turn in the side road and parked near the corner. Then, after a moment's hesitation, he got out and walked up towards the post office entrance. It was a foolhardy thing to do, but a theory was already taking solid form in his mind. He had used that trick himself. Mail anything you want to hide, addressed to yourself at a *poste restante* in any name you can think of: where could it be safer or harder to find?

She came out so quickly that he was almost caught. He turned in a flash and stood with his back to her, taking out his cigarette case and deliberating lengthily over his selection of a cigarette. Reflected in the polished inside of the case, he saw her cross the pavement again, still without looking round, and get back into the car.

But he had been wrong. As she came out she was putting an envelope into her bag, but it was only a small one—obviously too small and thin to contain such a dossier as Kennet must have given her.

His brain leaped to encompass this reversal. Her cloakroom story must have been true, then: she had simply given herself double cover, mailing the ticket to herself at the *poste restante*. His imagination bridged the gaps like a bolt of lightning. Without even turning his head to check his observations, without letting himself indulge in a further instant's vacillation, he started back towards his own car.

And in the middle of the next stride he stopped again as if he had run into an invisible wall.

Where he had left the Hirondel there was now another car drawn up alongside it—a lean drab unobtrusive car that hid its speedy lines under a veneer of studiously sombre cellulose, a car which to the Saint's cognisant eye carried the banners of the Mobile Police as plainly as the sails on a full-rigged ship, even before he saw the blue-uniformed man at the wheel and the other blue-uniformed man who had got out to examine the Hirondel at closer quarters. The dragnet was out, and this was the privileged one out of the hundreds of patrol cars that must even then have been scouring the city for him that had located its gaudy quarry. If he had waited in the car they would have caught him.

But his guardian angel was still with him. They must have arrived only a moment ago, and they were still too wrapped up in the discovery of the Hirondel to have started looking round for the driver.

The Saint had spun round as soon as he saw them. He was between two fires now, but Valerie Woodchester was the less formidable. He whipped out a handkerchief and held it over the lower part of his face as he started up the road again. The Daimler was pulling out from the kerb, moving on towards Kensington Gardens. On the opposite side of the road a taxi had pulled up to discharge its freight. Simon walked over towards it with long space-devouring strides that gave a deceptive impression of having no haste behind them. He climbed in the offside door as the passenger paid his fare.

"Go up towards the Park," he said. "And step on it."

The taxi swung round in an obedient semicircle and rattled north. As it came round the curve the Saint took a last look at the corner where he had so nearly met disaster. The blue-uniformed man who had got out of the police car was putting his hand on the Hirondel's radiator. He took it away quickly and said something to his companion, and then they both started to look round, but by that time their chance of immortal fame had slipped through their fingers. The Saint buried himself in the corner of the seat, and his cab bowled away on the second lap of the chase.

The policeman at the top of the road was stopping the north and south traffic, and the taxi had caught up to within a few yards of the Daimler's petrol tank when he lowered his arm. The driver slackened speed and half-turned.

"Where to, sir?"

"Keep going." The Saint sat forward. "You see this Daimler just ahead of you?"

"Yessir."

"There's two quid for you on top of the fare if you can keep behind it."

You may have wondered what happens in real life when the pursuing sleuth leaps into a cab and yells, "Follow that car!" The answer is that the driver says, "Wot car?" After this has been made clear, if it can be made clear in time to be of any use, he simply follows. He has nothing better to do, anyhow.

Whether he can follow adequately or not is another matter. Simon suffered a short interval of tenterhooked anxiety before he was assured that his guardian angel, still zealously concentrating on its job, had sent him a taxi that was capable of keeping up with most ordinary cars in traffic, and a driver with enough cupidity to kick it along in a way that showed that he regarded a two-pound tip as something to be seriously worked for. The whim of a traffic light or a point-duty policeman might still defeat him, but nothing else would.

Simon sat back and relaxed a little.

He had a brief breathing spell now in which to synopsise his thoughts on the recent visit from Comrade Fairweather which had dragged on to such a disastrous dénouement. He was sure that the dénouement had been no part of Fairweather's design. Fairweather, caught unprepared by Teal's presence and the things that had been going on when he arrived, had simply been improvising from start to finish—exactly as Simon's counter-attack had been improvised. What he had really meant to say when he came to Cornwall House had not even been hinted at. But Simon was sure that he knew what had been left unsaid. By that time Bravache and his satellites must have reported to headquarters, and all the ungodly must have known that their plans had done more than go agley. Fairweather would not have been sent to threaten—he was not the type. He had been sent to try diplomacy, possibly the kind in which the balance of power is a bank balance, perhaps more probably the kind which is meant to lead one party to that apocryphal place known to American gangdom as the Spot. Either way, it was a token of the ungodly's increasing interest which gave the Saint a stimulating feeling of approaching climax. He wished he could have heard what Fairweather really meant to say, but life was full of those unfinished symphonies . . .

They had slipped through the Park meanwhile and left it at Lancaster Gate. The Daimler threaded through to Eastbourne Terrace and parked there; the Saint's taxi driver, taking his instructions literally, stopped behind it. But luckily there is no vehicle on the streets of London so unlikely to draw attention to itself even by the weirdest manoeuvres as a taxi. Valerie Woodchester did not even look at it twice. She crossed the road and hurried away, heading for the gaunt grimy monstrosity known to long-suffering railway travellers as Paddington Station.

Simon unpacked himself from the depths of the cab into which he had instinctively retreated. He hopped out and poured two pound notes and some silver into the driver's palm.

"Thanks, Rupert," he said. "Pull down the street a little way and stick around for a bit—I may want you again."

He scooted on after Lady Valerie. She was out of sight when he rounded the next corner after her, but the station was the only place she could have been going into. He even knew what part of the station she would make for.

He stood inside the first entrance he came to and let his eyes probe around the gloom of the interior. It was so long since he had travelled by rail that he had almost forgotten the gruesome efficiency with which London railway terminals prepare the arriving voyager for the discomforts of his coming journey. The station, proudly ignoring the march of civilisation, had not changed in a single material detail since he last saw it, any more than it had probably changed since the days when trains were preceded by a herald waving a red flag. There were the same dingy skylights overhead, opaque with accumulated grime; the same naked soot-blackened girders; the same stark soot-blackened walls splashed with lurid posters proclaiming the virtues of Bovril and the bracing breezes of Weston-super-Mare; the same filthily blackened floors patterned with zigzag trails of moisture where some plodding porter had passed by with a rusty watering-can on a futile mission of dampening down the underfoot layers of dirt; the same bleak 'refreshment' rooms with cold black marble counters and buzzing flies and unimaginative ham sandwiches in glass cases like museum specimens; the same faint but pervading smell of stale soot, stale humanity, and (for no apparent reason) stale horses. Somewhere in that gritty grisly monument to the civic enterprise of twentieth-century London he knew he would find Lady Valerie Woodchester, and presently he saw her, looking amazingly trim and clean among the sweating mobs of holiday-departing trippers, coming away from the direction of the check room. And now she carried a bulky Manila envelope in one hand.

Simon ducked rapidly into a waiting-room that looked like the ante-room of a morgue, but she went straight to the ticket office selling tickets for the Reading and Bristol line. He saw her turn away with a ticket and walk briskly back towards one of the departure platforms.

The Saint declined for the window she had just left, but before he could reach it a large boiled-pink woman with two bug-eyed children clinging to her skirts was there in front of him. She was one of those women from whom no booking office ever seems to be free, who combine with the afflictions of acute myopia and deafness the habit of keeping their money in the uttermost depths of a series of intercommunicating bags and purses. Simon stood behind her and fumed on the verge of homicidal frenzy while she argued with the booking clerk and peered and fumbled with placid deliberation through the interminable succession of Chinese boxes in the last of which her portable funds were lovingly enshrined. A line of other prospective passengers began to form behind him. Unaware that the world was standing still and waiting for her, the woman began to count her change and reopen her collection of private puzzles to stow it lovingly away, while she went on to cross-examine the clerk about the freshness of the milk in the dining car on the train to Torquay. Meanwhile Lady Valerie had disappeared.

The Saint's patience came to an explosive end. He took hold of the woman by her raw beefy elbows and removed her from the window.

"Pardon me, madam," he said in a voice that the booking clerk was meant to hear. "I'm a police officer, and I'm busy."

He stuck his head down to the pigeonhole from which sixpenny excursion tickets are doled out at English railway stations with more grudging condescension than thousand-pound notes are passed out at the Bank of England.

"That young lady who was here just before your last customer," he said. "Where did she want to go to?"

Fortunately the clerk had a long memory.

"Anford, sir."

"Give me a ticket there—first class."

Simon slid the money under the grille and turned away, grabbing up his ticket. He shoved past the gaping queue and collared a porter who was mooning by.

"Which is the next train to Anford, and where does it go from?" he snapped.

"Anford, sir?"

"Yes. Anford."

"Anford," said the porter, digesting the name. "Anford."

"Anford," said the Saint gutturally.

"Anford," said the porter, keeping his end up without any sign of fatigue. "Where would that be, sir?"

"It would be in Wiltshire. You change at Marlborough."

"Ar, Marlborough." The porter scratched his head. "Marlborough. Marlborough. Then it's a Marlborough train you'd be wanting, sir."

Simon overcame a fearful impulse to assault him.

"Yes. I could manage with a Marlborough train."

"There's one just leaving from Platform Six," said the man laboriously, as though a dark secret was being dragged out of him, "but I dunno as how you'd have time to catch that one—"

The Saint left him to his own audience. He was off like a bolt out of a crossbow, plunging along towards an ancient smoky board that did its best not to reveal the whereabouts of Platform Six. And while he was on his way he was trying to orderlise this new and unexpected destination of Lady Valerie's. Was she going there because she was at Paddington and it was the first place that came into her head? Or was she subtle enough to think that it was the last place where she would be looked for? Or had she some positive purpose? Or . . .

Something seemed to go off like a silent bomb inside the Saint's chest. The concussion threw his heart off its beat, squeezed all the air out of his lungs; his legs felt as if the marrow had been sucked out of the bones. He kept on walking through nothing but sheer muscular automatism.

There was one thing he had forgotten, and he had almost walked straight into it.

A burly man in a dark suit was pacing bovinely past the entrance to the platform, methodically scanning the faces of all the passengers who came within his view. He had the trademarks of Scotland Yard stamped all over him, and Simon could have picked him out of a crowd at five hundred yards if he had not been too preoccupied to look for him. As it was, another dozen steps would have planted him squarely on the man's shinily booted toes.

The alarm had gone out in earnest. A searingly vengeful Chief Inspector Teal had covered every exit from London that it was in his power to cover. No doubt there were the same burly bovine men at every station in the metropolis. The Saint hadn't a snowflake's hope in hell of boarding the train that Lady Valerie had taken. He would be lucky enough to get out of Paddington without irons on his wrists.

CHAPTER SEVEN:

HOW SIMON TEMPLAR
CONVERSED WITH SUNDRY
PERSONS AND PC REGINALD
CONGRATULATED HIM

1

Simon kept on walking. How he managed it was one of those unsung victories of mind over matter, but he kept on. His steps remained outwardly unchanged, and to all ordinary appearances he was still only one of the undistinguished members of the crowd who scurried to and fro like well-trained movie extras providing background atmosphere for the picture of any busy terminus. None of them knew how easy it would have been for him to turn and run like a hunted fox.

But that would have singled him out at once. His only hope was to retain the anonymity which had so far given him divine protection. Quietly, evenly, without a trace of excitement, the Saint walked on, turning in a gradual curve that took him imperceptibly further away from the watching detective and finally reversed his direction entirely without ever including an abrupt movement that would have caught anyone's eye. Icy needles danced over his skin, but he completed the manoeuvre without a tremor. He knew that the detective had seen him and was looking at him; as he headed back towards the nearest exit, he could feel the man's eyes boring into the back of his neck . . .

God who in his infinite wisdom has ordained that all respectable English citizens shall go for their holidays to the same places at the same time, chose that moment to let a fresh horde of tourists loose in the station. Hot, sun-blistered, multitudinous, clutching their bags and parcels and souvenirs and progeny, they swarmed around the Saint and swallowed him up. Simon had never been glad of such inundations before, but he was so grateful for that one that he could have embraced each individual member of the motley mob. He let himself be carried along by the spate of humanity, and it held him in its midst and swept him through the exit he had been making for, and the rear-guard jammed in the doors behind him with a hearty unanimity that could scarcely have impeded pursuit more effectively if it had been organised.

Simon did not wait to see what happened. Perhaps the detective who had seen him was still not certain of his identification; perhaps he had at last made up his mind and was even then trying to struggle through the crowd, but in either event the Saint had no desire to linger. As soon as he was outside he set off at the speed of a racing walker, and felt as if he only began to breathe again when he had crossed Eastbourne Terrace with no sounds of a hue and cry behind him.

His taxi driver was still optimistically waiting, and he opened the nearest door as he saw the Saint approach.

Simon smiled and shook his head.

"Sorry," he said, "but I just came to tell you, you needn't wait any more."

"Orl right, guv'nor."

The driver looked dejected.

Simon tucked a ten-shilling note into the front of his coat.

"On your way. And have a drink with me when they open."

"That I will, guv'nor," said the man less glumly. "And I 'opes I see you again."

The Saint stood on hot bricks until the cab turned the next corner and passed out of sight.

Then he got into the driving seat of the Daimler.

It was his own car, anyway, although the taxi driver might not have appreciated that. And by the grace of good angels it was a car that he had always used for various nefarious purposes, and therefore it had been registered in a number of different names, but never in his own. It was one car whose number plates the Mounted Police would not be watching for. Perhaps more cogently than any of those things, it was the only car at his immediate disposal. It was not what he would have chosen for what he had to do, but he could not choose.

Lady Valerie had left the keys in the switch, and the engine was nicely warm. The Saint was away in four seconds after his taxi disappeared.

And on a trip like he had to make every second was vital. And he had to waste precious scores of them, feeling his way westwards out of London by devious and unfrequented back streets. The same dogged efficiency that had covered the railway stations was sure to have stationed watchers on the main traffic arteries leading out of London, but the labyrinthine ways of London and its suburbs are so many that it would have been impossible to cover every outlet. And Simon Templar had an encyclopedic memory for maps that would have staggered a professional cartographer. It was a gift that he had developed and disciplined for years against just such contingencies as this. He drove through back streets and suburban avenues and afterwards through country lanes, and did not join a main road until he came into Bracknell.

Then he gave the Daimler its head to the last mile an hour that could be squeezed out of it.

He drove with one eye on the road and the other switching between the mileometer and the dashboard clock. To race an express train in the

Hirondel was nothing, but to attempt it in that sedate and dowager-worthy limousine was something else. Mathematically it came out to be simply and flatly impossible. But Anford was a one-horse village on an antiquated single-track branch line over which trains shuttled back and forth with no great respect for time tables and never at even official intervals of less than an hour. The odds were all against Lady Valerie catching an immediate connection, and that uncertain margin of delay at Marlborough was all that the Saint could hope to race against.

A few days ago he had taken the Hirondel from Anford to London in an hour and twenty-five minutes. Risking his neck at least once in every two miles, he stopped the Daimler at Anford Station in three minutes under two hours.

He jumped out and went in.

It took him a little while to find a time table. Eventually he located one, pasted to a board on the wall and smudged and roughened with the trails of many grubby fingers that had painstakingly traced routes across its closely printed acreage before him. With difficulty he analysed the eye-aching maze of figures with which railway companies strive so nobly to preserve the secret of their schedules. The train which Lady Valerie had caught should have reached Marlborough thirty-five minutes ago, and there was a connection to Anford listed for three minutes later.

Simon searched the deserted premises and presently found the station-master weeding his garden.

"When does the next train from Marlborough get in?" he asked.

"The next train, sur? Urse been in already."

"What's that?"

The station-master pounced on a weed.

"I said, urse been in already."

"I mean the train that left Marlborough at four o'clock."

"Urse been in."

"But it couldn't!" protested the Saint. "It's never done that trip in forty minutes in its life!"

The station-master bristled.

"Well, urse done it today," he stated with justifiable pride.

"What time did it get in?"

"I dunno."

"But surely—"

"No, I dunno. It was five minutes ago be the clock, but the clock ain't been keepin' sich good time since we took the birds' nest outen ur."

"Thank you," said the Saint shakily.

"You're welcome, sur," said the station-master graciously, and resumed his weeding.

The Saint ploughed back through the station on what seemed to be lengthening into an endless pilgrimage. In the station yard he found a new arrival, in the shape of an automobile of venerable aspect against which leaned a no less venerable man in a peaked cap with a clay pipe stuck through the fringe of a moustache that almost hid his chin. Simon went up to him and seized him joyfully.

"Did you pick up a young lady here—a dark pretty girl in a light blue suit?"

The man cupped a hand to one ear.

"Pardon?"

Simon repeated his question.

The driver sucked his pipe, producing a liquid whistling noise.

"Old lady goin' on fifty, would that be?"

"I said a young lady—about twenty-five."

"I 'ad a young lady larst week—"

"No, today."

"No, Thursday."

"Today."

The man shook his head.

"No, I ain't seen 'er. Where does she live?"

"I want to know where she went to," bawled the Saint. "She got here on the last train. She may have taken a cab, or somebody may have met her. Did you see her?"

"No, I didn't see 'er. Mebbe Charlie seed 'er."

"Who's Charlie?"

"Yus."

"Who's Charlie?"

"There ain't no need to shout at me," said the driver resentfully. "I can 'ear perfickly well. Charlie 'as the other taxi around 'ere. This 'ill be 'im comin' along now."

A noise like a threshing machine had arisen in the distance. It grew louder. With a clatter like a dozen milk cans being shaken together in an iron box another venerable automobile rolled into the yard, came to a halt with a final explosion like a pistol shot, and stood there with its nose steaming."

"Oi," said the Saint's informant. "Charlie."

A very long man peeled himself out of the second cab and came over. He had two large front teeth like a rabbit, and one of his eyes stared at the bridge of his nose.

"Gennelman tryin' to find a lady," explained the man with the clay pipe.

"A dark pretty girl, about twenty-five, in a light-blue suit," Simon repeated.

"Hgh," said the long man. "I haw her."

"You saw her?"

"Hgh. Hungh hook her hu Hanghuh."

"You took her to Anford?" said the Saint, straining for the interpretation.

"Hgh."

"Where did you go?"

"Hanghuh."

"I mean, what part of Anford?"

"Hh Hohungh Hleeh."

"I'm sorry," said the Saint, with desperate courtesy. "I didn't quite catch—"

"Hh Hohungh Hleeh."

"I beg your pardon?"

"Hh Hohungh Hleeh."

"Oh, yes. You mean—"

"Hh Hohungh Hleeh," said the long man, with some asperity.

Simon felt the sweat coming out on the palms of his hands.

"Can you tell me where that is?"

"Hingh Hanghuh."

Simon looked imploringly at his first friend.

"You carn't miss it," said the man through his curtain of white whisker. "Straight through the Market Place, an' it's on yer left."

Simon clapped a hand to his head.

"Good God," he said. "You mean the Golden Fleece?"

"Haingh hagh hogh I heengh hehhigh hu?" demanded the long man scornfully.

The Saint smote them both on the back together.

"You two beauties," he said rapturously. "Why did the goblins ever let you go?"

He picked up the nearest hand, slapped money into it, and started back for the Daimler at a run. For the first time since the beginning of that long feverish ordeal he felt there was music in his soul again. Even the Daimler seemed to throw off its sedateness and fly like a bird over the short winding road that led from Anford Station into the town.

In its way, the Golden Fleece was such an obvious destination that he had not even considered it. And now again he wondered what was in Lady Valerie's mind . . .

But wondering was only a pastime when he was within reach of knowledge. He parked the Daimler around the next turning beyond the hotel, where it would not be too obviously in view, and walked back. At that lifeless hour before the English Inn is permitted by law to recommence its function for the evening, the lobby and lounge of the hotel were empty. There was not even any sign of tenancy at the office.

He moved quietly over to the desk and looked at the register. The last signature on the page said "Valerie Woodchester" in a big round scrawl. In the column beside it had been entered a room number: 6.

Simon flitted up the stairs. There was no one to question him. He moved along the upper corridor in effortless silence until he came to a door on which was painted the figure 6. When he saw it, it was like Parsifal coming to the end of his journey. He stood for several seconds outside, not moving, not even breathing, simply listening with ears keyed to hyper-normal receptiveness. The only sounds they could catch were occasional almost inaudible rustlings beyond the door. He took a quick cat-like step forward, grasped the handle and turned it smoothly, and went into the room.

Lady Valerie looked up at him from a chair on the far side of the room with her face blurring into a blank oval of dumbfounded amazement.

Simon locked the door and stood with his back to it.

"Darling," he said reproachfully, but with the hit of rapture still playing havoc with the evenness of his voice, "what was the matter with our hospitality?"

2

The room was one of those quaint dormitories which have always made the English country hotel so attractive to discriminating travellers. It was principally furnished with a gigantic imitation oak wardrobe, an imitation mahogany dressing-table with a tilting mirror, a black enamelled iron bedstead with brass knobs on it, and a marble-topped wash-stand bearing a china basin with a china jug standing in it, a soap dish with no soap, and a vase for toothbrushes. Under the marble slab were cupboard doors concealing unmentionable utensils, and under them stood a large china slop-pail. The pattern on the wallpaper had apparently been designed to depict one of the wilder horticultural experiments of Mr Luther Burbank, in which purple tulips grew on the central stems of bright green cabbages, the whole crop being tied together with trailing coils and bows of pink and blue ribbon. The dimensions of the room were so cunningly contrived that a slender person of normal agility could, with the exercise of reasonable care, just manage to find a path between them without being bound to bark his shins or stub his toes on any particular piece of furniture. Even so, there was no more than barely sufficient room to contain the chintz-covered armchair in which Lady Valerie was sitting, and behind which she had unsuccessfully tried to stuff away the sheaf of papers that she had been perusing when the Saint came in.

Simon's satiric eye rested on the ends of documents that still protruded.

"If you'd told us you wanted something to read," he said, "we could have lent you some good books."

He leaned against the door, clothed in magnificent assurance, as if he had been conversationally breaking the ice with an old friend from whom he was sure to receive a cordial welcome.

He got it. The stunned astonishment dissolved out of her face, and a broad schoolgirlish grin spread over her mouth.

"Well, I'm damned!" she said. "Aren't you marvellous? How on earth did you know I was here?"

He grinned in return. After all that he had been through to find her, he couldn't help it.

"Haven't you heard about me?" he said. "I do these tricks for my living."

"Of course," she said. "I always knew you were supposed to be frightfully clever, but I didn't really believe you were as clever as all that . . . Oh, well, we live and learn, and anyhow you haven't got it all your own way. I think I was pretty clever myself, the way I got away from your house. I worked it all out before I went to bed last night. Don't you think it was clever of me?"

"Very clever," he agreed, "But you see, it was just the way I expected you to be clever."

She stared at him.

"The way you. . ."

"Yes."

"But you don't mean you—"

"Naturally," he lied calmly. "I knew that if you got away, the first thing you'd do would be to get hold of those papers, wherever you'd left them. I wanted to know where they were, and I didn't want to have to beat it out of you. So I just let you get away and fetch them for me."

"I don't believe you!"

"Would you like me to tell you all about it? I was behind you all the time. You picked up the ticket at the South Kensington post office, and then you went on and collected the package from the cloakroom at Paddington. You took the first train down here, and you were driven up from the station by a bloke with no roof to his mouth and one of the oldest taxis on the road. Does that help?"

She looked as crestfallen as a child that has had a succulent lollipop snatched out of its mouth.

"I think you're beastly," she said.

"I know. Pigs move pointedly over to the other end of the sty when I come in. And now suppose you tell me what those papers were doing at Paddington."

"That's easy. You see, I had them with me when I was coming down here for last weekend, because of course I hadn't read them, and I was going to read them on the train and give them back to Johnny when I saw him. Then I thought if they had all these things in them that were so rude about Algy and General Sangore and the rest of them, perhaps I'd better not take them down with me, because Algy mightn't like it. So I just popped them in the cloakroom meaning to collect them on my way back. But then the fire happened, and . . . and everything, and I came back in Mr Luker's car, and what with one thing and another I forgot all about them until you started talking about them at the Berkeley. So after last night I thought I'd better see what they were all about."

"And what are they all about?"

"I don't know yet, but they look rather dull. You see, I'd only just started to look at them when you came in. I didn't like to open them on the train, because there were always other people in the carriage, and I didn't know if they might have seen something they shouldn't see . . . You can look at them with me if you like. As a matter of fact, I . . . I meant you to have them anyway."

Simon gazed at her with the admiration reserved for very special occasions.

"Darling," he said, "how can I ever have managed to misjudge you?"

"But I did, really. You don't think I'd have let Algy have them after what happened last night, do you?"

"Of course not—unless he paid you a much bigger price for compensation."

"Are you a beast?" she said.

The Saint sighed.

"Do we have to go into that again?"

She considered him, pouting.

"But you do really like me quite a lot, don't you?"

"Darling, I adore you."

"Well, I hope you do, because if you don't I'm going to scream for help and bring the whole town in. On the other hand, provided you're reasonable . . ."

The Saint put his hands in his pockets. He was patient to the point of languor, completely sure of the eventual outcome. He could afford to bide his time. These preliminaries were incidental illuminations rather than delays.

"Yes, if I'm reasonable," he said. "Go on. I'm interested."

"What I mean," she said, "is this. You can't get away from the fact that I'm just as much entitled to these papers as you are. If it comes to that, I'm probably more entitled to them, because after all Johnny gave them to me. So if I let you see them, I don't see why we shouldn't work together. You suggested it first, anyway, and after all you do make lots of money, don't you?"

He smiled.

"I keep body and soul together. But do you really think you'd like being shot at, and having people putting arsenic in your soup and blowing up bombs under your chair and all that sort of thing?"

"I might get used to it."

"Even to finding snakes in your bed?"

"Oh, but I expect you to look after me," she said solemnly. "You seem to survive all right, and I expect if I was with you most of the time I'd survive too. You've got to look after me now, anyhow. It stands to reason that if you got the papers they'll be bound to know you got them from me, and you can't just laugh lightly and walk away and leave me to be slaughtered."

"Suppose we decide about that after we've seen what these papers are," he suggested gently.

She seemed to sit more tightly in her chair, and her smile was very bright.

"You mean we are working together now?"

The Saint left the door. He was moving over towards her, still with his hands in his pockets, threading his way with easy nonchalance through the narrow footpaths between the furniture. The glimmer of lazy humour on his lips and eyes was cool and good-natured, but under it was a quiet ruthlessness that cannons could not have turned aside.

"Don't let's misunderstand each other again," he said pleasantly. "I came here just to see those papers. Now I'm going to look at them. There aren't any conditions attached to it. If you want a wrestling match you can have one, but you ought to know that you'll only be wasting your strength. And if you want to scream you can scream, but I don't think you'll get out more than half a beep before I knock you out. And then when you wake up you'll have a headache and a pain in your jaw, and I shall be very sorry for you, but by that time I shall have finished my reading. Does that make everything quite clear?"

Her eyes blazed at him. All her limbs were tense. She looked as if she was going to scream and risk the consequences.

The Saint didn't move. He had arrived in front of her, and there he waited. In his immobility there was a kind of cynical curiosity. It was plain that she could do what she liked: he was only interested to see what she would choose to do.

And he wasn't bluffing. His cynicism was not really unkind. He would hate hurting her, but he meant every word he had said. Circumstance had put him on to a plane where the niceties of conventional chivalry could have no weight. And she knew that it was not worth taking up the challenge.

Her lower lip thrust out petulantly.

"Damn you!" she whimpered, "Oh, *damn* you!"

"I'm sorry," he said, and meant it.

He bent over and took the sheaf of papers out of her hand, from behind her, and touched her mouth lightly with his own as he did so.

She got up and flung herself away from him as far as the topography of the room would let her. He watched her out of the corner of his eye, balanced for any action that might be forced upon him, but the moment of danger was past. She stood by the dressing-table, glowering at him and biting her lips in a way that he remembered. Her ill temper had something very childish and almost charming about it: she was like a little girl in a pet.

He sat down on the bed with the sheaf of papers in his hand.

"Are you going to Scotland for the grouse?" he inquired amiably.

She took her bag off the dressing-table, jerked out a packet of cigarettes, lighted one, and moved further away. She stood with her back to him, smoking furiously, tapping one foot on the threadbare carpet, the whole dorsal view of her expressive of raging contempt, but he observed that she was covertly watching him in the long mirror on the wardrobe.

The Saint lighted a cigarette himself, and turned the pages of the dossier that had disordered so many lives and ended at least two of them.

At once he seemed to have forgotten her existence. He read more and more intently, with a frown of concentration deepening on his face. His intentness shut out everything beyond the information he was assimilating. For a long time there was no sound in the room except the rustle of paper and the creaking of rusty bedsprings as he stirred to turn a page and the irritating tattoo of Lady Valerie's toe beating on the floor.

And as he read on, a curious empty chill crept over him.

Lady Valerie fidgeted with the catch on the wardrobe door. She breathed on the mirror and drew silly faces with her forefinger in the cloud deposited by her breath, and went on stealing furtive glances at him. At last she turned round in a final fling of exasperation and stubbed out her cigarette in a saucer on the dressing-table.

"Well," she said peevishly, "at least you might tell me what it's all about. Is it very interesting?"

"Wait a minute," he said, without looking up.

She pushed the saucer off the dressing-table with an exasperated sweep of her hand. Instead of providing a satisfactory smash, it landed on the carpet with a thick plunk and rolled hollowly away over the linoleum under the washstand.

The Saint went on reading.

And as he came towards the end of the manuscript, that dry deflated chill seemed to freeze the fire out of him and leave him numb with helpless bafflement.

For there was nothing in that bulky collection of documents that seemed to be worth much more than the paper it was written on in the way of powder and shot. There were the usual notes on the organisation of the arms ring, principally taken from the British end, but none of it was very new. Much of it could have been found in such detailed surveys as Merchants of Death. There were notes on Luker's background, the puppet directors of his various companies, the ramifications of their many subsidiaries, their international affiliations, their political connections, their methods of business, together with well authenticated samples of certain notable iniquities. It was all very interesting and highly scandalous, but it would cause no revolutions. Such exposés had been made before, but they had never done more than superficially ruffle the apathy of the great dumb populace which, might have risen up in its wrath and destroyed them. And under the laws made by governments themselves financially interested and practically concerned in the success of the racket, if not actually subsidised by it, there were not even grounds for a criminal prosecution. It was only the kind of oft-repeated indictment that caused a temporary furore, during which the racketeers simply laid low and waited for nature to take its course and the birth of sextuplets in Kalamazoo to re-possess the front pages of an indifferent press.

The latter part of the dossier was devoted to the Sons of France considered as part of a sales promotion campaign backed by Luker and his associates. There was an educative outline of the machinery of the organisation, some eye-opening copies of secret orders issued to members, specimens of its propaganda and declared objectives, in the usual Fascist jargon—'to eradicate Communism, Pacifism, and all such Jewish-inspired undermining of the heroic spirit of France . . . to institute State control, for the benefit of the people, over literature, art, motion pictures, radio, and all other means of disseminating culture . . . to build up the military, naval, and air strength of France so that French honour may be prepared to answer the insolence of the Hun.' There was good evidence of financial support given to the organisation by Luker and certain directors of the Fabrique Siebel des Armes de Guerre—but that, as Simon had pointed out to Teal, was probably not an offence under the law. There were a number of detailed records mostly made up from newspaper cuttings of certain rather revolting acts of violence and terrorism committed by alleged members of the Sons of France, but there was no evidence by which Luker and his associates could have been brought to book as their direct instigators. Certainly there was enough material to have brought down on Luker's head the moral indignation of the whole world, if the world had had any moral sense, but in the way of legal evidence of recognised crimes there wasn't enough to get him as much punishment as he would have earned by driving his car down Piccadilly at thirty-five miles an hour.

The last page of all was a sheet torn from a cheap memorandum book, on which someone seemed to have made a note of three functions or events, with their dates. The first and last were so heavily scored out as to be practically undecipherable, but the middle one was left plain and untouched in the centre of a frame of doodling arabesques such as a man draws on a pad during a conference. It read:

25 août: Ouverture de l'Hospice de Mémoire,
à Neuilly, par M. Chaulage.

Fastened to it with a detachable clip was a photograph of three men, one of whom was Luker, apparently talking in an office. And in the bottom corner of the memorandum sheet was pencilled in a different hand, so quick and careless as to require a clairvoyant to read it:

Remember the R—?

The last word eluded even the Saint's powers of divination. And that was all there was.

3

Simon Templar lighted another cigarette with the dispassionate detachment of a machine. He was more cold and grim than the girl had ever seen him, or had ever realised that he could be. He looked up at her with blue eyes that bit with the intolerable glittering cold of interstellar space.

"Come here," he said.

No power of mind that she could conceive could have disobeyed him.

She came over, in spite of herself, like a mindless robot. He took her hand and drew her down on to the bed beside him.

"Is this all there ever was in this package?"

"I . . . I think so."

"Have you taken anything out?"

"No."

He knew she was telling the truth. As he was then, she could never have made him believe a lie.

"Was the envelope sealed when you put it in the cloakroom?"

"Yes."

"It didn't look as if it had been tampered with when you got it out?"

"No."

But there he knew he was on the wrong tack. If Luker and Company had been able to get at the packet, they wouldn't have left any of it. And if they had known where it was, in order to tamper with it, they wouldn't have been going to such lengths to locate it.

This was all that there had ever been. And this was what Kennet and Windlay had died for.

He had expected that that dossier would give him a light that would make clear all mysteries, and instead it had only given him a darker riddle. He stared at that enigmatic last sheet with a glacial and immobile fury. Whatever Kennet and Windlay had been murdered for must be hidden there—he was as sure of that as he could be sure of anything, but that was no help to him . . . In a sudden uncontrollable defining of his belief, he ripped off the rest of the heavy batch of papers and tossed them into her lap.

"There you are," he said. "You can have 'em. If there's anything there that's worth a penny more than the News of the World would pay you for it, it'll take somebody a lot cleverer than me to dig it out."

"That's very nice of you," she said. "Anything that's no use, and you don't want, I can have. What's that page you're keeping?"

"I wish I knew."

"May I see it?"

She was sitting straight up, with a curious distant dignity.

He looked at her. In his mind was a nebulous puzzlement that he could not bring into sharp focus. She had not asked for terms then, nor did she go on to ask for them. But he didn't seem to have enough attention to spare for that.

He moved the paper a little, and she read it over his arm.

"'The twenty-fifth of August—Opening of the Hospital of Memory—'"

"'The Hostel of Memory, at Neuilly,'" he said. "I've heard something about it. It's an old château converted into a sort of Old Soldiers' Home, endowed by the French Government for disabled veterans of the Great War to end their days in in reasonably pleasant surroundings."

"'By Monsieur Chaulage,'" she read. "Isn't he the President, or the Premier, or something?"

He nodded, and a recollection struck him like a deadened blow.

"And tomorrow is the twenty-fifth of August," he said.

She stared at him with wide expressionless eyes. There was nothing definable that her eyes could have expressed. She was as nonplussed as himself. They gazed at one another in the barren communion of hopeless bewilderment, knowing that here was something that might make their blood run cold if they could understand it, and yet not knowing what to fear.

Presently she looked at the sheet again.

"What's the rest of it?" She leaned over further to peer at the spidery scrawl across the corner. "'Remember the—' What is it, Simon? It looks like 'Rinksty.'"

"You're as good a thought-reader as I am. Does it mean anything to you?"

"Nothing."

An idea crossed his mind.

"Do you know the handwriting?"

"Of course. It's Johnny's writing."

"Johnny's! Then you must know what it means—you must be able to read it—"

She shook her head.

"But I can't! Nobody ever could, when he wrote like that. Usually he wrote quite neatly, but when he was in a hurry he just scrawled things down like that and if you were lucky and you knew what he was likely to be writing about you could sometimes guess what the words were from the first letters and how long they looked."

"But he meant this for you. He scribbled it on the page to make you think of the point. 'Remember the Rinksty?'—or whatever it is. He thought it would mean something to you. Is it something that he'd told you about before when he was talking? Is it a ship? Is it a hotel? Is it a pet name of your own that you have for some place where you used to meet—some place where he might have told you about this? For God's sake, think!"

The Saint's voice hammered at her with passionate intensity; the grip of his fingers must have been bruising her arm. Somehow he was neither pleading nor commanding, but his fire would have melted stone. She was not stone. She twisted her fingers together and looked here and there, and her face was crumpled with the frantic effort of memory, but her eyes were big and tragic when they came to his face again.

"It's no good," she said. "It doesn't ring a bell anywhere. It isn't any place we went to, I'm sure of that—"

"Or anything he talked about?"

"He used to talk about so many things, but as I told you I never paid any more attention than I could help, because it all seemed so frightfully earnest and important and I'm much too young to start bothering about important things."

She couldn't have been lying, or trying to keep anything from him. If she had been, he must have known.

He stared at the paper as if by sheer physical and mental force he could drag out the secret that was wrapped up in that wandering trail of graphite particles. To have got so far and then to be stopped there was maddening; his brain couldn't accept it. He had never in his life been stopped by a puzzle that filled him with such a sickening feeling of impotence. This was no code or cipher or riddle that wit and patience might eventually solve. There were no invisible inks to develop or clues to put together. The answer was already there in black and white, exactly as Kennet had jotted it down without any intention to conceal it, wrapped up in the skeletal hieroglyphics which to him had been only hurried writing. Every kink and twist in that long squiggle that might have been 'Rinksty' or 'Ruckstig' or a dozen other things had stood for a definite letter when Kennet had traced his pencil over them, but he had finished writing and he would not come back to read out what he had written, and all the thought in the world wouldn't make one single kink one atom more distinct.

The Saint glared at it until it blurred under his eyes.

"Something happens at Neuilly tomorrow," he said savagely, "and this ought to tell us what it is. This is what Luker and the Sons of France are murdering scared of anybody getting hold of. Johnny must have thought you'd understand. If only you'd listened to him—"

"I know," she gulped. "I know I'm a silly little fool, b-but I'll go on trying to think of it . . . Is . . . isn't the photograph any help?"

"You see if it is."

He detached the print from the clip, and as he did so a scrap of celluloid perforated along the edges fluttered away. He picked it up and held it to the light. It was a Leica negative, obviously the original of the print he had been looking at.

He looked at the photograph again, over her shoulder. It was badly under-exposed, but now he could identify two of the men. On the left, seated at a desk, with his right profile to the camera, was a man with white hair and a thin under-slung jaw, and Simon knew that it was Colonel Marteau, Commandant of the Sons of France. In an armchair, further back, almost facing the camera, was Luker's square, granitic visage. The man on the right, who faced the desk as though being interviewed, was tall and gangling and shabbily dressed: his face looked coarse and half-witted, but that might have been due to the lighting or a slight movement when the picture was taken.

Simon touched him with one finger.

"Do you know him?" he asked.

"No. I'm sure I don't. I've never seen him before."

"You told me that Kennet was excited about a photograph. This must be it. What did he say about it?"

Her forehead was desperately wrinkled.

"I don't know . . . I told you I never listened. I've got a sort—sort of idea he said it would prove something about how Mr Luker was a murderer, but—Oh, I don't know!"

"Is that all you can remember?"

"Yes. Everything," she said despairingly. "But doesn't it help you? I mean, it's quite a lot for me to remember, really, and you're so clever, you ought to be able to think of something—"

The Saint might have hit her on the nose. He might have taken her neck in his two hands and wrung it out like a sponge. It stands to the credit of his self-control that he did neither of those things.

Instead he did something so free from deliberate thought that it might have been almost instinctive, and yet which afterwards he was tempted to think must have been inspired. He couldn't conscientiously pride himself on thinking so accurately and so far ahead. But he knew that photograph must be a vital part of the secret, if not the most vital part, and he knew that the negative mattered far more than the print. Of all things, that was what he must retain until he knew its secret. And retaining it might not be so easy. Even then, as he knew, all the police departments of England were hunting him, as well as the anonymous legions of the ungodly. Accidents could always happen, and at any moment one or the other might catch up with him, and then, whichever it was, the first thing that would follow would be that he would be searched. Luckily a Leica negative was not so hard to hide—

That was how he might have worked it out if he had thought so long. But he didn't. He simply got up and strolled over to the dressing-table with the negative held between his fingers. There, standing with his back to the girl, he took out his fountain pen, removed the cap, unscrewed the nib end, and carefully drew it out with the rubber ink sac attached. Then he rolled the negative gently with his finger and thumb, slid it down into the barrel of the pen, and replaced everything. It was not so good as the strong room of a safe deposit, where he would have liked to put it, but it was the best thing he could improvise at the moment, and the restrained mechanical occupation of his hands helped to liberate his struggling thoughts . . .

"What are you doing?" the girl asked fretfully.

"Thinking." He turned round empty-handed, the pen back in his pocket. She had seen nothing. "This seems like a good time and place for it." Again his eyes were narrowed on her like keen blades of sapphire probing for the first hint of deception, "And talking of places—what made you pick on this one to come to?"

"Oh, that was something else that I thought was pretty clever of me. I mean, if you hadn't been following me, which was sort of cheating, you'd never have thought of looking for me here, would you? And it all came to me in a flash, just like that, when I was at the cloakroom in Paddington. You see, I had to go somewhere, and I couldn't go to my flat because everybody knows where that is, and I knew you and Algy and the Sons of France and everybody else would be looking for me, so I had to find somewhere to hide, and then I suddenly remembered reading in a detective story once that the best place to hide was the most obvious place, because nobody ever thought of looking in it. So then I thought, well, I was only down here a few days ago, and lots of awkward things were happening down here then, and so nobody would expect me to come back here. So I just got on the first train and came back, and I got hold of a porter just before the train went out and gave him a telegram to send to Algy and told him if he wanted to talk to me any more about these papers he could put an advertisement in the *Morning Post* . . . What's the matter?"

The Saint was standing and gooping at her as if he had been hit on the back of the head. It was a few moments before he recovered his voice.

"You sent Fairweather a telegram before the train left?"

"Yes."

"From Paddington?"

"Yes. You see—"

"Never mind what I see. You poor little blithering feather-head, can't you see what you did?"

"Did I do anything wrong?"

The Saint swallowed.

"No, nothing," he said. "You only told him where to look for you. Haven't you realised that your telegram would be marked as handed in at Paddington? And do you think he's had a house here for all these years without knowing that Paddington is the station where you take off for Anford? And don't you think your telegram is going to remind him about it? And don't you think he's ever read any detective stories? And don't you think that that's just the half-witted break he'd credit you with at once from what he knows of you? He can afford the risk of being wrong, but where do you think is the first place he's going to look for you, just for luck? You . . . you female Uniatz, you've left him a trail a mile wide that leads straight to where you're sitting!"

At any other time her dismay might have been comical. She looked as if she was going to cry.

"D-do you really think he'll think of all that?"

"I know damn well he'll think of it. Has thought of it. There may be plenty of things about him I don't like, but he couldn't be where he is and be that dumb. And besides, he has Luker to help him think." Simon glanced at his watch. "By this time—"

He had no need to go into any further explanations of what might have happened by that time. A heavy knock on the door provided them for him.

The sound went down into the Saint's stomach as if he had swallowed a lump of lead. For an instant he felt as if all the blood stopped circulating in his veins, and his ears roared with the thunder of his own stillness. The knocking was so apt, so uncannily instantaneous on its cue, that for a fraction of a second he seemed to be jarred out of all power of movement.

And then he was very quiet and very cool. His glance whirled over the room: its masses of furniture provided half a dozen hiding places, but none of them was any good. He took one step aside, and looked out of the window. It opened on to the High Street, and the sidewalks were busy with people.

The Saint's eyes went back to Lady Valerie, and they were oddly, incredibly gay. But besides that reckless humour they carried something else that could only be described here in page after page of inadequate words. She stared at him in the frightened continuation of a stupor that had lasted longer than his own, while his eyes spoke to her with that queer vague message that awoke no less formless questions and answers in her brain, and the two of them seemed to be infinitely alone in a strange universe of their own where thoughts passed without words; all of that in an eternity that could only have lasted for a moment, before his lips were shaping inaudible syllables:

"Let them in."

She got up, and he moved behind her, and stood behind the door as she opened it, with his right hand resting lightly on the butt of his gun inside the breast of his coat.

A voice said, "Lady Valerie? May we come in?"

She stammered something, and stepped back. The Saint felt the edge of the bed against his knees and sat down quickly on it. The door, closing again, disclosed him to the arrivals at the same time as it revealed them to him. They were the police sergeant whom he had met before, in plain clothes, and the constable whose name was Reginald.

4

Whereupon quite a number of interesting jobs of looking proceeded to take place in various directions.

The Saint looked at the two arms of the Law, and his face broke into an affable and untroubled smile of welcome. He took his right hand out of the breast of his coat with his cigarette case in it.

The constable looked at the Saint, and his mouth sagged open. He said in a dazed and dumbfounded sort of voice, "Gorblimey, it's 'im." Then he went on staring, while his honest red face expressed an inward struggle between admiration and duty.

The sergeant looked at the Saint, and stiffened. He looked slightly frightened, but his uneasiness was clearly subservient to his sense of responsibility. He planted himself more firmly on his by no means ethereal feet, as if bracing himself to deal with trouble.

Then another thought seemed to cross his mind, distracting him. He tried to resist it, but it grew stronger. He frowned. He looked at Lady Valerie again, rather perplexedly.

Lady Valerie looked at him, and twitched a rather weak and uncertain little smile. Then she looked at the Saint.

The Saint looked at her. His face was cheerfully composed, but his eyes said again, for her alone, the same things that they had said when the two of them had looked at one another before he told her to open the door. It was as if they met her with a challenge, a suggestion, a request, a mocking invitation, a sardonic query, anything but a plea, and yet no other eyes on earth could have pleaded more compellingly. And now she understood some things she had not understood before.

She looked at the sergeant again.

The sergeant looked at the constable.

The constable looked at the sergeant, not very intelligently, perhaps, but with a dawning grasp of what was troubling his superior's mind.

Both of them looked at the Saint.

Both of them looked at Lady Valerie.

Both of them looked at the Saint once more.

The sergeant scratched his head.

"Well, I dunno," he announced helplessly. "There must be somethink barmy about this."

Simon had his cigarette case open. He took out a cigarette.

"What's on your mind, brother?" he inquired amiably.

The sergeant took another look round and apparently could only come to the same conclusion. As if in token of surrender, he took off his hat.

"Well, sir, it's like this. Just a few minutes ago we received a message from Scotland Yard saying as you'd kidnapped Lady Valerie Woodchester, an' she'd escaped from you, an' they 'ad reason to believe she might 'ave come here to Anford, an' you might be arfter 'er to try an' kidnap 'er again, an' we was to endeavour to trace 'er an' afford her every protection, an' if we found you hanging about there was a warrant for your arrest. Well, we tried the hotels first, and as soon as we rang up 'ere they told us that Lady Valerie 'ad just come in and taken a room. So I come along to see if she'd like to make a statement an' if she wanted a man to look arfter 'er, an' now you're here with 'er, and . . . Well," said the sergeant, plugging his initial thesis, "there must be somethink barmy about it."

"There's a warrant for my arrest?" Simon ejaculated. "What on earth is it for?"

"Kidnapping Lady Valerie. An obstructing the police in the execution of their duty."

Simon had wondered how Mr Teal would officially describe being locked up in a wardrobe with an ex-Cabinet Minister.

"Good Lord," he said, "does it look as if Lady Valerie was excited about being rescued?"

"That," said the sergeant, with lugubrious finality, "is wot looks so barmy."

The Saint grinned, and leaned back.

"Are you sure somebody hasn't been pulling your leg?" he suggested.

"I dunno. If anybody has, 'e'll be sorry he ever tried it, before I've finished with 'im. But it sounded all right; just like the regular communications we 'ave from the Yard when there's anythink doing." The sergeant turned his disappointedly bewildered eyes back to the girl. "Did Mr Templar kidnap you, miss?" he asked, like a drowning man clutching at the last straw.

Lady Valerie looked at the Saint again and back to the two policemen.

Simon put his cigarette between his lips and drew at it very slowly.

"Why," she said, "that's the funniest thing I ever heard!"

There was a silence in which no pins could have been heard dropping because nobody was dropping pins. The sergeant scratched another part of his head, and squeezed little wedges of coagulated dandruff from under his fingernails. He looked as unhappy as any public servant must look when confronted by a situation that fails to follow the dotted line. Simon took his cigarette out of his mouth and trickled the smoke out in a long leisured streamer through the unaltered quizzical curve of his lips. His gaze rested contemplatively on Lady Valerie as her glance returned to him. She looked coy and complacent, like a puppy that has got away with an unguarded plate of foie gras canapés. It was left to the constable to make the first constructive contribution. An expression of mingled relief and pride had ironed the wrinkles out of his countenance when he heard Lady Valerie's confirmatory denial: quite plainly he had been making a dutiful effort to convince himself that the Saint had actually been caught more or less red-handed, but he had never really made it stick hard enough to be able to let go of it, and it was distinctly cheering to him to be absolved from the strain of continuing to hold it down. Now he was free to indulge in his own theories, and the solution came to him with dazzling simplicity.

"I can see wot's 'appened," he proclaimed. "It's as clear as daylight. It's a gang. That's wot it is. One of these gangs which Mr Templar is always breakin' up 'as got it in for 'im, and they're tryin' to frame him for this kidnapping which he knows nothing about so as to get 'im out o' the way and leave 'emselves free to get on with their dirty work. That's wot it is."

The sergeant did not seem impressed.

"It isn't because any threats 'ave bin made to you in case you tell the truth, is it, Lady Valerie?" he persisted, as if hoping against hope. "Because if they 'ave, I can tell you that while we're here you need 'av no fear of any menaces, no matter ooze—"

"Of course not," said the girl. "Really, Sergeant, you're very kind, and I'm sure you mean well, and all that sort of thing, but this is getting too ridiculous for words."

"It's a gang," repeated the constable confidently. "That's wot—"

"Will you shut your mouth?" said the sergeant crushingly, and when his subordinate had obeyed he looked rather miserable and lonely. "Wot the 'ell," he said, giving way to forces stronger than official rank, "are we gain' to do about this?"

There was a pause of intense cogitation.

"Get 'old of Scotland Yard," said the constable, "and tell 'em wot Lady Valerie says."

"While we keep Mr Templar in custody," said the sergeant, seeing light.

"But you can't!" the girl said indignantly. "How can you lock Mr Templar up in your beastly prison for kidnapping me when I'm here to prove that he hasn't done anything of the sort? I mean, I'm the one who's supposed to have been kidnapped, so I ought to have some say about it. Who's got any right to say I've been kidnapped if I say I haven't?"

The sergeant wriggled wretchedly inside his coat.

"I dunno, miss," he said. "But those are the instructions we 'ad from London—"

"I won't hear of it!" she said tearfully.

She sat down on the bed beside the Saint and took hold of his arm. Her lovely brown eyes gazed at him with something like worship.

"Do you think we ought to tell them, Simon?" she said.

"Do you?" he replied, not knowing what she was talking about, but with an awful premonition.

"Yes." She flounced up, and took hold of the sergeant's arm. "You see," she said, "Mr Templar and I are going to be married."

Simon Templar leaned back on his elbows just a split second before he would have fallen back on them. His brain whirred like a clock preparing to strike.

The sergeant blinked.

The constable gulped, and then his face opened in a great joyful romantic beam.

He said, "Wot?"

She said, "Yes. You see, we only just fixed it up last night, when we found out we were in love. And . . . and we didn't want any publicity. I mean, you know what the newspapers would do with anything like that. So we thought we'd just run away. I suppose some of my friends have been trying to get hold of me, or something, and when they found I'd disappeared they thought something frightful had happened to me, and so they told Scotland Yard and started all this silly scare, but there's nothing in it really, and we've just eloped, and we're going to be married as soon as we can fix it up, and you can't arrest Mr Templar because that would spoil everything and it'd be in all the papers and we'd get all the limelight that we're trying to get away from. You do understand, don't you?"

The Saint lay completely back and closed his eyes, because he could think of nothing else to do.

And she had the nerve to sit down beside him and kiss him.

And then the constable was pumping his limp hand and saying, "Well, sir, may I 'ave the honour of being the first to congratulate you—"

"You may, Reginald," said the Saint feebly. "Indeed you may. And for all I know, you may be the last."

"Well, I dunno," said the sergeant, harping on his theme. "I suppose in that case all we can do is take a statement an' let both of you go."

"I'll take it down," said the constable.

He rummaged eagerly in his pocket and pulled out sheets of official foolscap. With his tongue protruding, he wrote laboriously at dictation.

"'My name is Lady Valerie Woodchester . . . I was not kidnapped by Mr Simon Templar. I am in love with him. We have eloped together . . . I eloped in secret because we did not wish any fuss . . .' Will you sign your name 'ere, miss?"

261

Lady Valerie signed.

"Mr Templar'd better sign it too," said the sergeant gloomily.

The Saint drew a deep breath, but he could say nothing. He took the pen, and wrote his name with a steady hand.

The sergeant read over the sheet, folded it, and put it in his pocket.

"Well," he said despondently, "that's all we can do. Will you be stayin' 'ere for some time, sir?"

"No," said the Saint definitely. "We were only spending a few hours before we went on to Southampton to catch a boat." He got up. "We'll go out with you."

They went out. The constable carried Lady Valerie's tiny valise. Simon paid the bill for her room at the desk. They left the hotel.

Simon steered the cortège along the street to the side turning where he had parked the Daimler. If Lady Valerie was surprised to see it, she gave no sign. He opened the near-side door and ushered her in with ceremonial courtesy. Just then he was too full of thoughts for words. He went round the car and got into the driving seat.

The constable leaned in at the window.

"Goodbye, sir," he said jovially. "And I 'opes all your troubles are little ones."

"So do I," said the Saint, from the bottom of his heart, and let in the clutch.

The sergeant and the constable stood and watched him go. Simon saw them receding in the driving mirror. The sergeant looked vaguely frustrated, as if he still thought he ought to have done something else even though he couldn't think of anything else he could have done. The constable looked as if he wished he had had a handful of confetti in his pocket.

Simon drove out of town and took the cross-country road that led towards Amesbury. His emotions were approximately those of a shell that had just been fired out of a gun. He had been shot into space with one terrific explosion, and now he was sailing along with the fateful knowledge that there was another almighty bang waiting at the other end of the journey. The old proverbial voyagings between frying pans and fires seemed like comparatively pale and peaceful transitions to him. He drove very carefully, as if the car had been made out of glass.

Lady Valerie snuggled up against him.

"Are you happy, darling?" she said.

"Beloved," said the Saint chokily, "I'm so happy that I could wring your neck."

"Don't you appreciate what I've done for you?"

"Every bit of it," he said, with superhuman moderation. "So much so that if I'd had the least idea what was in your mind—"

"Where shall we go for our honeymoon?"

Simon nursed the car round a corner like an old lady wheeling her granddaughter's pram.

"Listen," he said, "I don't particularly care where you go for our honeymoon, so long as it's no place where I'm going. If you have any sense, which is getting more doubtful every minute, you'll travel like smoke for the next few days and put the biggest distance you can between yourself and London, and you won't send your friends any picture postcards on the way to let them know where you are."

Her lips trembled slightly.

"I see," she said. "You . . . you've had all you want from me, and now you just want to get rid of me. Well, I've been too clever for you this time. I'm not going to be got rid of."

"Do you want to die young?" demanded the Saint exasperatedly. "Don't you see that I'm going to be much too busy to look after you? For Pete's sake, have a little sense. I'll let you off at Southampton, where there are lots of boats going to nice places like New Zealand and so forth—"

"And what are you going to do after you've ditched me?" she asked sulkily. "I suppose you'll go dashing back to your blonde girlfriend and tell her how clever you are."

"I don't have to tell her," said the Saint. "She knows."

"Well, you're not as clever as all that," flared the girl in open mutiny. "You heard what I told those two policemen. You didn't deny it then—anything was all right with you, so long as it helped you to get away. You . . . you signed your name to it. And I won't be ditched. If you try to get rid of me now, I . . . I'll sue you for breach of promise!"

Simon steadied himself. Now that the impending thunderstorm had broken, exactly as he had been nerving himself for it, he almost felt better.

"No jury would give you a farthing damages, sweetheart," he said. "As a matter of fact, they'd probably give me a reward for letting you out of an agreement to marry me."

"Oh, would they? Well, we'll see. It's all very well for you to go around breaking thousands of hearts and pushing around all the women you meet like a little Hitler bossing his tame dummies in the Reichstag—"

The car rocked with a force that flung her away from him.

The Saint straightened it up again somehow. He let go the wheel and thumped his fists on it like a lunatic.

He yodelled. His face was transfigured.

"My God," he yelled, "how did you think of it? Of course that's what it was. That's the answer. The Reichstag!"

She gaped at him, rubbing a bruised elbow where it had hit the door in that wild swerve.

"What's the matter?" she asked blankly. "Have you gone pots, or something?"

"The Reichstag!" he whooped deliriously. "Don't you see? *That's what Kennet wrote on that bit of paper. remember the Reichstag!*"

He was so dazed with understanding that he had not noticed a big black Packard which had crept up behind them, was hardly aware when it pulled out in the narrow road and raced level with the crawling Daimler. Almost unconsciously he swung in to let it pass.

Lady Valerie looked back over her shoulder, and suddenly screamed. With a quick panicky movement she turned and grabbed at the steering wheel and twisted it sharply. From the overtaking car came the crisp high-pitched crack of a gun, and the windscreen splintered in front of Simon's eyes. Then the Daimler lurched madly as its near-side wheels slithered and plunged into a gully at the side of the road. The bank that rose up from there to the bordering hedge seemed to loom directly ahead. Simon felt himself hurled forward helplessly in his seat; the steering wheel struck him a violent blow in the chest and knocked the wind out of him; then he rose into the air as if deprived of weight. Something struck him a fearful blow on the top of the head. Bright lights whirled dizzily before his eyes, and faded into a blackening mist of unconsciousness.

CHAPTER EIGHT:

HOW KANE LUKER CALLED A CONFERENCE AND SIMON TEMPLAR ANSWERED HIM

1

Obeying an urgent and peremptory summons, Mr Algernon Sidney Fairweather, Brigadier-General Sir Robert Sangore, and Lady Sangore, arrived at Luker's house a little before seven o'clock that evening. They were perturbed and nervous, and their emotions expressed themselves in various individual ways during the ten minutes that Luker kept them waiting in his study.

Nervousness made General Sangore, if possible, a little more military. He tugged at his moustache, and frowned out fiercely from under bristling white eyebrows; his speech had a throaty brusqueness that made his every utterance sound like a severe official reprimand.

"Infernal nerve the feller has," he rumbled. "Ordering us about as if we hadn't anything else to do but wait on him. Harrumph! I had a good mind to tell him I was too busy to come."

Lady Sangore was very cold and superior. Her face, which had always borne a close resemblance to that of a horse, became even more superciliously equine. She sat in an even more primly upright attitude than her corsets normally obliged her to maintain, bulging her noble bosom like a pouter pigeon and tilting her nose back as if there were an unpleasant odour under it.

"Yes, you were busy," she said. "You were going to the Club, weren't you? Much too busy to attend to business. Ha!" The word "ha" does not do justice to the snort of an irate dragon, but the limited phonetics of the English alphabet will produce nothing better. "You'd better stop being so busy and get your wits about you. Something must be seriously wrong, or Mr Luker wouldn't have sent for you like this."

Fairweather twittered. He fidgeted with his hands and shuffled his feet and wriggled; there seemed to be an itch in his muscles that would not let him settle down.

"I don't like it," he moaned. "I don't like it at all. Luker is . . . Really, I can't understand him at all these days. His behaviour was most peculiar when I told him about the wire I had from Lady Valerie this afternoon. He didn't even sympathise at all with what I went through with that man Templar and that boorish detective. He asked me a few questions, and took the wire, and rushed off and left me alone in his drawing room, and I just sat there until he sent the butler to tell me to go away and wait till I heard from him."

"I can't think why men get so excited about that girl," said Lady Sangore disparagingly, stabbing her husband with a basilisk eye.

The General cleared his throat.

"Really, Gwendolyn! You surely don't suspect—"

"I suspect nothing," said Lady Sangore freezingly. "I merely keep my eyes open. I know what men are."

She seemed to have made a unique anthropological discovery.

Fairweather leaned forward, glancing around him furtively as if he feared being overheard.

"There's something I . . . I must tell you before he comes," he said in a stage whisper. "We . . . I mean, there's good reason to suspect that

Lady Valerie is working with that man Templar against our interests, and unless something is done at once the position may become serious."

"So that's what it is," said Lady Sangore magisterially. "And what's Mr Luker going to do about it? The girl ought to be whipped, that's what I've always said."

Fairweather dropped his voice even lower.

"Last night he . . . he practically told me he meant to have both of them murdered."

"Good God!" exclaimed General Sangore in a scandalised voice. "But that's ridiculous—absurd! Why, she belongs to one of the best families in England!" He glared about him indignantly. "It's that bounder Templar who's led her astray. He ought to be severely dealt with. Dammit, if I'd ever had him in my regiment . . ."

He broke off as Luker appeared in the doorway.

Luker stood there for a moment and looked at them one by one. He did not seem in the least disturbed. Perhaps a faint flicker of surprise crossed his face when he saw that Lady Sangore was present, but he made no comment. His dark well-tailored suit fitted him like a cloth covering squeezed over a marble figure: he looked harder and stonier than ever, as though he would wear it out from the inside. His square rugged features had the insensitive strength of the same stone.

He moved deliberately across the room to his enormous desk, sat down in the swivel chair behind it, and faced them with almost taunting expectancy. They looked at each other and avoided his eyes, subdued in spite of themselves into hoping that somebody else would give them a lead.

General Sangore was the first to let himself go.

"What's this story of Fairweather's that you're planning to murder Lady Valerie Woodchester?" he blurted out.

Luker inclined his head unimpressionably.

"So you have heard—that will save some explanations. Yes, it has become very necessary that she and Templar should be eliminated. That is why I sent for you this evening."

"Well, if you think we're going to take part in any damned murder plots, you're damned well mistaken," stated General Sangore hotly. "I never heard of such . . . such infernal impudence in my life!"

He glanced at his wife as if for approval. Lady Sangore's lips were tightly compressed; her eyes were glittering.

"That girl ought to be well whipped," she repeated.

Luker stroked his chin thoughtfully. His manner was mild and patient. He spoke in the calm and reasonable tone of a man who states facts that cannot be disputed.

"I fear that whipping would scarcely be sufficient," he remarked. "We are not playing schoolroom games. Let me remind you of the circumstances. All of you are aware, I believe, that the French patriots have planned a *coup d'état* for tomorrow which if it is resisted may lead to a Fascist revolution."

His gaze passed questioningly over them, and arrived last at Fairweather. Fairweather dithered.

"Yes . . . That is, I may have heard rumours of it. I know nothing about it officially."

"During this change of governments, a number of people will quite definitely be killed," said Luker cold-bloodedly. "Would you call that a murder plot?"

"Of course not," boomed the General authoritatively. "That's quite a different matter. That's political. It's the same as war. Anyhow, as Fairweather says, we don't know anything about it—not officially."

"If the plot should fail, and if all the details should be discovered, I'm afraid we could not plead our official ignorance," Luker replied smoothly. "You see, before he was killed young Kennet gave certain papers to Lady Valerie. You know what was among them. She placed these documents, unread, in a cloakroom—from what has happened since, it seems likely that they were at Paddington. If we could have recovered them, it would have been all right; even if she had seen the one vital thing, I don't think she would have understood. I tried to make arrangements to deal with her and Templar last night, but those arrangements miscarried. Templar then appears to have kidnapped her. She escaped, returned to London, and presumably recovered the papers from where she had left them. From the telegram Fairweather showed me, I suspected that she might have gone to Anford. I sent two men down in a fast car. They reported to me by telephone that she was at the Golden Fleece, and that Templar had arrived soon after her."

"Probably they arranged to meet there," put in Lady Sangore. "I always knew she was a hussy. Whatever happens to her, she's brought it on herself."

"That thought will doubtless console her greatly," Luker observed. "However, Fairweather had meanwhile been stupid enough to show Lady Valerie's telegram to a detective who was with him when it arrived. Much later, Scotland Yard apparently also guessed, or discovered, that she had taken a train to Anford. They must have telephoned the Anford police, because two officers arrived at the Golden Fleece and went upstairs. I don't know what Templar told them, and I don't think he can have said anything about the documents which by that time he must have read, because not long afterwards the officers came out with Templar and Lady Valerie, all apparently on the most friendly terms, and allowed them to get into a car and drive away. My men overtook them on the road, carrying out my orders to recover the papers, to capture Templar and Lady Valerie alive if possible, and to hold them until I gave instructions how they were to be disposed of."

There was a stricken silence while Luker's point forced itself home. This time Fairweather was the first to regain his voice.

"But . . . but . . . for goodness sake, Luker, really, you can't murder a girl!"

"Why not?" Luker inquired blandly.

Sangore appeared to grope in darkness for an answer.

"It . . . Well, dammit, man—it simply isn't done," he said feebly.

Luker laughed. There was nothing hearty about his laughter. It was a silent, terrifying performance, as if a stone image had quaked with unholy mockery.

"You gentlemen of England, with your pettifogging conventions and your arrogant righteousness and your old school ties; you whitewashed dummies," he sneered, "You don't care what dirty work is done so long as you don't have to know about it 'officially;' you don't care how many people are murdered, so long as you can call it warfare, or dignify it with the adjective 'political.' You don't mind helping to start a civil war in France, in which it's quite certain that numbers of girls will be killed, do you?"

"I tell you, that's different," stormed the General. "Why . . . why, we've had civil wars in England!"

He said it as if that fact proved that civil wars must be all right.

"Very well," Luker went on. "And you didn't object to murdering Kennet and Windlay, did you?"

Fairweather said hoarsely, "We had nothing to do with that. In fact, I told you—"

Lady Sangore's face looked flabby. The powder cracked on her cheeks as her mouth worked. She stammered, "You . . . you . . . I never knew—"

"No doubt, like the others, you attributed those deaths to divine intervention," said Luker sarcastically. "I'm sorry to disillusion you. I gave orders for Windlay to be killed. I strangled Kennet myself, and started the fire under his room. Your husband and Fairweather knew I was going to do it; you yourself guessed. Therefore at this moment you are—all of you—already accessories to the crime of murder, unless you at once communicate your knowledge to the police. Of course, if you do that you may find it hard to explain your silence at the inquest, but the telephone is here on my desk if any of you would care to use it."

Nobody moved. None of them spoke. A paralysis of futility seemed to have taken hold of them, and Luker seemed to gloat over their strangulation. He gave them plenty of time to absorb the consciousness of their own moral impotence, while his own rock-like impassivity seemed to deepen with his contempt.

"In that case, I take it that you wish me to continue," he proceeded at length. "My instructions were carried out, in part. Templar and Lady Valerie have been captured. Their car was wrecked, and they were both stunned in the crash but otherwise not much harmed."

"Where are they now?" asked Fairweather limply. "Are they in London?"

Luker shook his head.

"No. My men rang up from Amesbury, asking for further orders. You see, while they recovered all Kennet's documents, the most important thing of all—the negative of a certain photograph—was not to be found, either in the car or on either of the captives. I therefore thought it advisable to question both of them about what had happened to it. You will understand that this may present some difficulties, since they may require—persuading. Meanwhile, they had to be kept in some safe place. Luckily I remembered that Bledford Manor was not far from Andover, which is not far from Amesbury. Knowing that the Manor was closed and the servants on holiday, I told my men to take them there."

Lady Sangore started to her feet as though she had been jabbed in the behind with a long needle.

"What?" she protested shrilly. "You sent them to my house? How dare you? How *dare* you!"

The General fought against suffocation. He made noises like an ancient car trying to start on a cold morning. His face was the colour of old bricks.

"Tchah!" he backfired. "Harrumph! By Gad, Luker, that's going a bit too far. It's monstrous. Tchah! I forbid it. I forbid it absolutely!"

"You can't forbid it," Luker said coolly. "It's done."

Fairweather pawed the air.

"This is nothing to do with us," he whined reproachfully.

"You're the only one in that photograph. Really, Luker, I—"

"I quite understand," Luker said, with imperturbably measured venom. "This was an attractive business proposition for you so long as somebody else took all the risk, but now that it isn't going so smoothly you'd like to wash your hands of it, the same as Sangore—of course from the highest motives and with the greatest regard for the honour of the regiment and the old school. I'm sorry that I can't make it so easy for you. In the past I have helped you to make your fortunes in return for nothing much more than the use of your honest British stupidity, which is so comforting to the public. Doubtless you thought that you were earning the just rewards of your own brilliance, but I assure you that I could have taken my pick from hundreds of distinguished imbeciles of your class. Now for the first time, in a small way, I really need your assistance. You should feel flattered. But in any event I intend to have it. And I can assure you that even if this particular photograph only refers to me, if I should be caught the subsequent investigation would certainly implicate yourselves."

He made the statement in a way that left them no doubt of how they might be implicated if the worst came to the worst. But they were too battered to fight back. His words moved like barbs among the balloons of their self-esteem. They stared at him, curiously deflated, trying to persuade themselves that they were not afraid.

Luker's square powerful hands lay flat on the blotter in front of him, palm downwards, in a pattern that symbolically and physically and quite unconsciously expressed an instinct of command that held down all opposition. He went on speaking with relentless precision, and with a subtle but incompatible change of manner.

"You, my dear Algy, have certain connections which will enable you to approach the Chief Commissioner at Scotland Yard. You will use those connections to find out exactly what Templar told the police in Anford, and report to my secretary here as soon as you have the information. I don't think he can have told them anything important, but it will be safer to find out. You"—he turned to General and Lady Sangore—"will go down to Bledford Manor. Since the house is supposed to be shut up, some local policeman may notice that there are people there and become inquisitive. You must be there to reassure him. You need not see the prisoners if it will embarrass you. I myself am going to Paris tonight, and I have arranged for Templar and Lady Valerie to be taken there—it will be easier to question them and dispose of them later on the other side. But there may be a slight delay before they can be moved, and I want you at Bledford as soon as possible as a precaution. You had better leave at once."

He did not consider any further argument. As far as he was concerned, there was no more arguing to be done. He simply issued his commands. As he finished he stood up, and before any of them could raise any more objections he had walked out of the room.

They sat still for some moments after he had gone, each knowing what was in the minds of the others, each trying to pretend that he alone was still dominant and unshaken.

Fairweather got up first. He pulled out a big old-fashioned gold watch and consulted it with a brave imitation of his old portly pomposity.

"Well," he said croakily, "I must be getting along. Got things to attend to—"

He bustled out, very quickly and busily.

The Sangores looked at one another. Then Lady Sangore spoke.

"It's all that little tart's fault," she said bitterly. "If she'd had any sense or decency at all we shouldn't be in all this trouble now. As for Luker, he ought to be kicked out of every club in London."

"I don't suppose he belongs to every club in London," said General Sangore dully.

His figure, usually so ramrod erect, was bowed and sagging; his shoulders drooped. Suddenly he looked very old and tired and pasty. He seemed bewildered, like a man lost in a chamber of unimaginable horrors; he seemed to be groping through the rusty machinery of his mind for one wheel that would turn to a task for which it had never been designed.

2

"Once upon a time," said the Saint, "there was a wall-eyed wombat named Wilhelmina, who lived in a burrow in Tasmania and grieved resentfully over the fact that Nature had endowed her, like all females of the marsupial family, with an abdominal pouch or sac intended for the reception and protection of new-born marsupials. Since, however, the strabismic asymmetry of Wilhelmina's features had always deterred discriminating males of her species from making such advances to her as might have resulted in the production of young wombats, she was easily persuaded to regard this useful and ingenious organ as an indecent excrescence invented by the Creator in a lewd and absent-minded moment, and she soon became the leader of a strong movement among other unattractive wombats to suppress all references to it and to decry its use as sinful and reprehensible, and invariably wore a species of apron or sporran to conceal this obscene conformation of tissue from the world. Now it so happened that one night a purblind male wombat named Widgery, of dissolute habits . . ."

He sat in the scullery of Bledford Manor with Lady Valerie Woodchester. They sat on the hard cold tile floor with their wrists and ankles bound with strong cord. A smear of blood had dried across Simon's face, and in spite of his quiet satiric voice his head was aching savagely. Lady Valerie's face was very dirty, and her hair was in wild disarray; she also had a headache, and she was in a poisonous temper.

"Oh, stop it!" she burst out jitterily. "You've got me into a hell of a nice mess, haven't you? I suppose you enjoy this sort of thing, but I don't. Aren't you going to do something about it?"

"What would you like me to do?" he asked accommodatingly.

"What are they going to do with us?"

He shrugged.

"I'm not a thought-reader. But you can use your imagination."

She brooded. Her lower lip was thrust out, her pencilled eyebrows drawn together in a vicious scowl.

"The damned swine," she said. "I'd like to see them all die the most horrible deaths. I'd like to see them burnt alive, or something, and jeer at them . . . My God, I wish I had a cigarette . . . Doesn't it seem ages since we were having dinner at the Berkeley? Simon, do you think they're really going to kill us?"

"I expect their ideas are running more or less along those lines," he admitted. "But they haven't done it yet. What'll you bet me we aren't dining at the Berkeley again tomorrow?"

"It's all very well for you to talk like that," she said. "It's your job. But I'm scared." She shivered. Her voice rose a trifle. "It's horrible! I don't want to die! I . . . I want to have a good time, and wear nice clothes, and . . . and . . . Oh, what's the good?" She stared at him sullenly in the dimming light. "I suppose you think that's frightful of me. If your girlfriend was in my place I expect she'd think this was an awfully jolly party. I suppose she simply revels in being rolled over in cars, and knocked on the head, and mauled about and tied up and waiting to be killed, and all the rest of it. Well, all I can say is, I wish she was here instead of me."

The Saint chuckled. He was not particularly amused, but he didn't want her nerve to crack completely, and he knew that her breaking point was not very far away.

"After all, you chose me for a husband, darling. I tried to discourage you, but you seemed to have made up your mind that you like the life. Never mind. I'm pretty good at getting out of jams."

"Even if we do get out, I expect my hair will be snow-white or something," she said miserably.

She blinked. Her eyes were very large and solemn; she looked very childish and pathetic. A pair of big bright tears formed in her eyes and roiled down her cheeks.

"I . . . I do hate this so much," she whispered. "And I'm so uncomfortable."

"All the same, you mustn't cry," he said. "The floor's damp enough already."

"It couldn't be any damper. So why shouldn't I cry? I can think of dozens of things I'd like to do, and crying's the only one of them I can do. So why shouldn't I?"

"Because it makes you look like an old hag."

She sniffed.

"Well, that's your fault," she said, but she stopped crying. She twisted her head down and hunched up one shoulder and wriggled comically, trying to dry the tears on her blouse. She drew a long shuddering sigh like a baby. She said, "All right, why don't you talk to me about something and take my mind off it? What were you getting so excited about when the car turned over?"

The Saint gazed past her, into one of the corners where the dusk was rapidly deepening. That memory had been the first to return to his mind when he painfully recovered consciousness, had haunted him ever since under the surface of his unconcern, embittering the knowledge of his own helplessness.

"The Reichstag," he said. "Remember the Reichstag. That's what Kennet wrote on that bit of paper, which he probably pinched from the headquarters of the Sons of France when he was a member. That's why he had to be cooled off. He knew one thing too much, among a lot of stuff that didn't matter, and if he'd lived that one thing might have wrecked the whole scheme."

"But what did he know?"

"Do you remember the Reichstag Fire in Berlin? That was the thing that started the Nazi tyranny in Germany. Of course the Nazis said that the Communists had done it, but, but a good many people have always believed that the Nazis arranged it themselves, to give themselves a grand excuse for what they went on to do afterwards. It seems pretty plain that the Sons of France have planned something on the same lines for tomorrow. That piece of paper was a list of various suitable occasions for a blow-up of that sort which had been jotted down and discussed and eliminated for various reasons until just one was left—the opening of the Hostel of Memory at Neuilly, by Comrade Chaulage. The scheme will be to have Comrade Chaulage assassinated during the proceedings. This of course will be the work of the Communists, like the Reichstag Fire, and it will not only be proof of what desperate and disgusting people they are, but it will also be evidence of their contempt for the Heroes of France, which is always a very strong point with the Fascist gang. The Sons of France will claim the assassination as a crowning example of the incompetence of the present Government to keep the Red Bandits in check; so they will mobilise their forces, seize the Government, and proclaim a dictatorship. And there you are."

"You mean the Sons of France are going to kill Chaulage," she said, "and Luker and Algy and General Sangore know all about it."

"That was my guess. And I still like it."

She seemed a little disappointed, as if she had expected something more sensational than that. Her brief silence seemed to argue that after all there were millions of Frenchmen, and one more or less couldn't matter as much as that.

"I think I saw a picture of Chaulage in the paper once," she said, with almost polite indifference. "A funny little fat man who looks like a retired grocer."

"He is," said the Saint. "He also happens to be Prime Minister of France. And funny little fat Frenchmen who look like retired grocers often have ideas, particularly when they get to be Prime Ministers. Of course that would never be allowed in this country, but it happens there. And one of Comrade Chaulage's ideas is a bill to take all the private profit out of war, which is naturally very unpopular with Luker and Fairweather and Sangore and the directors of the Siebel Factory. So that makes Comrade Chaulage a doubly suitable victim. And when the Sons of France seize power his bill will be firmly forgotten, people will march about and wave flags, bigger and better armaments will be the cry, the people will be told to be proud of going without butter to pay for bombs, and the people who sell the bombs will be very happy. Hitler and Marteau will scream insults at each other across the frontier like a couple of fishwives, and pretty soon everything will be lined up for a nice bloody war. Some millions of men, women, and children will be burned, scalded, blistered, gassed, shot, blown up, and starved to death, and the arms ring will sit back on its foul fat haunches and rake in the profits on a turnover of about five thousand pounds per corpse, according to the statistics of the last world war."

"Would that photograph have something to do with it, too?"

"That's probably the most damning evidence of all. It seems to me that there's only one thing it can possibly mean. The half-witted-looking warrior on the right—you remember him?—he must be the martyr who's going to do the job. Some poor crazy fanatic they've got hold of who's been sold on the idea of how glorious it would be to give his life for the Cause; or else some ordinary moron who doesn't even know or care what it's all about. It must be that, or the photograph doesn't mean anything. God knows how Kennet managed to take it—we never shall. He risked his life when he did it, and the risk caught up with him in the end, but it's still a photograph that might make history. It would probably swing all except Marteau's most fanatical sympathisers against him if it was published; under any government that Marteau wasn't running it could send Luker to the guillotine. . ."

He went on talking not because he wanted to, but to give her the distraction she had asked for. It grew darker and darker until he could no longer see her at all. The time dragged on, and presently he had nothing new to say. Her own contributions were only short strained apathetic sentences which left all the burden of talking to him.

Presently he heard her stirring in an abrupt restless way which warned him that the sedative was losing its effect. He was silent.

She shuffled again, coming closer, until her shoulder touched his. He could feel her trembling. It would have helped if he could have held her. But his wrists were bound so tightly that his hands were already numb; long ago he had tried every trick he knew to release himself, but the knots had been too scientifically tied, and anything with which he might have cut himself free had been taken from him while he was unconscious.

Because there was nothing else he could do, he kissed her, more gently than he had ever done before. For a while she gave herself up hungrily to the kiss, and then she dragged her lips desperately away.

"Oh, hell," she sobbed. "I always thought it'd be so marvellous if you ever did that, and now it just makes everything worse."

"I know," he said. "It must be dreadful to feel so safe."

Then she giggled a little hysterically, and presently her head drooped on his shoulder and they were quiet for a long time. He sat very still, trying to strengthen and comfort her with his own calm, and the truth is that his thoughts were very far away.

In the kitchen, two men sat smoking moodily. The plate on the kitchen table between them was piled high with ash and the ends of stubbed-out cigarettes.

One of them was Pietri. He was not coloured in tasteful stripes any more, but a certain raw redness combined with an unusually clean appearance about his face testified to the labour with which they had been removed. The shaven baldness of his head was concealed by a loud tweed cap which he refused to take off. The other man was quite young, with close-cropped fair hair and a prematurely hardened face. In his coat lapel he wore the button badge of the British Nazis.

He yawned, and said in the desultory way in which their conversation had been conducted for some hours, "You know, it's a funny thing, but I never thought I'd have the job of putting the Saint out of action. In a way, I used to admire that fellow a bit at one time. Of course, I knew he was a crook, but he always seemed a pretty sound chap at heart. When I read about him in the papers, I used to think he'd be worth having in the British Nazis. Of course he deserves what's coming to him, but I'm sort of glad I haven't got to give it to him myself."

Pietri yawned more coarsely. He had no political leanings: he simply did what he was paid to do. To him, the British Nazis were nothing but a gang of half-hearted amateur hooligans who got into scraps with the police and the populace without the incentive of making money out of it, which proved that they must be barmy . . .

"You're new to this sort of thing, ain't you?" he said pityingly.

"Oh, I don't know," said the other touchily. "I've beaten up plenty of bastards in my time." He paused reminiscently. "I was in a stunt last Sunday, when we broke up a Communist meeting in Battersea Park. We gave them a revolution, all right. There was an old rabbi on the platform with long white hair and white whiskers, and he was having a hell of a good time telling all the bloody Reds a lot of lies about Hitler.

285

He's having a good time in the hospital now. I got him a beauty, smack in the mouth, and knocked his false teeth out and broke his jaw." He sat up, cocking his ears. "Hullo—this must be Bravache at last."

He got up and went out of the kitchen and across the hall. His feelings were mixed: they were compounded partly of pride, partly of a sort of uneasy awe. He was a picked man, chosen because the leaders of the movement knew that his loyalty and efficiency could be absolutely relied on; he was one of the first to be entrusted with the business of liquidating an enemy. In future he would probably be detailed again for similar deadly errands. He was one of the storm troops, the striking force of the movement, and their duty was to be merciless. As he opened the front door, the young British Nazi saw himself being very strong and merciless, a figure of iron. It made him feel pretty good.

A two-seater sports car had drawn up beside the black Packard that was parked in the drive, and Bravache was already stumping up the steps. Dumaire followed him. Their faces, like Pietri's, looked scoured and tender, and they also kept their hats on. Bravache raised his hand perfunctorily as the British Nazi came to attention and gave a full Fascist salute.

"The prisoners?" he said curtly.

"This way, Major."

The young British Nazi led the way briskly through the kitchen, opened the scullery door, and switched on the light. Lady Valerie stirred and gave a little moan as the sudden blaze stabbed her eyes. Bravache bowed to her with punctilious mockery, his lips parting in the unhumorous wolfish smile that Simon remembered.

"Much as I regret to disturb you, mademoiselle, your presence is required at the headquarters of the Sons of France."

Dumaire came past him and kicked Simon savagely in the ribs. Then he bent over, grinning like a rat, and lightly touched the dried bloodstains on Simon's cheeks.

"Blood is a better colouring than paint," he said.

He closed his fist and hit Simon twice in the face.

"Bleed, pig," he said. "I like the colour of your blood."

"It is red, at any rate," said the Saint unflinchingly. "Yours would be yellow."

Dumaire kicked him again, and then Bravache pushed him aside.

"Enough of that," he said. "We have no time to waste now. But there will be plenty of time later. And then I shall enjoy a little conversation with Mr Templar myself. We have several things to talk over."

"You must let me give you the address of my barber," said the Saint affably.

Bravache did not strike him, or make any movement. His cold fishy eyes simply rested on the Saint unwinkingly, while his teeth glistened between his back-drawn lips. And in the duration of that glance Simon knew that all the mercy he could expect from Bravache was more to be feared than any vengeance that Dumaire could conceive.

Then Bravache turned and flicked his fingers at the British Nazi and Dumaire, and at Pietri who had followed him to the door.

"Bring them out," he ordered briefly. "We must be going."

He went back to the hall, and as he arrived there he saw a door move. He went over to it and pushed it wide, and found General Sangore standing there just inside the library beyond it, like an eavesdropper caught at the keyhole, with a large glass of whisky clutched in one hand.

"My apologies for troubling you, General," Bravache said with staccato geniality in which there was the faint echo of a sneer. "But I'm afraid we shall need you to guide us to the place where our aeroplane is to meet us. I was told to ask for 'the long meadow'—Mr Luker said you would know it. He also said that you wished to avoid being seen by the prisoners. That will be easily arranged. They will be in the back of the Packard, and if you put on a hat and turn up your coat collar they will not recognise you in the darkness. Personally I should call it a needless precaution. By this time tomorrow, the Saint and all his associates will be beyond causing you any anxiety."

"All?" Sangore repeated stupidly.

He gulped at his drink. He still seemed to be in the same daze that he had been in when he left Luker's house. For perhaps the first time in twenty years the rich cerise and magenta tints of his complexion looked grey and faded.

Bravache nodded, drawing his gloves up tighter on his hands. His swaggering erectness, the cold confident glitter of his eyes, the cruel curl of his lips, were personal characteristics which he wore like the accoutrements of a uniform, the insignia of a new breed of soldier compared with whom Sir Robert Sangore even at his most militaristic was a puffing anachronism.

"Yes. We have been able to find out from Scotland Yard that the Sûreté have traced Mr Quentin, Miss Holm, and two others of his gang to the Hotel Raphael, in Paris. Unfortunately Scotland Yard now have no charges on which to ask for their arrest. But the delay is only temporary. Within a few hours the Sons of France will be giving their own orders to the Sûreté."

Simon Templar heard most of the speech as Pietri and the British Nazi were dragging him roughly through the hall and out to the waiting car, and it rang in his ears like a jeering refrain through the short drive and the longer wait which followed. As he was dragged out of the car again and thrown into the big cabin monoplane which swooped out of the dark to land by the light of the Packard's headlamps he could still hear it. It was the bitterest torment that he had to bear. He had not only lost his fight and condemned Lady Valerie to the penalties of his own defeat, but Patricia and Peter and Hoppy and Orace were included in the price of his failure.

3

Simon could not guess exactly how long they flew, but since he knew approximately where they were going the time was of no great importance. He lay awkwardly in the space behind the two bucket seats in which Bravache and Dumaire were sitting behind the pilot, where they had dumped him with no regard for his comfort, and Lady Valerie was huddled partly beside him and partly on his legs. They seemed to be sprawled all over one another, and it was impossible for them to move. The girl did not try to speak any more, but at intervals he felt the violent shudders that ran through her.

At last the roar of the engine ceased, and there was only the swift whirr of their wings gliding through the wind. After a while the engine snarled again in a couple of short bursts; then they hit the ground with a slight bump, settled, and trundled joltingly along with a creaking of undercarriage springs and the throaty drone of the engine turning at low speed. Then even that stopped. They were in France.

Men in a uniform of black riding breeches and shirts of horizon blue swarmed round the machine. Bravache and Dumaire got out; Simon and Lady Valerie were dragged out ungently after them. They felt the cool night air on their faces, and had a brief glimpse of stars and a dim line of poplars somewhere in the distance; there was no sign of the lights or buildings of a regular airport. Then bandages were tied over their eyes, and hands fumbled with the ropes on their ankles. With their legs freed, they were hustled away and pushed into another waiting car.

The drive that followed lasted about half an hour before the car stopped again. There was the sound of other footsteps round it, a brief mutter of voices. Then the Saint and Lady Valerie were hauled out again. Two men seized the Saint, one of them holding each of his arms. A voice said, *"Allez!"*

Simon was shoved on. He tripped over a step, marched for some distance in devious directions over a stone or tiled floor; then he was halted. There was a pause, and he heard a faint click. They went on.

From the manner in which his guides huddled close to him, and from the dank cold smell of the air, they seemed to pass into a fairly narrow underground passage. Several footsteps rang and reverberated hollowly in the confined space.

The passage led steeply downwards, then levelled off. Simon counted his steps. After twenty paces they turned sharply, and the passage seemed to widen. Thirty paces beyond the turn they stopped again, and there was a peculiar knocking and a brief delay while another door was opened. Simon was led through it, marched a few more paces, turned round a number of times, and halted once more. The men who were holding his arms released him. He heard the same manoeuvres being repeated after him, and guessed that Valerie's steps were among them. There were other movements, and the almost inaudible swish of a heavy door being silently closed. The air seemed warmer, but there was the same damp tang in it. Then the blindfold was taken off his eyes, and he could look about him.

He seemed to be in a spacious underground cellar. It must have been part of a very old building, for even the warmth of an electric fire built into one wall could not altogether dissipate the damp chill which pervaded it. A large tricolour hung on the wall facing him, above a long table behind which stood three plain wooden chairs, the only furniture there was. There were various doors in all four walls with nothing about them by which he could identify the one through which he had been brought in. He had been turned round enough while he was blindfolded to lose his bearings completely.

Valerie was beside him, and the four uniformed Sons of France who had formed their escort were drawn up on either side of them and behind them.

Bravache was there also. He emphasised his own importance by stopping to very deliberately draw off his gloves before he strolled across to one of the doors that opened off the room where they were. He knocked, turned the handle, and clicked his heels in the doorway as he raised his arm in salute.

"*Les prisonniers, mon Commandant.*"

"*Très bien,*" answered a voice from the room beyond, and even in those two words the Saint recognised the harsh strident tones that he had heard on the radio in his car—at least a hundred and fifty years ago.

Bravache turned away from the door and clicked his heels again.

"*Garde à vous!*" he barked.

The escort sprang to attention, but without taking their hands from the butts of their revolvers.

Out of the room, striding past the stiffly drawn up figure of Bravache, came a tall grey-haired man of about fifty-five. He wore the same uniform as the escort, except that there was a double row of coloured ribbons on his breast and his blue shirt had six gold bars on each shoulder. No Frenchman would have needed any introduction to him. That long narrow face with the low forehead and the black piercing eyes and the chin that stuck out like the toe of a boot had been caricatured by a score of artists who tomorrow might be wishing that their talents had been otherwise employed. It was Colonel Raoul Marteau, prospective Dictator of France.

And after him came Kane Luker.

Luker glanced at the prisoners without expression, as if he had never seen them before, while Marteau ceremoniously returned the escort's salute. He followed the Commandant as he went on to take one of the chairs behind the long table, and the Saint's old dauntlessly irreverent smile touched his bruised lips.

"You know," he remarked to Valerie, "if Luker only had a barrel organ he'd still be a bloated Capitalist. An ordinary organ-grinder thinks himself lucky if he's just got one monkey."

Marteau glanced at Luker inquiringly. Apparently he did not speak English. Translating for him, Luker looked almost amused. And Simon realised that to try and bait Kane Luker was not even worth the waste of breath. He was that uncommon type of man for whom abuse or insolence simply had no meaning: they were inane puerilities, incapable of making the slightest difference to any material issue, therefore not worth the loss of an atom of composure.

Marteau was different. His eyes burned darker, and he rasped an order through thin tense lips, and the escort on Simon's right turned and struck him brutally in the face, and returned woodenly to attention.

The force of the blow staggered the Saint back a pace before he recovered his balance, and the girl gasped and whimpered, "You bloody swine!" The blood boiled in Simon's veins, and his cords cut into his wrists against the fierce strain that tautened his muscles, but it was not the blow that hurt him so much as the humiliation of knowing that any courage he could show would only whet the sadistic contempt of these shining crusaders who made a fetish of their own courage. Yet he kept his face set in its mask of indomitable derision, while his mind said pitilessly, "Presently it'll be over, but they'll never be able to say that they made me crawl."

Ignoring him after that swift and callous retaliation, Marteau had turned to Bravache.

"They have been searched?" he was asking in French.

"Oui, mon Commandant."

"Did you find the photograph?"

"Only a print, *mon Commandant.*"

Marteau nodded and sat back with a rudimentary but sufficient gesture towards Luker, and Luker sat forward.

He clasped his hands on the table in front of him and said quietly, with his eyes fixed passionlessly on the Saint, "Mr Templar, among the papers which you secured from Lady Valerie there was a photograph and the negative of that photograph. Where is the negative?"

There was a short silence.

"Go on," said the Saint encouragingly.

"That is all I want you to tell me."

"But you haven't finished yet. Don't you know the formula: You have to describe all the hideous things that'll happen if I don't tell you, and make my blood run cold. The audience expects the thrill."

Luker's expressionlessness did not change. He answered in the same passionless voice.

"A number of hideous things may happen to you in due course, Mr Templar. But for the present I am not concerned with them. I know quite well that you have a temperament which would probably resist interrogation for a long time, and at the moment time is precious. We shall therefore start with Lady Valerie, whose powers of resistance are certainly less than yours. The Sons of France have an excellent treatment for obstinacy. Unless we are given the information we require, Lady Valerie will be tied up over there"—Luker pointed with one hand—"and flogged until we do get it."

The Saint's eyes travelled in the direction indicated by Luker's hand. In the wall to which Luker was pointing there were two iron rings, a yard apart, cemented into the stone about seven feet from the ground. The wall around them was stained a different colour from the rest, and in spite of his jest the Saint felt as if cold fingers crept up his spine.

Lady Valerie looked in the same direction, and her breath caught in her throat.

"But I don't know," she cried out quiveringly. "I don't know what happened to the negative. Simon, I don't know what you did with it!"

"That's true," said the Saint, in a voice of terrible sincerity. "Leave her out of it. She doesn't know. She couldn't tell you, even if you flogged her to death."

He might as well have appealed to a graven image. Luker was not even interested.

"In that case I hope that your natural chivalry will induce you to spare her any unnecessary suffering," he said. "You will of course be allowed to watch the proceedings, so that your sympathies may be fully aroused. A word from you at any time will save her any further— discomfort." He brought his hands together again with an air of finality. "Since I understand that you were proposing to marry Lady Valerie, your affection for her should not encourage you to hesitate."

Simon looked at the girl. She stared back at him, her eyes wide with terrified entreaty.

"Oh, Simon, must I be flogged?" she said faintly.

Her face was white and terror-stricken; her lips trembled so that the words would hardly come out. And yet in a queer way it was plain that she was only asking him to tell her, whatever he might say.

The Saint felt that everything inside him was cold and stiff, as if the rigor of death had already touched him. But somehow he kept all weakness out of his face.

He spoke to Marteau in French.

"*Monsieur le Commandant*, I ask nothing for myself. But you have ideals, and you would wish to be called a gentleman. Will you be proud to record the torture of a helpless girl as the glorious beginning of the revolution in which you believe?"

Marteau's face flushed, but the arrogant unyielding lines deepened around his mouth.

"The individual, monsieur, is of no more importance than an ant compared with the destiny of France." His dark eyes glowed with a mystic light. "Tomorrow—today—we make history, and France takes her rightful place among the nations of Europe. I can give way to no sentimental reluctance to do anything that may be necessary to safeguard the trust which is in my hands. Those who are not with us are our enemies." The glow faded from his eyes, leaving only the hard lines still shifting about his mouth. "As a man, I confess that I should prefer to spare mademoiselle, but that responsibility is yours. As a Leader, with the destiny of France in my care, my own course cannot falter."

"I see," said the Saint softly, "And if I told you what you want to know, I suppose we should be murdered just the same, only without the trimmings."

Marteau's face grew cold and more distant.

"I should like you to understand, monsieur, that the Sons of France do not commit murder. Although your guilt is perfectly evident, you will receive a fair trial by court martial; naturally, if you are found guilty, you must expect to suffer the due penalty."

"Exactly." Luker spoke, in English, and the old ironical gleam was back in his eyes. "You'll get a fair trial by court martial, and you'll be shot immediately afterwards. The day after tomorrow we shall probably start court-martialling traitors in batches of twenty. I'll try to arrange for you both to be in the first batch. But you must agree that that will be far preferable to the same inevitable result with the preliminary addition of what I think you called the trimmings."

"Of course," said the Saint. "You're so generous that it brings a lump into my throat."

But his smile was very tight and cold.

His shoulders ached with a weary hopelessness. No one except himself, not even Luker, could guess what dregs of defeat he had to taste. Death he could have met carelessly: he had lived with it at his elbow so long that it was almost a friend. He had fenced and bantered with it, and light-heartedly made rendezvous and broken them, but never without the calm knowledge that the day must come, however distant, when they would have to sit down together and talk business. Death with trimmings, even, would not have made him cringe: he had faced that too, and other men had gone through it, men many of them forgotten and nameless now, who had endured their brief futile agony that was swept away and obliterated like a ripple in the long river of time.

But here he was not alone. He had to sentence the girl in the acceptance of his own fate.

And there was nothing to give it even a plausible ultimate glory. They died, anyway. And if he died, and let the girl die, without speaking under any torture, it achieved no more than just that. It was not a question of keeping the photograph safe for what might be done with it. There would be no one left to do anything with it, after Patricia and the others had been rounded up in the morning. And even if they escaped, there would be nothing to be done. The negative would remain where it was hidden, in his fountain pen, and would probably be destroyed along with his body and the clothes he was wearing; or at the best someone would appropriate it, and the most likely person to appropriate it was one of the Sons of France, and even if he found it, it would alter nothing. If the Saint was silent and it was never found, it would only mean that Luker and Marteau would be worried about it for some time, but nothing would happen, and their anxieties would ease with every day that went by, and soon they would be too strong to care. How could he condemn the girl to that extra unspeakable ugliness of death for no better reason than to leave Luker and Marteau with a little unnecessary trepidation, and to give his pride the boast that they had never been able to make him talk?

But the bitterness of surrender fought against letting him speak.

He saw Luker watching him steadily, and knew that the other was following almost every step in his inevitable thoughts. Luker's eyes were hardening with the cold certainty of triumph.

"Perhaps you would like to discuss it with your fiancée, Mr Templar," he said. "I shall arrange for you to be given five minutes alone. I'm sure that that will be sufficient for you to reach the only conclusion that two sensible people can come to."

4

They were in a tiny box of a cell furnished with a small wooden table, a wooden chair, and a wooden cot with, a straw palliasse; all the articles of furniture were securely bolted to the floor. It smelt sour and musty. A faint dismal light came through an iron grille over the door which seemed to be the only means of ventilation.

Valerie dropped limply on to the cot and leaned back against the wall in an attitude of supreme weariness.

"Alone at last," she said. And then, "My God, I'm tired."

"You must be," said the Saint. "Why don't you go to sleep?"

She smiled weakly.

"With a man in my room? What would the dear vicar say?"

"Probably the same thing that the bishop said to the actress."

"What was that?"

"'It is a far bedder thing—'"

"'—I do now than I have ever done,'" she said, and then her voice broke.

She said huskily, "Simon . . . will it hurt dreadfully?"

The Saint's mouth felt dry, but the palms of his hands were wet. He knew exactly how cruelly shrewd Luker had been in giving them those few minutes to think. If he had had any doubts before, he could not have kept them long.

The only thing left to discover was what else might be done with the postponement.

He went over and sat down on the end of the cot, beside her, and against the wall. The wall was of baked bricks, roughly laid, and age had moulded the mortar in many of the courses and neglect had let it crumble away. He felt the surface behind him with his numbed fingertips. It seemed to be harsh and abrasive . . .

"Does dying frighten you very much?" he asked gently.

Her head was tilted back against the wall and her eyes were half-closed.

"I don't know . . . Yes, I'd always be terrified. But I don't think I'd mind so much just being shot. This . . . being flogged—to death—it makes me go sort of shuddery deep inside. I want to scream and howl and weep with terror, and . . . I can't . . . I'm afraid I'd never have been any good to you, Simon. I suppose your girlfriend would go to it with a brave smile and her head held high and all that sort of thing, but I can't. I'm afraid I'm going to disgrace you horribly before it's over—"

He was rubbing his bound wrists against the brickwork behind him, tentatively at first, then with a more determined concentration. He could feel the dragging resistance against each movement, could hear the slurred grating sounds that it produced . . . He bent his head towards her until his lips were almost touching her ear.

"Listen," he whispered. "You're not going to be flogged. We can prevent that, at least. But you heard what Luker said. Whatever else happens, we're booked for the firing squad within the next couple of days. So we have to be shot, anyway. Personally I'd rather be shot on the run, and at least give them a fight for their money. I'm going to try to make a getaway. I don't suppose it'll make a damn bit of difference, but I'm going to try it."

She looked at him quickly, as if all her muscles had stiffened. And then they relaxed again.

"Of course—you couldn't take me with you," she said wistfully. "I'd only be in the way."

It was hard to keep the rope pressed firmly enough against the brick and at the same time keep his flesh away. There seemed to be more protruding bones in his hands and wrists than he had ever dreamed of, and his skin was much less tough than the rope. Fierce twinges of rasping agony stabbed up his arms, but he could not allow himself to heed them.

He said, "If you feel the same way that I do, and you'd like to take a chance, we'll have a shot at it together."

She had begun to stare at the curious rhythmic twitching of his shoulders.

"What are you doing?"

The sweat was standing out in beads on his forehead, although she could not see that, and his teeth were clamped together in stubborn endurance of the torture that he was inflicting on himself while he tore the flesh off his bones as he fought to fray off the strands of hemp that tied his hands. But his heart was blazing with a savage exaltation that partly deadened pain.

He said, through his clenched teeth and rigid lips, "Never mind. We haven't got much longer. When they fetch us out again, I'm going to try to break loose. You give way to all your impulses—scream your head off, and fight as hard as you can to break away. Anything to keep their attention occupied. Leave the rest to me. I expect all we'll get will be two bellyfuls of bullets, but I may be able to kill Luker and Marteau first."

She was quite still for a moment, and then she said in a strange strained voice, "Okay. I'll do everything I can."

He laid his face against hers as she leaned towards him, and went on sawing his wrists against the wall in a grim fury of torment. He only spoke once more.

"I'm sorry about this, Valerie," he said. "We might have had such a lot of fun."

Five minutes was no time at all. It seemed to be only a few moments before the big iron key rattled in the lock and the door opened again.

Bravache bowed in the doorway, his teeth shining in the set sneering grin that sat so naturally on his cold haughty face.

"You are ready?" he inquired.

It was a second or two before Lady Valerie got up.

The Saint rose to his feet after her. For all that he had suffered, the cords still held his wrists. But he had his strength, saved and stored up through all the hours when it had been useless to struggle: he had always had the strength of two or three ordinary men, and at this time when he had need of it all for one supreme effort his own will might make it greater. If only that was enough . . . Now that the last sands were trickling away he was conscious of a curious inward peace, a great stillness, an utter carelessness in which his nerves were like threads of ice.

He let the girl go first, and followed her back into the big barren room from which they had been taken.

Luker and Marteau still sat at the long table under the flag. Marteau was drawing nervous fingers on the bare wood with a stub of pencil, but Luker was outwardly untouched by anxiety. Simon and Valerie were marched up in front of the table, and the escort of Sons of France reformed around them, and Luker looked up at them with nothing but confidence on his square stony features.

"Have you made up your minds?"

"Yes," answered the Saint.

"Well?"

"We have made up our minds," said the Saint unhurriedly, "that besides the barrel organ you might do well with ice cream as a side line."

Luker's expression did not change. It only became glassy and lifeless, as if it had been frozen into place. He moved one of his hands less than two inches.

"Tie up the girl," he ordered in French, and the two nearest Sons of France grabbed Valerie by the arms.

Perhaps she was only acting. Or perhaps her nerve really broke then; perhaps her brain in the stupidity of terror had never quite grasped what the Saint had said while they were alone. But she fought wildly, crazily, even with her hands tied behind her back, bucking and staggering against them as they tried to drag her over to the iron rings in the wall, kicking out madly so that they cursed her until the third Son of France had to go over and help them. And that left only one on guard beside the Saint—the one who had slammed his fist into Simon's face only a little while before.

"You can't do this to me!" she was shrieking deliriously. "You can't . . . you filthy brutes . . . you can't . . .!"

Perhaps she was only acting. But the shrill shaky intensity of her voice stabbed through the Saint's brain with a rending reminder of how real it might have been.

He had half-turned to watch her, and as he stood still no one was paying much attention to him. But in that volcanic immobility his arms hardened like iron columns, strained across the fulcrum of his back like twisted bars of tempered steel. The muscles writhed and swelled over his back and shoulders, leapt up in knotted strands like leathery hawsers from his shoulders down to his raw and bleeding wrists; a convulsion of superhuman power swept over his torso like the shock of an earthquake. And the ropes that held his hands together, weakened by the loss of the few strands that he had been able to rub away in the few minutes that had been given him, were not strong enough to stand against it. There was a snap as the fibres parted, and his arms sprang apart with the jerk of unleashed tension. He was free.

Free but unarmed—for the few instants in which an unarmed man might move.

The guard beside him must have sensed the eruption that had taken place at his elbow; or perhaps his ears caught the thin crack of separating cords—too late. He began to turn, and that was his last conscious movement, the last flash of awareness in his little world.

He started to reach for the revolver in its holster on his hip. But another hand was there before his, a hand of lean sinewy fingers that whipped the weapon away from under his belated groping. An ear-splitting detonation crashed out between the cellar walls, and a shattering blow tore through his chest and gave him only an instant's anguish . . .

Simon Templar turned square to the room as the man folded down to his feet with an odd slowness. The barrel of his revolver swerved over the others in a measured quadrant.

"Any of you can have what your friend got," he said generously. "You've only got to ask."

None of them asked. For that brief precarious spell they were incapable of any movement. But he knew that every passing second was against him. He spoke to the girl, his voice razor-edged and brittle.

"Valerie, come over here—behind me. And keep well out of the line of fire."

She started towards him, staying close against the walls. He didn't watch her. His eyes were darting like wasps over the six men that he had to deal with, probing with nerve-wracked alertness for the point where the fight would start. The three remaining members of the escort, grouped fairly close together where they had been struggling with the girl. Bravache, further away, with a skeletal grin pinned and forgotten on his face. Colonel Marteau, white-lipped and rigid. Luker, heavy and petrified, but with his brain still working behind unblinking eyes.

And in his mind the Saint did ruthless arithmetic. Six men. And unless he was holding a five-chambered gun, he should have five shots left. Even if he could drop one man stone cold with every single shot, that would still leave one armed man against him at the end. Even if no other Son of France elsewhere in the building had heard his first shot and would be coming in at any moment to investigate . . . It couldn't be much longer now before other heads made the same calculation. Whatever happened, if they called for a showdown, he couldn't win. The only choice he had left was where he should place his shots—while he had time to choose.

And yet he didn't want to take that suicidal vengeance while there was still even a spider-thread of hope.

He said to the room at large, "Which is the way out of here?"

Nobody had time to answer, even if anyone had decided to.

Colonel Marteau stood up.

"Anyone who tells him," he stated harshly, "is a coward and a traitor."

"Will you set the example?" asked the Saint silkily. "Or would you rather be a dead hero?"

"I shall not tell you."

Simon knew that he had lost an infinitesimal point. But his face gave it no acknowledgement. The steel hardened in his eyes.

"Maybe we can change your mind for you," he said, without a flicker of apprehension in his voice. "Valerie, slip round behind these guys and bring me their guns."

He did not hear any movement.

"Go on," he rapped.

"But how can I?"

"If you try it, I think you'll be able to twist your hands round enough."

But he had lost another point. Those few words between them must only make plainer the ultimate hopelessness of his position. And with every point lost the score was creeping up against him with frightful speed. He would fight every inch of the way with the stubbornness of despair, but he knew in his heart that the battle could only end one way. If he could have made one of the men tell him the way out at once, they might have made a dash for it with a faint sporting chance of shooting their way through, but that had always been a far-fetched hope. The enemy would never be made to talk so easily. And delay was on their side. Sooner or later their confidence would return. It could only be a matter of seconds now. It was already returning. Sooner or later, with the eye of his Commandant upon him and his brain swimming with dreams of glory, one Son of France would screw up his nerve to the crucial fatal heroism that would point the way to a swift inevitable ending . . .

Valerie had moved round on the Saint's left. She was beside the nearest Son of France, twisting her hands round to reach the revolver in his holster.

Simon's eyes raked the man's face. Was this the one who would first find the courage to take his chance? If not, with two guns instead of one in the Saint's hands, the odds might be altered again. Or would it be one of the other? Other faces loomed on the outskirts of the Saint's vision. Which of them had the courage to call for a showdown?

And then a door opened stealthily on the Saint's right.

He saw the movement out of the corner of his eye at the same time as the soft sound reached his ears, and irresistibly he turned partly towards it. The muzzle of his revolver turned with him. He saw a tall scrawny figure, a vacant idiot's face lighted by pale maniacal eyes, and knew at once where he had seen it before. It was the face and figure of the killer in Kennet's photograph, and it had an automatic clutched in one bony hand.

And at that moment Lady Valerie cried out, and the Saint knew what must have happened in the fractional instant while his vigilance was drawn away.

He fired before he turned.

He knew that his shot scored, but he could not be certain where. A glimpse of the killer sagging in the middle flashed across his retina as he whirled to the left. Then he could see only the scene that was waiting for him there.

The Son of France whose gun Lady Valerie was trying to take had seized his chance while he had it, and made a grab at her, trying to throw her in front of him to shield his body. But her backward start had momentarily marred the completion of his manoeuvre, and there was about twelve inches of space between them. Through those twelve inches the Saint sent a bullet smashing into the man's breastbone, so that he staggered and let go and drooped back until the wall kept him from falling. But by that time, in the grace that they had been given, four other guns were out. Every gun except Luker's—if Luker had a gun. And the Saint knew that he could never silence them all.

Quite coolly and deliberately he levelled his sights between Luker's eyes. Other gun muzzles were settling upon him, other eyes crisping behind the sights, other fingers tightening on triggers, but he seemed to have all the time in the world. Perhaps he had all the time in eternity . . . But whatever happened he must make no more mistakes. This was the last thing that he could do. His body was braced against the shock of lead that must soon be ploughing from four directions through his flesh and bone, but none of that must stir his aim by as much as a summer breeze. Not until he had placed exactly where he wanted them the two shots that had to stand as the last witness to

THE SAINT PLAYS WITH FIRE

everything to which he had given his tempestuous life . . . He did not feel any doubt or fear.

He squeezed the trigger, and the revolver jumped in his hand. A round black mark appeared in Luker's forehead, and while Simon looked at it the rim of it turned red.

And then the room seemed to be full of thunder.

The Saint felt nothing. He wondered, in a nightmarishly detached sort of way, whether he had actually been hit or not. But he was able to turn and align his sights without a quiver on their next target.

And that was when he really felt that something must have snapped in his brain. For Colonel Marteau was not even looking at him. He was standing stiffly upright, his right arm down at his side and the muzzle of his gun resting laxly on the table, and a strangely drawn and bloodless expression on his face. And somewhere a little further off Bravache seemed to be sliding down the wall, like a lazy figure whose knee-joints have given way. And there was a blue-shirted figure squirming on the floor and making queer moaning noises. And another pair of blue-sleeved arms raised high in the air. And another door open, and grim-visaged armed men swarming in, men in plain clothes, men in the uniforms of gendarmes and agents de police and the black helmets of the Gardes Mobiles. And among them all two men who could only have been the ghosts of Peter Quentin and Hoppy Uniatz with automatics smoking in their hands. And another man, short and dapperly dressed with a blue chin and curled moustaches and bright black eyes, who seemed to be armed only with a cigarette in an amber holder, who strode up between them and bowed to the Saint with old-fashioned elegance.

"Monsieur Templar," he said, "I only regret that your message reached me too late to save you this inconvenience."

The Saint had no idea what he was talking about, but he could never have allowed the Prefect of Police of Paris to outdo him in courtesy.

"My dear Monsieur Senappe," he said, "really it's been no trouble at all."

EPILOGUE

"That's a nice bit of chinchilla," said the Saint.

"It is, isn't it," said Lady Valerie Woodchester, rubbing her cheek luxuriously on her shoulder.

They had met quite by chance in Piccadilly. Simon took her into the Berkeley and bought her a sherry.

"By the way," she said very casually, "I think I'm going to be married soon."

"Quite right too," he approved. "A healthy good-looking girl like you ought to get married. Who's the unlucky man?"

"Don Knightley—Captain Knightley. You remember him, don't you? He rescued me from the fire."

"So he did." The Saint laughed quietly, but it was a rather thoughtful kind of laugh. "Dammit, that was less than a month ago."

"Is that all?" she said. "It seems ever so much longer than that. Just think—only a month ago everything was ordinary, if you know what I mean, John and Ralph and Luker were alive, and General Sangore . . . Why do you think General Sangore shot himself?"

"I suppose he thought it was the best way out for him," said the Saint soberly. "Probably he wasn't so far wrong, at that. Anyway, let's drink to him."

He raised his glass.

She looked at him curiously.

"It's funny that you should do that," she said.

"Is it? I don't think so. We shouldn't be having this drink together now if it hadn't been for him."

"I don't understand."

"Don't you? I thought perhaps you might. But haven't you ever wondered why all those policemen poured into that cellar in the nick of time, just like the last instalment of a Pearl White serial?"

"Well, I heard what Senappe said. He got a message from you—"

"How do you think he got it?"

"I don't know. I never really thought about it. But I suppose you did one of those frightfully clever things that you're famous for and got it to him somehow. Anyway your friend Peter and that Mr Uniatz were there, so I knew everything was all right, and all I can say is I thought it was pretty mean of you to keep it up your sleeve and let me go through that perfectly paralysing emotional orgy—"

"I didn't put you through any emotional orgy," he said steadily. "You see, I never sent anybody any message."

She stared at him.

"You never—"

"Of course not. If you think a bit, you'll see that I never had the chance to."

"Then—"

"Sangore sent it."

Her face was blank almost to incredulity.

"But—"

"I know all the 'buts,' darling. And I don't suppose I shall ever know much more. I can only imagine that when Luker told the others exactly what was meant to happen to us, and even had the nerve to tell Sangore that we were being stored at Bledford Manor—that's where we spent half the night, if you didn't know it—it was a bit too much even for Sangore to swallow. The Old School Tie rose up and pointed accusing fingers at him, if you can follow the metaphor."

The Saint's flippancy was only in his words. His voice was not flippant, and his eyes were very clear and unlaughing.

"Anyway, I only know what happened. Sangore rang up Peter at the Raphael that night. It must have been some time after we were taken away from Bledford. He told him what had happened to us, and where we were being taken, and what was going to happen to us, and all about the secret way into the Sons of France's headquarters, through the back of a cheap café a couple of blocks away. And he told him all about the plot against Chaulage and the rest of it, and gave him enough dope to make the police sit up and take notice. It was Sangore who told him to go to the Prefecture. It was about the one thing that convinced Peter that the whole thing wasn't a trap. Peter was in a pretty tough spot, but he knew that he couldn't hope to take over that headquarters with just Hoppy and Orace to help him, and he figured that if Sangore really wanted him to go to the police there must be something in it. So he took his chance. Fortunately it wasn't too hard to make the Prefecture sit up, partly because a few rumours of a *coup d'état* had been leaking out and bothering them, and partly because Senappe doesn't like the Sons of France at all and he'd just been praying for a break like that. The only other thing Sangore did was to make Peter swear that he'd report the message as having come from me and leave Sangore himself right out of it. As far as I can make out, the old boy must have shot himself as soon as he rang off. I suppose he knew that he was in for it after that, anyway, and he preferred to go out without any mud on him. That's why none of us ever said anything. But I think you ought to know." He touched the lapel of his coat. "I suppose, in a sort of way, he's the one who really ought to have worn this."

She looked at the narrow red ribbon in his buttonhole, and could not say anything just then.

The Saint gazed at the pale straw-tinted wine in his glass, and lived again through unforgettable hours, not all of them only his own. And he felt a restlessness for which there was no accounting. It was hard to believe that that chapter had been finally closed. So much had been done, but for how long would there be peace? . . .

"Anyway," he said abruptly, "here's luck."

"I saw in the paper that Colonel Marteau and a lot of others are going to be tried next week," she said at last. "You don't think they'll get off, do you?"

He shook his head.

"They haven't a hope. The French are very practical in these matters. Luckily I didn't quite kill that bloke who was going to do the assassination, and they got a statement out of him before he slid off . . . It's a pity they couldn't get anything definite on Fairweather, though. I hate to think of him being the only one to get away with it, even if he was the least important of the lot."

"I think you're very vindictive," she said. "There's no harm in Algy, really. I've still got quite a soft spot for him."

"Maybe I'll try to develop some sort of spot for him myself," said the Saint meditatively. "Let's not bother about him now. Tell me more about your marriage."

She frowned.

"What do you want to know about it? You don't object or anything, do you?"

"Not at the moment. I'm only waiting to see my solicitor and find out what chance I'll have of suing you for breach of promise. I've still got the evidence, you know, and I think it must have been Reginald who told the newspapers—anyway, they all printed it, and I shall have a lot of questions to answer if you jilt me."

She looked at him rather sadly.

"I mean, you aren't really entitled to object, are you? It isn't as if you wanted to marry me yourself, or anything like that."

"Of course I want to marry you myself. But since your heart belongs to another I shall be a strong silent man and keep a stiff upper lip and—"

"I wouldn't marry you, anyway," she said. "I admit you did rather steal my girlish heart away at one time, but after that night when everything happened I decided I just couldn't stand the pace. After all, spending one's whole time being lugged about and threatened with floggings and firing squads and being generally manhandled isn't much of a life for a girl, is it? All the same, I hope you'll come and see me after I'm married, whenever you aren't doing anything in particular. I mean, there must be some evenings now and again when you haven't got a gang of desperadoes after you, and Don will be away quite a bit, you know."

"I think you ought to make him very happy," Simon remarked, a little sardonically.

She gazed at him, wide-eyed and innocent.

"Why, naturally I shall. After all, nobody wants an unhappy man moping about the place. I think I'll have him made a general in a few years."

"Just like that," said the Saint. "And how will you set about it?"

She shrugged.

"It oughtn't to be very difficult. I mean, I know all the right people, and he knows all the right people, and he's rather stupid in the right sort of way, and I'm rather clever, and if a man's stupid in the right sort of way, and his wife's rather clever, and they both know the right people, it isn't very difficult for him to be made a general."

Simon regarded her with honest Admiration.

"You know, I'm beginning to believe you really are clever," he said. "And if he's as stupid as you think he is—in the right sort of way, of course—I'm sure you'll make him very happy."

He ordered another drink and considered her speculatively.

"Have you by any chance started making him happy by allowing him to buy you that nice bit of fur?" he asked.

"Oh, no," she said. "I bought this myself with my own hard-earned money."

Simon sat up with impudently interrogative eyebrows.

"What hard-earned money?"

"The money from my memoirs," she said simply. "You see, I thought it would be a good idea to write my memoirs and sell them to one of the Sunday papers. They'd have been awfully thrilling, with all about you and Luker and Algy and everybody and all our adventures, and I thought they'd be a great success. I told Algy about it, and he thought so too. In fact, he offered to buy them from me himself."

"Oh, did he?" said the Saint. "And how much did he give you for them?"

"He's given me ten thousand so far," she said artlessly, "but I expect he'll give me quite a generous wedding present as well. It's saved me a lot of trouble, too, because he doesn't actually want me to write them just yet, and I must say I wasn't actually looking forward to that because my spelling is lousy."

For several moments the Saint glared at her speechlessly.

"Damn you, young woman," he exploded. "Do you realise that Algy was my only chance of collecting any boodle out of this party? And after all I've done for you, you have the nerve to step in and knock him off under my nose!"

"I don't know about that," she said diffidently. "After all, I did find him first."

Simon Templar surrendered. He lay back and laughed helplessly.

"You win," he said. "You know, I'm beginning to think that Luker and Marteau and Company made a pretty clean getaway after all. If they'd been at large, they'd probably have found that they'd fallen into the arms of a monster that would have made them suffer a lot more. Algy is the really unlucky guy."

She lowered her eyes demurely.

"If by monster you mean me, I can tell you that there are quite a lot of men who wouldn't consider themselves a bit unlucky to fall into my arms."

"The trouble is," said the Saint, "I'm afraid I could almost be one of them."

PUBLICATION HISTORY

A condensed version of this story was first published in the May 1938 edition of *Cosmopolitan* magazine under the title *Prelude for War*. A UK serialisation of the story started in *Answers* magazine the following month and ran past the July debut of the hardback novel.

Reviewers loved it, with one reviewer commenting that "The Saint goes on and on and on—and seems to get better; each time . . . Here is something to tingle your nerves with its vicarious dangers and excitement. And Mr Charteris is not slow to smack Nazism, Fascism and Dictatorship quite resoundingly. Swell!"

It was Triangle Books—again—who were responsible for the change of title, christening the book *The Saint Plays with Fire* for its July 1942 reprint with Hodder & Stoughton, using the title from the 1950s onwards.

The book was quickly banned in Italy and Germany, which objected to its antifascist undertones. It may well have been the inspiration for a note that Charteris's first biographer, W. O. G. Lofts, would find some thirty years later. He reported that ". . . the Nazi Party had a list of famous people to 'dispose of' once victory was complete. No. 1 was

Winston Churchill and way down on the list was Leslie Charteris . . ."
The book was finally published in Italy in 1974.

Foreign translations eventually materialised; the Hungarians were
first off the mark, with *Lesújt az angyal* in 1941, and the French
published the book under the title *Le Saint joue . . . et gagne* once the
war was over in 1946. A Dutch edition appeared under the title *Pro en
contra èn de Saint* in 1950.

The novel was adapted by John Kruse for *The Saint* with Roger
Moore, airing under title of "The Saint Plays with Fire" and first
broadcast on Thursday, 28 November 1963. The episode, which is
generally considered one of the best from the show's long run, featured
Joseph Fürst as Kane Luker, and Justine Lord as Lady Valerie; it was
directed by the show's producer, Robert S. Baker.

The novel was also adapted by Neville Teller for BBC Radio 4. It
was one of three dramatizations and starred Paul Rhys as the Saint, first
airing in the summer of 1995.

---

* *Winnipeg Free Press*, Saturday, 20 August 1938

ABOUT THE AUTHOR

I'm mad enough to believe in romance. And I'm sick and tired of this age—tired of the miserable little mildewed things that people racked their brains about, and wrote books about, and called life. I wanted something more elementary and honest—battle, murder, sudden death, with plenty of good beer and damsels in distress, and a complete callousness about blipping the ungodly over the beezer. It mayn't be life as we know it, but it ought to be.

—Leslie Charteris in a 1935 BBC radio interview

Leslie Charteris was born Leslie Charles Bowyer-Yin in Singapore on 12 May 1907.

He was the son of a Chinese doctor and his English wife, who'd met in London a few years earlier. Young Leslie found friends hard to come by in colonial Singapore. The English children had been told not to play with Eurasians, and the Chinese children had been told not to play with Europeans. Leslie was caught in between and took refuge in reading.

"I read a great many good books and enjoyed them because nobody had told me that they were classics. I also read a great many bad books which nobody told me not to read . . . I read a great many popular scientific articles and acquired from them an astonishing amount of general knowledge before I discovered that this acquisition was supposed to be a chore."[1]

One of his favourite things to read was a magazine called *Chums*. "The Best and Brightest Paper for Boys" (if you believe the adverts) was a monthly paper full of swashbuckling adventure stories aimed at boys, encouraging them to be honourable and moral and perhaps even "upright citizens with furled umbrellas."[2] Undoubtedly these types of stories would influence his later work.

When his parents split up shortly after the end of World War I, Charteris accompanied his mother and brother back to England, where he was sent to Rossall School in Fleetwood, Lancashire. Rossall was then a very stereotypical English public school, and it struggled to cope with this multilingual mixed-race boy just into his teens who'd already seen more of the world than many of his peers would see in their lifetimes. He was an outsider.

He left Rossall in 1924. Keen to pursue a creative career, he decided to study art in Paris—after all, that was where the great artists went—but soon found that the life of a literally starving artist didn't appeal. He continued writing, firing off speculative stories to magazines, and it was the sale of a short story to *Windsor Magazine* that saved him from penury.

He returned to London in 1925, as his parents—particularly his father—wanted him to become a lawyer, and he was sent to study law at Cambridge University. In the mid-1920s, Cambridge was full of Bright Young Things—aristocrats and bohemians somewhat typified in the Evelyn Waugh novel *Vile Bodies*—and again the mixed-race Bowyer-Yin found that he didn't fit in. He was an outsider who preferred to make his own way in the world and wasn't one of the privileged upper class. It didn't help that he found his studies boring and decided it was more fun contemplating ways to circumvent the law. This inspired him to write a novel, and when publishers Ward Lock & Co. offered him a three-book deal on the strength of it, he abandoned his studies to pursue a writing career.

When his father learnt of this, he was not impressed, as he considered writers to be "rogues and vagabonds." Charteris would later recall that "I wanted to be a writer, he wanted me to become a lawyer. I was stubborn, he said I would end up in the gutter. So I left home. Later on, when I had a little success, we were reconciled by letter, but I never saw him again."[3]

X Esquire, his first novel, appeared in April 1927. The lead character, X Esquire, is a mysterious hero, hunting down and killing the businessmen trying to wipe out Britain by distributing quantities of free poisoned cigarettes. His second novel, *The White Rider*, was published the following spring, and in one memorable scene shows the hero chasing after his damsel in distress, only for him to overtake the villains, leap into their car . . . and promptly faint.

These two plot highlights may go some way to explaining Charteris's comment on *Meet—the Tiger!*, published in September 1928, that "it was only the third book I'd written, and the best, I would say, for it was that the first two were even worse."[4]

Twenty-one-year-old authors are naturally self-critical. Despite reasonably good reviews, the Saint didn't set the world on fire, and Charteris moved on to a new hero for his next book. This was *The Bandit*, an adventure story featuring Ramon Francisco De Castilla y Espronceda Manrique, published in the summer of 1929 after its serialisation in the *Empire News*, a now long-forgotten Sunday newspaper. But sales of *The Bandit* were less than impressive, and Charteris began to question his choice of career. It was all very well writing—but if nobody wants to read what you write, what's the point?

"I had to succeed, because before me loomed the only alternative, the dreadful penalty of failure . . . the routine office hours, the five-day week . . . the lethal assimilation into the ranks of honest, hard-working, conformist, God-fearing pillars of the community."[5]

However his fortunes—and the Saint's—were about to change. In late 1928, Leslie had met Monty Haydon, a London-based editor who was looking for writers to pen stories for his new paper, *The Thriller*—"The Paper with a Thousand Thrills." Charteris later recalled that "he said he was starting a new magazine, had read one of my books and would like some stories from me. I couldn't have been more grateful, both from the point of view of vanity and finance!"[6]

The paper launched in early 1929, and Leslie's first work, "The Story of a Dead Man," featuring Jimmy Traill, appeared in issue 4 (published on 2 March 1929). That was followed just over a month later with "The Secret of Beacon Inn," starring Rameses "Pip" Smith. At the same time, Leslie finished writing another non-Saint novel, *Daredevil*, which would be published in late 1929. Storm Arden was the hero; more notably, the book saw the first introduction of a Scotland Yard inspector by the name of Claud Eustace Teal.

The Saint returned in the thirteenth issue of *The Thriller*. The byline proclaimed that the tale was "A Thrilling Complete Story of the Underworld"; the title was "The Five Kings," and it actually featured Four Kings and a Joker. Simon Templar, of course, was the Joker.

Charteris spent the rest of 1929 telling the adventures of the Five Kings in five subsequent *The Thriller* stories. "It was very hard work, for the pay was lousy, but Monty Haydon was a brilliant and stimulating editor, full of ideas. While he didn't actually help shape the Saint as a character, he did suggest story lines. He would take me out to lunch and say, 'What are you going to write about next?' I'd often say I was damned if I knew. And Monty would say, 'Well, I was reading something the other day . . .' He had a fund of ideas and we would talk them over, and then I would go away and write a story. He was a great creative editor."[7]

Charteris would have one more attempt at writing about a hero other than Simon Templar, in three novelettes published in *The Thriller* in early 1930, but he swiftly returned to the Saint. This was partly due to his self-confessed laziness—he wanted to write more stories for *The Thriller* and other magazines, and creating a new hero for every story was hard work—but mainly due to feedback from Monty Haydon. It seemed people wanted to read more adventures of the Saint . . .

Charteris would contribute over forty stories to *The Thriller* throughout the 1930s. Shortly after their debut, he persuaded publisher Hodder & Stoughton that if he collected some of these stories and rewrote them a little, they could publish them as a Saint book. *Enter the Saint* was first published in August 1930, and the reaction was good enough for the publishers to bring out another collection. And another . . .

Of the twenty Saint books published in the 1930s, almost all have their origins in those magazine stories.

Why was the Saint so popular throughout the decade? Aside from the charm and ability of Charteris's storytelling, the stories, particularly those published in the first half of the '30s, are full of energy and joie de vivre. With economic depression rampant throughout the period, the public at large seemed to want some escapism.

And Simon Templar's appeal was wide-ranging: he wasn't an upper-class hero like so many of the period. With no obvious background and no attachment to the Old School Tie, no friends in high places who could provide a get-out-of-jail-free card, the Saint was uniquely classless. Not unlike his creator.

Throughout Leslie's formative years, his heritage had been an issue. In his early days in Singapore, during his time at school, at Cambridge University or even just in everyday life, he couldn't avoid the fact that for many people his mixed parentage was a problem. He would later tell a story of how he was chased up the road by a stick-waving typical

English gent who took offence to his daughter being escorted around town by a foreigner.

Like the Saint, he was an outsider. And although he had spent a significant portion of his formative years in England, he couldn't settle.

As a young boy he had read of an America "peopled largely by Indians, and characters in fringed buckskin jackets who fought nobly against them. I spent a great deal of time day-dreaming about a visit to this prodigious and exciting country."[8]

It was time to realise this wish. Charteris and his first wife, Pauline, whom he'd met in London when they were both teenagers and married in 1931, set sail for the States in late 1932; the Saint had already made his debut in America courtesy of the publisher Doubleday. Charteris and his wife found a New York still experiencing the tail end of Prohibition, and times were tough at first. Despite sales to *The American Magazine* and others, it wasn't until a chance meeting with writer turned Hollywood executive Bartlett McCormack in their favourite speakeasy that Charteris's career stepped up a gear.

Soon Charteris was in Hollywood, working on what would become the 1933 movie *Midnight Club*. However, Hollywood's treatment of writers wasn't to Charteris's taste, and he began to yearn for home. Within a few months, he returned to the UK and began writing more Saint stories for Monty Haydon and Bill McElroy.

He also rewrote a story he'd sketched out whilst in the States, a version of which had been published in *The American Magazine* in September 1934. This new novel, *The Saint in New York*, published in 1935, was a significant advance for the Saint and Leslie Charteris. Gone were the high jinks and the badinage. The youthful exuberance evident in the Saint's early adventures had evolved into something a little darker, a little more hard-boiled. It was the next stage in development for the author and his creation, and readers loved it. It became a bestseller on both sides of the Atlantic.

Having spent his formative years in places as far apart as Singapore and England, with substantial travel in between, it should be no surprise that Leslie had a serious case of wanderlust. With a bestseller under his belt, he now had the means to see more of the world.

Nineteen thirty-six found him in Tenerife, researching another Saint adventure alongside translating the biography of Juan Belmonte, a well-known Spanish matador. Estranged for several months, Leslie and Pauline divorced in 1937. The following year, Leslie married an American, Barbara Meyer, who'd accompanied him to Tenerife. In early 1938, Charteris and his new bride set off in a trailer of his own design and spent eighteen months travelling round America and Canada.

The Saint in New York had reminded Hollywood of Charteris's talents, and film rights to the novel were sold prior to publication in 1935. Although the proposed 1935 film production was rejected by the Hays Office for its violent content, RKO's eventual 1938 production persuaded Charteris to try his luck once more in Hollywood.

New opportunities had opened up, and throughout the 1940s the Saint appeared not only in books and movies but in a newspaper strip, a comic-book series, and on radio.

Anyone wishing to adapt the character in any medium found a stern taskmaster in Charteris. He was never completely satisfied, nor was he shy of showing his displeasure. He did, however, ensure that copyright in any Saint adventure belonged to him, even if scripted by another writer—a contractual obligation that he was to insist on throughout his career.

Charteris was soon spread thin, overseeing movies, comics, newspapers, and radio versions of his creation, and this, along with his self-proclaimed laziness, meant that Saint books were becoming fewer and further between. However, he still enjoyed his creation: in 1941 he indulged himself in a spot of fun by playing the Saint—complete with monocle and moustache—in a photo story in *Life* magazine.

In July 1944, he started collaborating under a pseudonym on Sherlock Holmes radio scripts, subsequently writing more adventures for Holmes than Conan Doyle. Not all his ventures were successful—a screenplay he was hired to write for Deanna Durbin, "Lady on a Train," took him a year and ultimately bore little resemblance to the finished film. In the mid-1940s, Charteris successfully sued RKO Pictures for unfair competition after they launched a new series of films starring George Sanders as a debonair crime fighter known as the Falcon. But he kept faith with his original character, and the Saint novels continued to adapt to the times. The transatlantic Saint evolved into something of a private operator, working for the mysterious Hamilton and becoming, not unlike his creator, a world traveller, finding that adventure would seek him out.

"I have never been able to see why a fictional character should not grow up, mature, and develop, the same as anyone else. The same, if you like, as his biographer. The only adequate reason is that—so far as I know—no other fictional character in modern times has survived a sufficient number of years for these changes to be clearly observable. I must confess that a lot of my own selfish pleasure in the Saint has been in watching him grow up."[9]

Charteris maintained his love of travel and was soon to be found sailing round the West Indies with his good friend Gregory Peck. His forays abroad gave him even more material, and he began to write true-crime articles, as well as an occasional column in *Gourmet* magazine.

By the early '50s, Charteris himself was feeling strained. He'd divorced his second wife in 1943 and got together with a New York radio and nightclub singer called Betty Bryant Borst, whom he married in late 1943. That relationship had fallen apart acrimoniously towards the end of the decade, and he roamed the globe restlessly, rarely in one place for longer than a couple of months. He continued to maintain a firm grip on the exploitation of the Saint in various media but was writing little himself. The Saint had become an industry, and Charteris couldn't keep up. He began thinking seriously about an early retirement.

Then in 1951 he met a young actress called Audrey Long when they became next-door neighbours in Hollywood. Within a year they had married, a union that was to last the rest of Leslie's life.

He attacked life with a new vitality. They travelled—Nassau was a favoured escape spot—and he wrote. He struck an agreement with *The New York Herald Tribune* for a Saint comic strip, which would appear daily and be written by Charteris himself. The strip ran for thirteen years, with Charteris sending in his handwritten story lines from wherever he happened to be, relying on mail services around the world to continue the Saint's adventures. New Saint books began to appear, and Charteris reached a height of productivity not seen since his days as a struggling author trying to establish himself. As Leslie and Audrey travelled, so did the Saint, visiting locations just after his creator had been there.

By 1953 the Saint had already enjoyed twenty-five years of success, and *The Saint Detective Magazine* was launched. Charteris had become adept at exploiting his creation to the full, mixing new stories with repackaged older stories, sometimes rewritten, sometimes mixed up in "new" anthologies, sometimes adapted from radio scripts previously written by other writers.

Charteris had been approached several times over the years for television rights in the Saint and had expended much time and effort during the 1950s trying to get the Saint on TV, even going so far as to write sample scripts himself, but it wasn't to be. He finally agreed a deal in autumn 1961 with English film producers Robert S. Baker and Monty Berman. The first episode of *The Saint* television series, starring Roger Moore, went into production in June 1962. The series was an immediate success, though Charteris himself had his reservations. It reached second place in the ratings, but he commented that "in that distinction it was topped by wrestling, which only suggested to me that the competition may not have been so hot; but producers are generally cast in a less modest mould." He resented the implication that the TV series had finally made a success of the Saint after twenty-five years of literary obscurity.

As long as the series lasted, Charteris was not shy about voicing his criticisms both in public and in a constant stream of memos to the producers. "Regular followers of the Saint saga . . . must have noticed that I am almost incapable of simply writing a story and shutting up."[10] Nor was he shy about exploiting this new market by agreeing to a series of tie-in novelisations ghosted by other writers, which he would then rewrite before publication.

Charteris mellowed as the series developed and found elements to praise too. He developed a close friendship with producer Robert S. Baker, which would last until Charteris's death.

In the early '60s, on one of their frequent trips to England, Leslie and Audrey bought a house in Surrey, which became their permanent base. He explored the possibility of a Saint musical and began writing some of it himself.

Charteris no longer needed to work. Now in his sixties, he supervised the Saint from a distance whilst continuing to travel and indulge himself. He and Audrey made seasonal excursions to Ireland and the south of France, where they had residences. He began to write poetry and devised a new universal sign language, Paleneo, based on notes and symbols he used in his diaries. Once Paleneo was released, he decided enough was enough and announced, again, his retirement. This time he meant it.

The Saint continued regardless—there was a long-running Swedish comic strip, and new novels with other writers doing the bulk of the work were complemented in the 1970s with Bob Baker's revival of the TV series, *Return of the Saint*.

Ill-health began to take its toll. By the early 1980s, although he continued a healthy correspondence with the outside world, Charteris felt unable to keep up with the collaborative Saint books and pulled the plug on them.

To entertain himself, Leslie took to "trying to beat the bookies in predicting the relative speed of horses," a hobby which resulted in several of his local betting shops refusing to take "predictions" from him, as he was too successful for their liking.

He still received requests to publish his work abroad but had become completely cynical about further attempts to revive the Saint. A new Saint magazine only lasted three issues, and two TV productions—*The Saint in Manhattan*, with Tom Selleck look-alike Andrew Clarke, and *The Saint*, with Simon Dutton—left him bitterly disappointed. "I fully expect this series to lay eggs everywhere . . . the only satisfaction I have is in looking at my bank balance."[11]

In the early 1990s, Hollywood producers Robert Evans and William J. Macdonald approached him and made a deal for the Saint to return to cinema screens. Charteris still took great care of the Saint's reputation and wrote an outline entitled *The Return of the Saint* in which an older Saint would meet the son he didn't know he had.

Much of his time in his last few years was taken up with the movie. Several scripts were submitted to him—each moving further and further away from his original concept—but the screenwriter from 1940s Hollywood was thoroughly disheartened by the Hollywood of the '90s: "There is still no plot, no real story, no characterisations, no personal interaction, nothing but endless frantic violence . . ." Besides, with producer Bill Macdonald hitting the headlines for the most un-Saintly reasons, he was to add, "How can Bill Macdonald concentrate on my Saint movie when he has Sharon Stone in his bed?"

The Crime Writers' Association of Great Britain presented Leslie with a Lifetime Achievement award in 1992 in a special ceremony at the

House of Lords. Never one for associations and awards, and although visibly unwell, Leslie accepted the award with grace and humour ("I am now only waiting to be carbon-dated," he joked). He suffered a slight stroke in his final weeks, which did not prevent him from dining out locally with family and friends, before he finally passed away at the age of eighty-five on 15 April 1993.

His death severed one of the final links with the classic thriller genre of the 1930s and 1940s, but he left behind a legacy of nearly one hundred books, countless short stories, and TV, film, radio, and comic-strip adaptations of his work which will endure for generations to come.

> *I was always sure that there was a solid place in escape literature for a rambunctious adventurer such as I dreamed up in my youth, who really believed in the old-fashioned romantic ideals and was prepared to lay everything on the line to bring them to life. A joyous exuberance that could not find its fulfilment in pinball machines and pot. I had what may now seem a mad desire to spread the belief that there were worse, and wickeder, nut cases than Don Quixote.*
>
> *Even now, half a century later, when I should be old enough to know better, I still cling to that belief. That there will always be a public for the old-style hero, who had a clear idea of justice, and a more than technical approach to love, and the ability to have some fun with his crusades.* [12]

---

1 *A Letter from the Saint*, 30 August 1946
2 "The Last Word," *The First Saint Omnibus*, Doubleday Crime Club, 1939
3 *The Straits Times*, 29 June 1958, page 9

4 Introduction by Charteris to the September 1980 paperback reprint of *Meet—the Tiger!* (Charter), the last ever print edition.

5 *The Saint: A Complete History*, by Burl Barer (McFarland, 1993)

6 PR material from the 1970s series *Return of the Saint*

7 From "Return of the Saint: Comprehensive Information" issued to help publicise the 1970s TV show

8 *A Letter from the Saint*, 26 July 1946

9 Introduction to "The Million Pound Day," in *The First Saint Omnibus*

10 *A Letter from the Saint*, 12 April 1946

11 Letter from LC to sometime Saint collaborator Peter Bloxsom, 2 August 1989

12 Introduction by Charteris to the September 1980 paperback reprint of *Meet—the Tiger!* (Charter).

WATCH FOR THE SIGN
OF THE SAINT!

THE SAINT CLUB

*And so, my friends, dear bookworms, most noble fellow
drinkers, frustrated burglars, affronted policemen, upright
citizens with furled umbrellas and secret buccaneering
dreams that seems to be very nearly all for now. It has been
nice having you with us, and we hope you will come again,
not once, but many times.*

*Only because of our great love for you, we would like
to take this parting opportunity of mentioning one small
matter which we have very much at heart . . .*

—*Leslie Charteris,* The First Saint Omnibus *(1939)*

Leslie Charteris founded The Saint Club in 1936 with the aim of
providing a constructive fanbase for Saint devotees. Before the War, it
donated profits to a London hospital where, for several years, a Saint
ward was maintained. With the nationalisation of hospitals, profits
were, for many years, donated to the Arbour Youth Centre in Stepney,
London.

In the twenty-first century, we've carried on this tradition but have
also donated to the Red Cross and a number of different children's
charities.

The club acts as a focal point for anyone interested in the adventures of Leslie Charteris and the work of Simon Templar, and offers merchandise that includes DVDs of the old TV series and various Saint-related publications, through to its own exclusive range of notepaper, pin badges, and polo shirts. All profits are donated to charity. The club also maintains two popular websites and supports many more Saint-related sites.

After Leslie Charteris's death, the club recruited three new vice-presidents—Roger Moore, Ian Ogilvy, and Simon Dutton have all pledged their support, whilst Audrey and Patricia Charteris have been retained as Saints-in-Chief. But some things do not change, for the back of the membership card still mischievously proclaims that . . .

The bearer of this card is probably a person of hideous antecedents and low moral character, and upon apprehension for any cause should be immediately released in order to save other prisoners from contamination.

To join . . .

Membership costs £3.50 (or US$7) per year, or £30 (US$60) for life. Find us online at www.lesliecharteris.com for full details.

Made in the USA
San Bernardino, CA
14 March 2017